THE DREAMER'S CURSE

Book Two of the Artifactor

HONOR RACONTEUR

🐎 Raconteur House

Published by Raconteur House
Murfreesboro, TN

THE DREAMER'S CURSE
Book Two of the Artifactor

A Raconteur House book/ published by arrangement with the author

Sometimes, the strength to get back on one's feet after defeat is more important than the strength that makes one invincible.

- Kyou Shirodaira, Spiral: Suiri no Kizuna

Sevana had both hands entwined in a particularly hairy trap mechanism for zippels when Big announced, *Two intruders.*

Two? Sevana had thieves show up here every now and again, lured by the idea of raiding her storerooms and selling her magical items on the black market for a pretty price. But they usually showed up in large groups or all alone. She rarely had small parties. "Are they inside?"

Main tunnel, Big responded.

"Well, you know what to do. Is Baby helping this time?" Sometimes when they had intruders, Baby and Big would tag team so that Big would create tunnels that infinitely looped and Baby would happily chase them until they miraculously stumbled across an exit.

No, Big denied, sounding a little glum.

Well, the cat might be out hunting, or even napping, considering it was still early in the day. Well, early for Sevana at least. With a shrug, she refocused on her work and didn't spare another thought for the hapless intruders inside of her mountain.

It had been a peaceful almost-three months since Bel and company finally left. In that time, the government had slowly stabilized with Aren back in control. She'd gone back to her normal routine now that she didn't have a dozen people trying to claim her attention. Her eternal Artifactor's License had arrived not a month after the victorious return to Lockbright Palace, and she had framed it and displayed it prominently in her workroom. (The better to gloat about, of course.)

The trap nearly sprung itself twice as she set it, which made her think that her design for this really needed to be simplified before she accidentally lost a hand. Frustrated, she tossed it into a corner, where it made a very satisfying *crash*, and lifted her arms above her head in a long stretch. Alright. Maybe she should go look at that task list Kip had written up for her yesterday. Who knew? There might be something urgent written on it.

But as she rose from her chair and headed for her research room, she noticed that the floor had risen a few inches, blocking the door. Big had developed this simple way of alerting her to danger and to keep people from carelessly entering the hallways while he played with the stupid intruders.

"Big? Are the intruders still here?"

Yes, Big rumbled, agitated. *Outside main door.*

Outside the main door? Her head canted to the side. She'd had a variety of overly ambitious and stupid thieves visit here over the years, but she hadn't yet met one brazen enough to sit outside of her main door in *broad daylight*. Hmmm. Maybe Big had jumped to conclusions too quickly about the nature of their guests. Perhaps these were not thieves at all.

"Let me out."

Big moved the floor back to its normal position so she could open the door. Beyond curious, she headed up to the top level, snagging her sword and a shielding wand on the way. When she exited out onto the clearing at the very top of Big, she closed the door firmly before walking down a side trail that meandered toward the bottom of the mountain. She'd actually worn this trail herself, as she found it necessary on a regular basis to come out and see for herself who stood in front of her door. The trail abruptly ended at a rather large tree growing out the side of the mountain, right above the door, and it gave her the perfect way of perusing her guests without them seeing her.

The air still felt nippy, even though winter had more or less passed. She saw signs of spring as she walked through the trees: blossoms starting to bud, leaves regaining their strength under the pale warmth of the sun. It took some care on her part to avoid the leftover leaves of fall. They were perfectly dry and brittle, ready to give away her position if she put a careless foot down. In fact, she had to focus on the trail so much that she couldn't spare more than a glance upwards now and again toward her destination, and so didn't see her visitor until she finally reached the thick oak tree.

With her hands against the rough bark, she leaned into the solid trunk and put her head around it just enough to get a good look.

A man in his early twenties sat directly in front of the door, legs crossed comfortably, hands on his knees. His straight dark hair had been closely shaven on the lower half of his head, the top layer grown out to collect in a ponytail high at the crown. He possessed the strong nose, jaw, and cheekbones of a Kindin, but his white shirt, simple leather vest, and dark pants said Windamere. At his waist, strapped to his back, and in his boot, he carried a variety of daggers; one sword; and a bow lying on the ground beside him. She didn't need clairvoyance to know this man's occupation: hunter.

At his other side sat one of the largest wolves known in Mander. His fur was black as midnight, eyes a golden topaz that shone like old gold. He wore an earring in one ear, and the way he sat scanning the area around him with eyes and nose, spoke of high intelligence.

A hunter and a wolf. What a fascinating combination to find on one's doorstep.

The wolf's nose twitched, several times, then his head came up and around as if homing in on her location. She knew the instant he spotted her for he shifted into a standing position and gave a soft huff.

His master took instant notice and also looked up, his dark eyes finding her with unerring accuracy. These two had clearly spent too much time together.

Spotted, she gave up on hiding and came around the tree into full view, moving down three steps so that she stood directly above her own door.

"You are not a thief," she observed.

"I am not," he responded, voice deep enough to vibrate rocks. "Are you an Artifactor?"

So, he had indeed come to see her, and wasn't here because of some silly mistake in directions. "I am."

"Good." He gained his feet effortlessly, gathering up his bow as he stood and settling it over his shoulder with the ease of long habit. "My name is Decker. I'm here with a job request for Artifactor Sevana Warran. You match her description. Do I have the right person?"

"You do." She cocked her head, still studying him from head to toe. She knew that accent. She'd heard it before—on the very edge of Windamere's borders, to be precise. The clothes and looks fit, too. She'd bet her eye teeth he came from the Kindin-Windamere border. "Most people, you know, go to my business manager with job requests."

"He's a mite difficult to track down at the moment and I didn't have time to chase after him," Decker responded. His tone remained level as he spoke, but lines of strain and fatigue deepened around his eyes.

This man had come a very long way to speak to her directly. Whatever had sent him here wasn't trivial. "You've succeeded in getting my attention, Hunter." With a casual hop, she jumped the seven feet to the ground and landed easily. "First thing—is that an Illeyanic wolf?"

Decker blinked, the first sign of surprise he'd shown in front of her. "He is. Most people aren't familiar enough with the breed to recognize him on sight."

She didn't bother to explain that Master had a wolf of the same breed and that she had spent enough time around him to know that this breed of wolves had more intelligence than most people. She just turned and addressed the wolf directly. "Wolf." When he looked at her, she continued, "I have a mountain lion that claims this place as his territory. I'd take it kindly if you didn't start a fight with him."

The wolf cocked an ear at her and gave a soft whine of understanding.

"Well enough." To Decker, she waved a hand toward the door. "Come inside. I'll hear your request."

He hadn't lost his tense posture, but he let out a short breath of relief. "Thank you."

Sevana led the way inside, shutting the door behind them. These two moved well—if not for the slight scuff of boot heels on stone floors, she would not have known they were there. They didn't ask her anything as she escorted them into the main room. "Take a seat."

Decker took the love-seat, not sitting so much as dropping into it. She hadn't seen a horse, but he might very well have left it in the village before making his way up here. The way he sank into the couch made her think he'd ridden hard and long to get here quickly.

She paused long enough to throw another two logs on the fire before folding herself into her favorite armchair. The wolf chose to lie down at his master's feet, but he watched her every bit as carefully as she did him. Yes, a very interesting pair. This man had to be very successful to dress as well as he did, not to mention own a wolf as expensive as this one. But successful or not, why would he come here with a job request? Hunters dealt with their own business, usually, and didn't look for outside help.

"Alright, Hunter, what's the request?"

"I come here on behalf of my village." The way he started made it sound as if he had rehearsed this a hundred times in his head. "We are under a curse."

She put up a hand to stop him. "Wait, wait, the *whole* village is cursed? You're not speaking of the majority?"

"All of us, except four men," he answered grimly. "And I'm included among those four. Only the hunters are unaffected, although I'm not sure how long that will last."

Why only the hunters…? She waved him on, eager to hear the whole story.

"The curse has been in effect roughly four months, although we didn't realize it was a curse at first. The curse is this: whenever someone dreams of a place, they wake up in that actual place. They are physically transported there."

Sevana blinked at him, her mind not quite able to accept what her ears had just heard. "So if a person lies down to sleep, and dreamed of being in the middle of the ocean—"

"Then he would wake up in the middle of the ocean come

morning," Decker finished, expression tight. "Every single person in the village, from the youngest child to the oldest elder, has experienced this at least once. Most of them, multiple times."

"How far are they transported?"

"The range is increasing. At first, it was just a mile or so. We thought it nothing more than a case of sleepwalking and took measures against it. But then it became obvious it was more than that—that some other power had to be at work. The current record is seventy-five miles."

Seventy-five *miles*?! Sevana's mouth dropped open, eyes bulging. The man must be pulling her leg. Transporting someone that far took an insane amount of magical energy! "How long ago was this?"

"The morning I left." Decker grimaced in a humorless smile. "Actually, that was the catalyst that made me leave. I knew that if we didn't get an expert soon, someone that could truly help us, the situation would only get worse. And I don't want to see how bad it can get."

She steepled both hands in front of her mouth, mind whirling. A transportation spell that could take someone seventy-five miles away, one that grew with every passing day, that could affect an entire village. She had never heard of such a thing. Even during the days of the great magic, spells like that were only used very rarely, and never on such a scale. "Where is your village precisely?"

"It's called Chastain. It's near—"

"The Kindin-Windamere border," she finished his sentence this time with a quirk of her brows. "Some ten miles from Vanorman, isn't it?"

He sat back and gave her a slow, acknowledging nod of approval. "You know your geography."

"Not really. But I do know Chastain. They are the best and most consistent suppliers of pelts in Windamere. I am a faithful customer of your village." Not that she had ever been there personally, but she regularly had things shipped to her from there. "But if someone was transported from Chastain 75 miles out, then where did they end up?"

"Ence," he replied. "Fortunately. If they had landed in Kindin, it would have been very troublesome to get them back. So far, everyone has been taken to some part in Windamere or just along its borders. I don't expect our luck to hold in that regard."

As he shouldn't.

"We hunters have spent day after day hunting our missing people down and bringing them back. It's getting harder to find them, so much so that we've had to hire magicians to help us. But no one could do more than trace their whereabouts. They couldn't tell us what caused the curse, or how to stop it, or even how to contain it. The last magician we spoke to suggested hiring an Artifactor, as you would be better suited to solve the puzzle. Then I heard of what you did in the Child Prince's case—he had been abandoned as a lost cause too, but you broke his curse." Decker leaned forward, eyes and voice intense. "Help us. Please."

Sevana felt inclined to take on the job just because it sounded like a marvelous challenge. After Bel's case, she hadn't had any fun riddles to unravel at all. She would probably do it for free just for the sheer intellectual excitement. But Kip had drilled it into her to never say such a thing and always get a price upfront. "What's your price?"

"One year's worth of pelts, at your discretion and choosing," he offered without a second of hesitation.

Ooooh, spiffy. What a good price. That would save her a lot of money. "Alright." She hit the armrests with both hands and levered herself nimbly to her feet. "I'll take the job."

Decker's eyes closed in relief. "Thank you," he said huskily.

"Don't thank me yet," she warned cheerfully. "I've never heard of anything like this and I have no idea if I can help at all. But yours is the first good challenge I've heard yet this year, so I'll tackle it. Hmmm. But if we're going to Chastain, I'll need to pack a few things and make some preparations." She'd have to send a note to Kip telling where she was headed (he threw fits if she didn't warn him), lock up her storerooms to prevent anything from spoiling, get the skimmer out, pack enough food for two people and a wolf to get north—wait, come to think of it…. "Did you ride here?"

"Yes." Decker stood as well, adjusting the bow to ride over his shoulder again. "I left Roki in the village, as I wasn't sure if I'd be able to see you today or not."

"Go get him," she ordered. "We're not going to travel by land, but by skimmer. Pick up any supplies you want to travel with while you're in the village. I have a few loose ends to tidy up and some packing to do, but I think we can leave in about two hours."

Decker actually smiled at her, teeth flashing white in his tanned skin. "You're willing to leave today?"

"Oh, on this sort of thing, I don't give curses time to create more havoc. Leaves more of a mess to clean up." She shooed him out, following as he left the room.

As she stepped into the hallway, Big whispered, *Caller.*

"Caller?" Oh, right, she'd left it in the research room. "Who is it?"

Decker and the wolf seemed unnerved by this bodiless voice and were craning their necks around, frantically trying to identify the source.

Pierpoint.

Oh? Pierpoint only called her with magical questions or impossible requests. Sevana headed for the Caller, having just enough pity to explain over her shoulder, "The voice belongs to the mountain. He's sentient."

Decker snapped around, eyes wide, but said, "Oh," as if he had expected that answer. She placed a bet with herself that she'd make him crack before long.

By the time she reached the Caller, it had already assumed Pierpoint's features and was pacing agitatedly back and forth across the small tabletop's surface. When she stepped inside, the Caller abruptly stopped, and Pierpoint's tiny voice said, *"Finally! Sevana, do you know anything about the village of Chastain's curse?"*

She froze in midstep. "I just learned of it. But how did you hear of it?"

"Well, the thing is, there's a little girl here in the palace that's from that village. She told me some fantastical tale about waking up in the library here, of all places. She also says that you're working on breaking the curse."

Sevana felt a chill go up her spine. Lockbright Palace sat a good hundred miles away from Chastain Village. To be transported that far…. "Wait a minute, Pierpoint." Ducking back outside, she called, "DECKER!"

It took a few seconds, but he rounded the corner and gave her a look askance. "Yes?"

"You'll need to hear this," she told him grimly, waving him to come inside. "Pierpoint, this is Decker, a hunter from Chastain Village. He just hired me on for the job of breaking the curse. Decker, this is Pierpoint, the court magician at Lockbright." Meeting Decker's eyes, she added, "He's calling here because a little girl from your village was found in the palace library today."

"*What*?!" Decker dove for the Caller before abruptly checking himself, apparently realizing that grabbing the Caller would do no good. Instead he hovered, arms half-stretched toward the white figurine on the table. "Who?"

"She said her name is Clari. Clari Hanh."

Sevana watched with interest as the color just drained from Decker's face, leaving him looking a remarkable shade of pale yellow. "Someone you know?"

"My niece," he responded hoarsely, putting a shaking hand over his eyes. "Sir, tell me she's alright."

"Oh, she's fine. We found her an hour ago in the library, sitting on top of a stack of books with another open in front of her. Apparently she had every intention of finding someone and telling them what was going on, but the pretty books distracted her." Pierpoint chuckled in rich amusement. "Quite the little girl, your niece. She's now having a grand time with Princess Hana, I understand, having an outdoor tea party while I figure out the situation."

"Sitting on top of books," Decker repeated in a mutter. His hand dropped, the color returning to his skin as his terror faded. "Why am I not surprised…wait, she's with the princess?"

"Hana's a sensible sort," Sevana assured him absently, as her mind spun in a different direction entirely. "She's from Milby, actually, and

I trust her more with a child than the rest of the palace put together. Pierpoint, did you take any sort of magical reading on her?"

"I did, first thing. That's what made me believe that she wasn't just spinning tales. The magical signature on her…I've never seen the likes of this, Sevana. I've never even heard a legend that described something like this. Just what is going on?"

"I don't know, not yet. I haven't even had a chance to get to the village yet and do an inspection." And why, why didn't she have a portal anywhere in that area? The border area to the north had a lot of poorer villages, none of them rich enough to afford her clocks. Maybe she should cut them a good price, just to get one or two in that area… not that it really mattered at this particular juncture. She still had a wolf, horse, and a hunter to transport with her. "Pierpoint, sit on the girl. I'll be there in two days to get her. And be a friend—take daily readings on her for me."

"I most certainly will. You do realize that as soon as you get here, King Aren and Prince Bellomi will want to talk about the situation."

"Yes, yes," she flapped her hands at him. "Shoo. I'll be there as soon as I can."

"I'll tell them." He turned to Decker and said kindly, "Your niece will be well taken care of until you come for her, Master Decker. I promise you. And she's truly well—there's not a bruise on her. In fact, she's having the time of her life here. Do not worry for her."

Decker gave the man a deep bow. "I am in your debt, sir. Thank you."

"Think nothing of it. But do be prepared to speak to the king and prince when you come. They will want the full tale from you."

"I will."

"Good. Sevana—I suggest hurrying."

"I suggest going away so I can pack," she responded mock-sweetly.

Pierpoint gave a snort, but the Caller fell back into its seated position, becoming a faceless figurine again.

Sevana shortened her mental list of tasks and said to Decker, "We leave in one hour."

The man didn't even attempt to argue, he just nodded, worry and relief clashing on his face, spun, and sprinted out the door, his wolf at his heels.

Sevana followed at a similar pace. "Big! Get the skimmer out!"

A hundred miles. *A hundred miles.* No spell, curse or magical artifact that Sevana knew of could do that kind of magic without some serious repercussions. Doing such a thing would leave quite the aftermath in its wake, showing in the land itself—or at least it should. Decker had described it as a curse.

Sevana knew better. It was a disaster of epic proportions waiting to happen.

Sevana sat at the front of the skimmer, guiding it along as they travelled east over Windamere, and even though her back was to her passengers, she could feel Decker's eyes studying her intently. He'd likely heard some fairly fantastic rumors about her, most of them contradictory. Kip would sometimes regale her with the more outlandish ones that he heard while travelling. But she wasn't the monstrous woman that the rumors painted her to be. She really didn't look like some overpowering woman, just a slender blonde with a pretty face and a no-nonsense attitude. Because she didn't care for frippery of any sort, she dressed like a man, with trousers, long sleeve shirt, vest and boots. For Windamere culture, this style of hers was odd but most didn't dare to comment on it.

Most probably didn't care for her brisk manner of dealing with people, but Decker hadn't complained about it. He seemed thankful for her quick reaction, but it clearly also worried him. She reacted to this curse as more than a job, more than a challenge, but a real threat that she wanted to subdue as quickly as possible. Judging from that intent stare, he likely wondered what she knew or had guessed but hadn't shared with him.

He didn't try to ask questions as they had loaded on board her 'skimmer.' He did pause and give it a long study before approaching it, though. For him, it probably looked oddly familiar but strange all at once. It looked like a barge with railing on all sides, a wall of wooden cabinets in the back, and angled, billowing sails out at the sides. It had taken considerable coaxing to get Roki on board and even now the stallion looked about with wide eyes, feet braced on the decking. She'd given them both an amused smirk at their caution (which Decker hadn't all appreciated). Well, since they were high up in the sky, with a good five or six hundred feet between them and solid ground, he had cause for that unease. He himself sat in the middle of the skimmer, well away from the sides, with Gid at his side. (The wolf didn't care for this height any more than the stallion did.)

At one point, she turned and gave them a glance, smirk lifting the corners of her mouth. "Nervous bunch, aren't you?"

Yes, and you're enjoying our discomfort, his expression said. But the words he spoke were, "How safe is this…vessel, Artifactor Warran?"

"Perfectly safe unless lightning strikes us or we're caught up in some major storm."

He relaxed a tad.

"Although I did crash it once," she added, almost as an afterthought.

He froze again. Licking dry lips, he ventured, "Do I want to know how that happened?"

"Probably not." Her smirk became an outright evil smile.

He gulped, lifted his eyes to the heavens, and crossed his fingers from mouth to heart in a quick prayer.

With his prayer winging its way to heaven, he inquired, "Do you mind if I ask some questions?"

"It's going to be a long trip if you don't talk."

Encouraged, he pointed at the grandfather clock tied securely to the very back of the deck. "Why the clock?"

"It's a magical portal." She turned her eyes back toward the sky and the land, shooting off another stream of clouds. "It will connect back to Big. I didn't want to pack up my research room or laboratory, but I have a feeling I'll need access to both."

Decker turned and gave it closer scrutiny. "The way you reacted to my description of the curse makes me think that this is more dangerous than we'd assumed."

The humor on her face faded, mouth flattening into a grim line.

"Yes. It is certainly that. Decker, I'm no historian and I don't pretend to be, but my Master is. He told me that there's only a handful of documented cases where large transportation spells were used. And those were from the days of great magic, not from recent times."

"Then this curse…."

"Isn't normal by any stretch. I also highly doubt it's a curse. I rather think that it's a spell, or an inscribed incantation, or even an abandoned artifact that your village has somehow activated." She shook her head, unhappy at her own conjectures. "The power level alone necessary to transport anyone *a hundred miles* is mind boggling."

"It worries you?"

"No, it scares the light right out of me," she confessed bluntly. "Power like that can destroy a whole landscape, a nation even."

Swallowing hard, he repeated the prayer gesture. "Which do you think it really is?"

"An artifact," she responded instantly. "But I'm not jumping to conclusions until I get there and can properly investigate. Now, let's put your time to proper use." She jerked a thumb at the cabinets in the very back. "There's quill, ink and paper in there. Draw me a map of your village, and include every detail. I want to know if there are any ruins nearby, where the underground streams are, if there are any deposits of minerals, any ancient trees, *all of it*."

He obediently fetched everything, and although he didn't have the best artistic skills, he sat on the deck and drew everything out carefully. This proved slightly tricky as the wind kept ruffling the paper, so that he had to draw with one hand and hold it down with the other.

"Mark where everyone lives, too," she added.

As he drew, he asked, "Can you put up some sort of magic that will prevent people being taken away?"

"I have to figure out what's causing it first. Magic doesn't just counter magic because the castor wants it to. We have to know what's causing something to counter it."

He glanced up at her. "Then you have no way of knowing how

long this will take to solve, either."

"Not the slightest clue." She shrugged, as this didn't bother her. "But I can do some damage control when I arrive. I can put locating charms on everyone so that I can easily fetch them, and even put shield charms on them to prevent them from being hurt. If we really do have someone that dreams of being in the ocean, the shield charm will keep them from drowning until I can get to them."

He let out a breath of relief, a taut line of tension bleeding out of his shoulders. "You have no idea how relieved I am to hear that."

"Oh, I might." She gave him a quick look over her shoulder, eyes trying to see everything in an instant. "Hunters are also the protectors of a village because of their skills with weapons."

She left unsaid, W*hich is why you look worn out.* Truly, he was and couldn't feign otherwise. It didn't take a genius to guess why, either. Aside from running all around the countryside fetching friends and family home again, he'd been half-afraid to sleep himself for fear that he too would fall to the curse. After all, who guards the guardians?

Over the next day and a half, she quizzed him on anything and everything related to the village. The map that he drew for her gave her a preliminary sense of the lay of the land, as well as the village layout, but she knew she wouldn't get a good grasp of everything until she stood looking at it with her own eyes. While she thought on things, she had him write out a rough timeline as well, listing every major event that he could think of that had happened within the past five months. Everything from births to renovations of the village to major weather storms that had passed through. Decker at first couldn't think of much, but as his mind turned to it, things occurred to him and the timeline gradually grew from a half page to four full pages of cramped words.

Sevana glanced over both map and timeline as she navigated their way to Lockbright. Nothing leaped out at her—no odd events, major storms, or anything suspicious had happened. She could see well now why the magicians Decker had consulted with had advised hiring an Artifactor. It would take one to see past this seemingly ordinary course of events of village life.

The fact that interested her greatly was that the hunters didn't all live outside of the village's boundaries. She'd assumed they must, simply because they were the only ones unaffected. But two of them lived in the village itself and two of them lived well outside of it.

Curioser and curioser.

She could hardly dwell on the mystery and safely navigate at the same time. (A fact she had learned painfully well the first and only time she had crashed the skimmer.) So she set the papers aside with only an errant glance here and there until they settled on a clear patch of lawn in the palace courtyard.

The skimmer moved slow enough, and attracted enough attention, that they had a greeting party outside one of the side doors by the time they landed with a solid *thump*. Sevana had a bet going on with herself on who would manage to escape the confines of the skimmer first—stallion aside, Decker and Gid could easily jump the railing and abandon ship. She put her mental money down on the wolf getting out first.

They'd no sooner touched earth when Gid hopped to his feet, and with a quick lunge, cleared the railing, landing lightly on the manicured lawn. Decker looked after the wolf with longing eyes, clearly wanting to do the same thing, but he restrained himself and dutifully led his stallion clear first.

Sevana chuckled under her breath. Yes, good, she knew Decker wouldn't abandon his poor horse on the skimmer. So now that she'd won that bet, what would she do? Hmmm, perhaps buy that rather expensive book she'd had her eye on? Yes, that sounded like a fine plan.

As she skipped off the deck, a little girl of about ten flew out of the palace, black hair trailing along in the air, arms outstretched. She didn't look a thing like her uncle, with that slightly upturned nose and clear blue eyes, and Sevana knew very well that the pink ruffled dress she had on must have been a gift from Hana. No way a village girl could afford to wear something like *that*.

"Uncle Deck!"

Decker took two long strides to her, before catching her with a grunt. "Clari," he said with a long sigh of relief.

She hugged him around the neck for a brief second before drawing back and saying with animated excitement, "Uncle Deck, I've had *so much fun*! Princess Hana and Prince Bel let me read whatever book I wanted to, and I've had tea parties with them, and I even danced with the king last night, and they let me play Captured Princess in the tower and sleep in a biiiig—" her arms stretched out to either side as far as she could reach "—princess bed with a canopy and everything."

He gave her a wry smile. "Well, I'm glad you had fun, sweets. How many books did you end up reading?"

"I lost count," she confided in a loud whisper.

Shaking her head, Sevana walked past the reunion, heading up the small staircase where Bel, Hana, Aren and Pierpoint stood waiting. Bel surprised her by walking down the three steps and meeting her partway. Then he surprised her again when he wrapped both arms around her waist and lifted her off her feet in a strong, affectionate hug.

"Sevana," his deep voice said against her ear. "I missed you."

Beyond flustered at this totally bizarre greeting, she put both hands against his shoulders and tried to push him away. "Bel! Sweet mercy, put me down."

Laughing, he did just that, eyes crinkled at the corners. He'd grown another inch since she'd seen him last, and filled out a tad more, looking more adult than teenager. With enough application of some hot irons and thumb screws, she might be willing to admit aloud that she enjoyed seeing him, too, especially so hale and hearty. But for now, she gave him a suspicious look and edged away.

Her expression didn't deter anyone, as Hana followed her husband's example and also swooped down the stairs and gave her a warm hug. "Despite what you might think, Sevana," the princess pulled back enough to give her a smile, "we *do* miss you. We even like being around you."

Sevana fended her off. "What is this? Some sort of hugging disease going around the capital?"

"Nothing of the sort," King Aren assured her, stepping around his son. He extended a hand, smile warm but also wry. "Sevana."

Grateful for a more normal greeting, she clasped his arm in turn with a firm grip. "Aren," she said with a nod. The arm under hers was firm and steady, nothing like the shakiness or thinness he'd had after his curse broke. He didn't look like an animated skeleton anymore either. He had flesh in his cheeks, a hint of sun on his skin, and the clothes he wore fit right instead of hanging off of him. Seeing him steadily recuperate from ten years of being a somewhat invalid relieved her.

There was a distinct silence behind her. She reclaimed her hand and turned, gesturing Decker forward. "Well come on, man, you can introduce yourself."

Decker shot her an anxious look, head shaking minutely. He obviously did *not* want to speak directly with royalty if he could help it.

Bel took the option right out of his hands. He went directly to Decker and held out a hand, a disarming smile on his face as he offered, "Bellomi Dragonmanovich."

The hunter blinked at him, caught off-guard for a long moment, but cultural reflex kicked in and he took the prince's arm in a warrior's clasp. "Decker of Chastain Village."

"A pleasure, Master Decker." Bel's smile became particularly charming, one that Sevana knew he'd learned from Kip. "I'm sure you've travelled a very long way in a short amount of time, and would prefer to rest, but I do need to speak with you."

Clari hung on to Decker's free hand and looked up at both adults. "Bel's been waiting to talk to you, Uncle Deck. I told him about the curse and he said he'd help us. But he said he needs to know more. I couldn't tell him much."

"I *do* need more details," Bel agreed.

"Your Highness, I will tell you everything I can," Decker responded gratefully, thawing from his nervousness. "But I'm afraid what I know can be easily summed up in a few sentences. I doubt I can add much to what Clari has already said."

"Regardless, come inside and tell me your take on this," Bel invited with a wave of the hand. "Sevana?"

"I'll be talking with Pierpoint," she informed him. "He has some information for me. Be warned, I plan to leave here in an hour, so make your questions quick and to the point."

Bel's attention on her sharpened. "Is the situation that grave?"

"I don't dare give this—whatever it is—more time to escalate."

Bel's eyes searched her expression for a moment and found whatever answer he needed. He nodded curtly. "I think I see. Then we'll convene back at these steps in one hour."

"What is this?" Sevana whispered, voice shaking. She stared at the readings that Pierpoint had taken for her, grateful that she sat on a chair in his cluttered office, and wasn't standing. She felt so shaken that her knees would likely have given out and sent her straight to the floor. The number written on the page in his scrawled handwriting wavered in front of her eyes. Numbly, she looked up at Pierpoint. "This must be a mistake. You *had* to have made a mistake."

He looked back at her soberly, eyes tight with worry. "I thought the same thing. I convinced myself the first two times I took the readings that I did something wrong. But I couldn't convince myself the third time. It's not wrong, Sevana."

She slammed the thick, leather-bound book down, making everything on the table jump and rattle. "This is so wrong that it's beyond words! Sixteen. *The power rating is sixteen!* That's simply unheard of, Pierpoint!"

"I know."

Unable to contain herself, she shot to her feet and started stalking from one end of the room to the other. This proved a little difficult, with all of the cluttered worktables, bookshelves, and chairs crammed into the room, leaving a very narrow walkway. She batted away some of the herbs hanging from the ceiling as well, not slowing her pace, trying to escape the icy tendrils clawing at her spine. She didn't have a lot of experience with this emotion, but she recognized it—raw fear.

"This is unheard of," she repeated, speaking more to herself than to him. "Even the anti-spells don't go over fourteen. I've never seen anything more powerful than a fourteen! And those spells are ridiculously hard to create. They're usually so unbalanced that they tear themselves apart before they can even do what they're created to. How in the wide green world can anyone create something with a power level of *sixteen* and make it balanced enough to work?!"

"That I don't know." Pierpoint dropped heavily into an armchair, making the springs squeak. He put his head in his hand, letting out a long sigh. "But our modern understanding of magic is limited compared to our ancestors. In the days of great magic, they could do something like this."

True. She paused mid-stride. "You think that this—whatever this is—is a relic from that time?"

"It has all the earmarks of it. The only transportation magic that could move people over this kind of distance existed in those times. We certainly can't do it now."

She opened a hand, silently acknowledging his point. That he had made the same assumption as she didn't surprise her much. She stared sightlessly out of the narrow window, thoughts whirling. "But why would it activate now, almost five hundred years after the days of great magic? Why lie dormant for so long and then suddenly start working again?"

"That, you'll have to discover." Pierpoint finally raised his head, his attempted smile strained and forced. "I don't envy you the job. The book you just threw down is your copy, by the way. I have my own of the readings."

She grimaced at him, glancing back at the now closed book. The residual readings of a completed spell didn't tell much. It would give the overall power level of the spell, perhaps a hint of what kind of magic it was—casted, cursed, or charmed—but little else. She would have to track down the source of this thing in order to divine what elements were used to make the transportations possible. "How much do the royals know?"

"I explained what I knew. They understand that this is unheard of, perhaps dangerous, but I don't think it really sank in *how* dangerous until they saw your reaction downstairs." Pierpoint shook his head.

"After all, nothing rattles you."

"This just did." She blew out another breath, trying to become calm. Panicking wouldn't help anyone.

"You're going to need help on this one," he informed her, not unsympathetic.

"If you mean *good* help, then yes." She wouldn't say something like 'I'll take any helping hand at this point' because bad help was no help at all.

Pierpoint glanced at the grandfather clock tucked in between two bookshelves and heaved himself to his feet, making the chair squeak again. "We need to go back down. Our hour is nearly up."

She caught up her book with the readings, tucking it into her pouch at the waist as she followed him out the door and down the winding stairs. Pierpoint lived and studied at the top of the east tower (people always wanted to put magicians at the top of towers for some reason), so it took a considerable hike to get back down to the main level of the castle and to the courtyard where they had left a horse and parked skimmer. Bel, Aren, Hana, Decker and his niece Clari were already waiting in the courtyard. They turned almost in unison as the two magicians arrived.

Aren took a slight step forward, hand raising to catch their attention. "Pierpoint, Sevana, I have a better grasp of the situation now. Sevana, what can we do to help?"

"I need several things," she informed him as she passed through the open doorway and into the sunshine. "First, I want magicians. I can put locating and shielding charms on everyone in the village so we can find them easily, but it'll still take time to run them all down and bring them back. That's time I don't have. I need to focus on the problem at hand and not be constantly distracted."

"So you need magicians to retrieve the villagers," Bel summed up.

"Not just any magicians," she corrected, lifting a finger. "Magicians who specialize in retrieval or transportation magic. I imagine that Pierpoint would know where to find them."

Pierpoint nodded in support of this. "Indeed, yes. I can think of several off the top of my head, in fact."

"Call them in," Aren commanded him. "I want them there as quickly as possible. I'm declaring this a state of emergency and I want people to act accordingly."

Thank all mercy he saw the direness of the situation and she didn't have to beat that into him. For one thing, she didn't have the time to spare to beat it into him right now. "Second thing: I'm going to need expert help. I have never heard of or seen something like this before. But I do know two people who might know something about it. Aren, give me an unlimited purse to work with. These two men are good but they're certainly not cheap."

"You have it," he answered without hesitation. Turning to his son, he said, "Bel, get me a royal seal for her to use." As Bel took off in a sprint back inside, Aren explained, "It'll work like a purse for you. Just write me a letter or quick note about whom this person is and what you owe, press the seal onto the paper, and send it to me. I'll see it's paid for."

Good enough. "One last thing. I left a note for Kip, but I didn't know just how bad this situation was at that point. If he comes to you with questions, answer them, but do *not* let him follow me in there. I have no idea what's going on in that village and can't predict what will happen if a stranger stays there."

"Worried about his safety?" Hana asked, tone and expression sympathetic.

"I just don't want this dreamer's curse affecting him too and giving me someone *else* to track down every morning," Sevana grouched. "Now. Where's Bel with that seal?"

"Here!" he called from behind her. Bel skidded to a stop not a moment later, not at all winded or flushed, and handed the seal to her.

It looked impressively genuine with the embossed coat of arms of the Dragonmanovich family in a ceramic disk that filled her entire palm. It also had a surprising bit of weight. Sevana dropped it into her waist pouch and gave him a nod. To Aren she added, "I think I can reach Chastain in a day, perhaps even by late tonight. I'll take over finding people once I arrive, but I don't want to do that for long. Get those magicians up there as quickly as possible."

"We will," he promised her.

She'd done all she could here. With a nod to the whole family, she spun on a heel and headed straight for the skimmer, gesturing for her passengers to follow as she walked. "Load up, people."

It took some serious coaxing to get both wolf and stallion back on board. Sevana didn't even try to help Decker during this process, just sat in her chair and impatiently tapped out an irritated rhythm against the wooden deck. The worst delay was Clari, who had to say proper goodbyes to her hosts, but eventually the little girl climbed on board too.

Satisfied that everyone had settled enough to not fall off, Sevana lifted the skimmer off the ground with a slight scrape and groan. Clari clapped her hands and laughed aloud. "Uncle Deck, we're *flying*!"

Oh? Sevana cast a quick glance over her shoulder. Unlike her uncle, Clari apparently had no fear of heights and was looking around with wide-eyed wonder. She kept asking questions on how this all worked, and wasn't satisfied with the one word answer of "Magic" that her uncle gave her, either.

Sevana lost track of their conversation as she navigated their way around the top parts of the palace and higher into the air, then pointed due north. It always felt exhilarating up here, with the wind rushing past her skin and ruffling her hair. This season of the year, it carried hints of spring and growing things that tickled her nose and cleared her head. As scary as the "curse" was, she couldn't focus on it entirely and lose focus of everything else. She inhaled a deep lungful and let it out again, feeling better for it.

"Clari, *please* don't go so close to the edge," Decker pleaded nervously.

Sevana hooked the skimmer up to a long stream of clouds before daring to half-turn in her seat. Clari stood right at the railing, both hands on the top, and her head leaning out over the side to see the ground below. Decker had grabbed her by the ankles and was insistently tugging at her, trying to draw her back toward the center.

"Uncle Deck, I'm alright," she insisted, not letting go of the railing.

"You're *not* alright," he shot back. "What if you fall?"

"She can't," Sevana piped up, finding the sight humorous. When Decker shot her a confused look, she elaborated, "There's a charm on this vessel that prevents people from falling. She can't go more than three inches before the charm will activate and push her back inside."

"An anti-falling charm," he grumbled not quite under his breath as he released his hold on Clari's ankles. "*Now* she tells me."

Sevana cackled.

They picked up a tailwind from the south and made better time than Sevana had dared hope for. They arrived at Chastain just as the sun was setting. She got a very good bird's-eye view as they slowly reduced their altitude, coming in to land at the village's outskirts. From the air, it certainly didn't look like much. It had that interesting blend of Kindin and Windamere architecture—the bold colors of the trimming on the houses were pure Windamere, but the bases were made of stone and brick instead of the usual thatch and wood. This village hadn't just grown every which way as most did, but had a semblance of order to it. Actually, it looked like a giant spider web. The center had a very large fountain that gushed water endlessly with a courthouse, bank, church and meeting hall around it in a small circle. Then from there were short streets that connected to four long streets, all with either businesses or homes, all of which glowed with lamplight at this late hour. It seemed like a very peaceful, unassuming place.

Pity appearances were so deceiving.

Even at this hour, someone noticed them coming in, and a loud bell rang out three times in quick succession. Several people poured out of their homes and rushed toward the edge of town, all of them carrying weapons of various sorts. Considering recent events, and the interesting neighbors they had in Kindin, Sevana didn't blame them for their caution. "Decker, shout out a word before someone tries to shoot arrows at us."

He didn't get the chance before his niece beat him to the railing, leaned out, and called down in a surprisingly loud voice, "Don't worry! It's us!"

From below a voice called back faintly, "CLARI?!"

"Yes, it's me! Uncle Deck's here too!"

A lot of chattering went around in the group below, but no one tried to get more information until Sevana found a clear spot to land. Most of the area seemed to be farmland with a smattering of trees here and there. She found a spot big enough for the skimmer quite easily and set it down with a solid thump. As she furled in the sails and secured the charts at the desk, her passengers gratefully got off, the horse more so than anyone.

Seven men crowded around, all of them firing off questions in quick succession. Sevana stepped onto the cool grass slowly, eyeing each one of them in turn. In this group, she would say two men were hunters (both older than Decker), one of them a butcher (judging from that wicked knife in his hand), one retired soldier, and three other burly men that she couldn't quite pin a profession to offhand. One of the men took Clari by the hand and escorted her directly into the village, and likely to her very anxious parents.

"This is Artifactor Sevana Warran. She's agreed to help us," Decker said to the others.

"Gentlemen," she greeted with a general nod to the group. "I need to speak to the mayor or whatever leader you have in this village."

"We have an ombudsman," Decker volunteered. "He's our mayor, of sorts."

"That's fine. Take me to him. We have things to do this very night to prevent mischief happening tomorrow." Oh, wait. Snapping her fingers, she pointed at the grandfather clock still on the skimmer. "And I need two men to carry that."

"Ummm…" the butcher looked at the grandfather clock with misgiving. "Begging pardon, Miss Artifactor, but two men can't be carrying the likes of that."

"It has a weight cancellation charm on it," she explained impatiently. "It's not heavy, just awkward. *Move.*"

Decker, at least, understood the importance of the clock well enough to instantly climb back on board. With his lead, two other men climbed inside after him and assisted in moving the clock out of the skimmer. As they carefully maneuvered the clock free, Sevana directed, "Take it to whatever inn or house that I'm staying in while I'm here. I'll set it up properly in a minute. For now, take me to the ombudsman."

One of the huntsmen extended a hand to her, his craggy features somewhat undiscernible in this twilight lighting. "I'm Muller, Miss Artifactor. If you'll follow me."

She accepted the arm. "Sevana. Call me Sevana. Let's go."

He waved her onto a gravel road that led directly to the main street, from the look of things. She hadn't parked far from the village so it took bare minutes to reach the outskirts. As she walked, a heavyset man with white hair ran toward them, tugging on a jacket as he moved.

"Krause!" Muller raised a hand and waved, getting the other man's attention.

Krause waved back but didn't say anything until he lumbered to a stop. "I heard Clari's back," he said to Muller, his eyes on Sevana. "Who's this?"

"Sevana Warran, an Artifactor," Muller introduced succinctly. Krause's eyes lit up with relief and pleasure. "Sevana, this is Krause, our Ombudsman."

"Sir," she greeted. "I'll make this short as we have a lot to do tonight. I'm going to put locating and protective charms on every man, woman and child in this village. I need you to call them all. *Now.*"

He didn't even think to question her. He just gave a short sigh of relief before promising, "They'll be at the main square within a half hour."

"Good. Go." As Krause ran back through the village, calling out to people as he went, she turned to Muller and said, "I need a place to set up. Somewhere quiet where I can work and think."

Muller stroked his chin for a moment and thought. "How much

room do you need?"

"A single room will suffice." If she needed any more room than that, she could always retreat to Big and work there for a day. But she didn't think it would come to that.

"Then the court building has a back room that's fairly empty. Just a table and some chairs in there."

"Perfect." She turned to see that the clock was steadily catching up with her. "The clock needs to go in there. I have to fetch some things before I meet with everyone in the village."

Muller looked at her blankly, not following at all. "How do you fetch things with a clock?"

She smirked at the man. "Watch and be amazed, huntsman."

The room they gave her to work in could not have been more bland. Four dark paneled walls, a threadbare carpet on the floor, and that simple rectangular table with eight chairs Muller had mentioned to her. But it suited her needs down to the ground. She didn't have to worry about shoving someone else's clutter out of the way to make room for her own.

Sevana spent the majority of the night setting up shop, so to speak. She calibrated the clock to connect to the one in Big, went through to fetch her charms, and then stayed up until well past midnight attaching them to every person in the village. As she put the charms on them, the glow board she'd tacked onto the wall updated and kept not only a running tally for her, but a precise location. It was this map board that she would use in the future to determine where people had been randomly transported to.

Of course, the children just liked to stare at the board because it was glass and had pretty lights shining on it.

The charms were the least of what she fetched to Chastain. If the time with Bel had taught her anything, it was this: she needed more than two modes of land transportation. The far-see glasses worked perfectly as long as she limited it to one person. The skimmer worked just fine for groups of people but moved slower than frozen honey. If she wanted a quick method of travelling over land with just two or three people, she didn't have a good solution. Or she *hadn't* at least. After Bel and company had left Big, Sevana turned her mind to the problem and developed a smaller version of the skimmer which could comfortably carry two people or three in a pinch.

She got up early that morning, even though she had been up most of the night, and went through the clock portal back to Big. Most of the equipment in her workroom she left alone as she still didn't quite know what she needed yet. But she went up immediately to the second storage room, where she put all of her vehicles, and grabbed her mini-skimmer, dubbed *Cloud Putter*. Even though she had made this as slender and portable as possible, she still had a devil of a time hauling it downstairs and she thought she'd *never* get it through the narrow confines of the clock. It actually left skid marks on the sides of the wood, it was that tight of a squeeze. Huffing, puffing, and cursing aloud, she finally managed to shove it through and out the other side. Then she just lay on it for a while, breathing hard and blowing loose strands of hair out of her face.

"Uh, Sevana?"

Half-draped over the mini-skimmer, she looked up into Decker's perplexed face and growled, *"What?"*

He took a long look at the situation and asked, "It's too late to offer help, isn't it?"

"Worlds too late," she informed him crossly. "Unless you want to carry it outside for me." Which was help that she wouldn't turn down at the moment.

Being an intelligent man, Decker beamed at her and gave her a bow. "It would be my great pleasure to do so."

Amused despite herself, she rolled off of it and got to her feet, rolling her shoulders as she moved to work some of the building tension out.

He paused with his arms outstretched and looked it over from stem to stern. "If I can ask…what is it?"

"Think of it as a miniature skimmer."

His eyebrows rose dubiously. "This is?"

Well, alright, maybe it didn't look like it. It was shaped like an oval tube with narrowing ends on the front and the back, a hole going straight through the center with an iris that could open and close at her command via a lever on top. Carved into the tube were two seats, a leather cushion stitched in, with a folding compartment in the very back that could hold two bags or a small person. From the sides were collapsible sails that had wind charms sewn into them that would catch the wind and ride it, keeping the vehicle aloft. But it remained true to the skimmer in general principle if not in looks—clouds propelled it forward. Best yet, it moved at three times the speed of the skimmer.

"It looks like a large dragonfly," Decker muttered as he picked it up with both arms, awkwardly holding it at an angle.

"That's actually where I got the idea," she admitted. "It moves faster than the skimmer so I thought it best to fetch it now before figuring out who got transported last night."

"About that…" Decker paused in the doorway and looked back. "I actually came to tell you. Denni is the one that you need to fetch. Quickly as you can too."

She didn't like the tone of his voice or the concern she saw. "Why quickly?"

"He's two."

"Stone the crows!" she swore aloud. Could this morning get any more complicated or frustrating?! "How often do the children get transported?"

"As often as the adults," Decker said grimly.

In other words, far too often. "His parents?" she demanded, already grabbing up different wands, potions and crystals and shoving them into her bag. "Where are they?"

"Waiting outside."

Sevana lost no time in opening the door, leaving it wide so that Decker could get through. A young mother and father stood waiting, agitated and gripping each other's hands tightly. Sevana hadn't a child of her own, but she was far enough apart in years with her brother that she was half-sister, half-mother, so she had an inkling what these people must be feeling. It gave her an unusual sense of sympathy, enough so that the first words out of her mouth were, "He's fine. The protective charm I put on him last night will make sure of that. I can fetch him back quickly." They relaxed a hair, but tears were still standing in the mother's eyes and Sevana didn't blame her for them.

"Is there anything I can bring with me that will calm him?" Sevana asked. "A favorite blanket or toy?" The last thing she needed was to deal with a squalling child while bringing him back.

The mother rallied enough to say shakily, "Yes. He has a blanket he loves."

"Get it," Sevana ordered. "I'll take a look at the board and get his location."

The dark-haired father moved quickly, turning and sprinting back down the narrow street. Sevana spun just as quickly and darted back inside, looking for the boy's name on the side panel first to find his color. Pure white, eh? Alright, then…she scanned the board's surface and found him in a second. Phew. Not as far as Clari had flown.

While she did this, Decker had taken *Putter* out and come back in to ask, "Find him?"

"Yes." Without trying to explain anything to him, she moved around the table and back outside, her mind whirling as she walked. The area between Chastain and the boy was level grassland and farms. She could move just as fast, if not faster, using the far-see glasses. Did she dare strap a two year old onto the mini-skimmer and expect him to not somehow wiggle free and fall off?

Years of experience with her younger brother said no.

As soon as she hit the door, the father skidded to a stop in front of her, panting for breath but with a small blue and white quilt clutched in his hand. Sevana took it from him as she explained, "He's just outside of Gerrety and safe. I can have him back before lunch."

Both parents did a silent prayer of thanks.

Pointing to the mini-skimmer, she told Decker, "Put that back inside. I don't dare use it with a two year old."

He blinked at her. "I thought your vehicles have anti-falling charms on them?"

"That one doesn't, not yet. Just the straps to hold you in place and I know two year olds—they have this uncanny ability to do things they're not supposed to. It's safer to use the glasses for this trip." There. That would have to suffice as she didn't want to stand around yakking while the child was stranded somewhere alone. Tucking the blanket under one arm, she extracted the glasses from her pouch, put them on her nose, and did a quick hop out to the main street. The feel of cool morning air passed by her in a blur as well as scents of food that came and went too quickly for her to properly identify. Once she came to the main thoroughfare, she spotted a place out of town and closed the shades again, going to the edge of the village within seconds.

She repeated this process several times over the next hour, flying through planted fields, passing crops of trees, and over unending grassland that she knew the look of very well after flying over it yesterday. According to the charm's locating dot, the kid should have ended up just north of Gerrety City. Sevana thanked any god listening for that small favor. Having to search a large city for a small child did *not* rank among her favorite pastimes. Once she saw Gerrety on the horizon, she slowed down slightly and took smaller leaps, taking the time in between to scan the area and see if she could spot the kid. Sevana had almost reached the outer wall of Gerrety before she found Denni, not by sight, but by sound. She could hear his terrified wailing for his parents quite clearly.

"Denni!" she called out, walking in the direction that she heard his voice. "Denni! Answer me, kid!"

The wailing stopped for a second, as though he was hiccupping for breath. "W-who?"

"You met me last night, remember?" Reasoning with upset two year olds didn't always work out well, but Sevana was game to try as long as he listened. "I put the charms on you. Your parents sent me to fetch you home." She waited a beat. No response to that. Hmm, alright, switch tactics. "Your father gave me your favorite blanket. You want it?"

That got a response. Denni shot up out of his hunched posture in the grass, finally coming within line of sight of her, and dashed forward on chubby little legs. Kid certainly looked a sight what with that snotty face and bed-mussed hair. His mother had apparently anticipated he might be taken as she hadn't put him in a nightgown but sturdy trousers, a blue shirt and thick socks.

Sevana untucked the blanket and waved it in front of her as if enticing a bull. It worked like a charm. Denni didn't so much as grab the blanket as tackle both her *and* the blanket, ending up fetched against her legs. She took advantage of the opportunity and picked him up under the arms, slinging him onto one hip with ease. Kid was *so* much lighter than Bel had ever been. "You set?" she asked him, unable to see his face as he burrowed into his quilt. "I'll have you home for lunch."

"Home?" he asked, daring to peek up out of his blanket.

"Home," she repeated firmly, relieved he wasn't in the mood to keep squalling. "Just hang tight."

Denni grabbed her shirt with a fist, other arm full of his blanket, and hunkered into her like a mole burrowing into his den. Sevana turned to face north, opened the shutters on her glasses, and took the first long leap back toward Chastain.

The boy didn't know what to make of this at first. When she stopped, he let out a huge breath of pent-up air, more taken aback than scared. But after the second long leap, he let out a squeal of excited delight. Sevana paused and looked down at him. He nearly bounced in her arms, waiting for her to do it again. Come to think of it…Bel had enjoyed this too. "Having fun?"

"Ya!" he said, Kindin accent slipping through his speech. "Again!"

Again, huh? Chuckling, Sevana obliged. Perhaps she hadn't needed to worry about taking the mini-skimmer with Denni after all. If this was how the kid thought of thrills, he'd have taken to the air like a homing pigeon. Ah well. The glasses were faster anyway.

He never got tired of the jumps and squealed and laughed and bounced in her arms so that an ache developed in her right side from holding on to him. Sevana reached the main street of the village and, with outright relief, put the kid down on his own feet.

"Awwww," Denni complained, trying to climb back on her.

"You can do it again the next time you get transported in your dreams," she assured him dryly.

He thought about that quite seriously for a moment. "After my nap?"

Sevana couldn't help but laugh even as she groaned. Children really had no sense of time or patience, did they? Although his question did bring up an interesting point—would naps be enough to trigger the curse or did it take a full night's sleep to do it?

"DENNI!" a frantic mother's voice called.

Sevana prudently stepped back as two worried parents dove for their child and picked him up. Denni, not seeing anything to worry about, beamed at them and said in baby-babble, "Fun *zoom*! Again, Mama, again!"

"Zoom?" his father repeated blankly.

Not in the mood to explain, she headed for the main street and a much delayed breakfast. The couple would likely hunt her down later and offer thanks of some sort—they seemed like the type—but right now all she wanted was a full belly and some answers to the questions buzzing around in her head.

Sevana didn't do anything elaborate for breakfast. Actually, she ate and worked at the same time. She held a diagnostic wand in one hand, scanning anything and everything in her path, and bought food from various bakeries and shops so that she could eat with the other. As absolutely nothing had shouted *power being used!* to her during her short time here, she started at the very outer edges of the village and started walking around in an ever-closing spiral that would eventually end at the center of town. If she didn't find anything after searching here, she would start looking outside the village proper. But she didn't think it would be outside. These village streets seemed to hum somehow, as if every part of them had been touched with magic, only she wasn't quite sensitive enough to see it for herself.

The ombudsman, Krause, caught up with her before she could make it completely around the edge of the village, huffing and puffing as he came. He dabbed at the sweat dewing on his forehead with a handkerchief, skin ruddy with exertion. In proper lighting, he looked like a grandfather with that snow white hair and stout frame. "Sevana," he called as he jogged toward her. "Have you found anything?"

She rolled her eyes. "Krause, if it was that easy to figure out, those other magicians you called in would have been able to solve it."

He slowed to a stop, expression slightly dismayed. "Is it truly that difficult?"

Motioning him to fall in step with her, she tried to explain it in layman's terms with the hopes that if she explained it to *him* he would explain it to *everyone else* and she wouldn't end up repeating herself a hundred times.

"Think of magic as strong wind. When it's active, you can feel it and see the effect it has on the things around you. It's easy to see that the wind is there. But when it's not active, there's nothing to feel, nothing to see. You might see traces of it left behind, if it was strong enough, but you'd have no idea which direction it came from or really how strong it was. I know that this curse is strong, diabolically so, because traces of it lingered behind on the people it transported. But right now, our metaphorical wind is not blowing, so I'm going to have to track it down the hard way."

Krause, thankfully, followed this explanation closely. "I believe…I see. So you are now tracking it down?"

"Trying to. This wand," she waved it a little in the air, "is a tool I use for such cases. I'll walk around the entire village first. If I don't find the source here, then I will go outside of it."

"I quite understand." He gave her a game smile in support although his eyes were still worried. "Is there anything we can do to help?"

"Not at the moment." Rethinking that, she added, "Did Decker tell you what Aren promised?"

"About sending other magicians to help? Yes, he told me."

"When they arrive, notify me. I need to coordinate with them." Solely so that she could hand the troublesome task of rescuing people over to someone else.

"I will do so," he promised. Then, as if sensing he was doing nothing but hampering her, he gave a deep bow of the head and retreated back the way he had come.

Sevana kept walking, wand scanning in front of her from side to side, similar to the motion that a blind man with a cane would use. She felt blind too, as if she were just feeling her way around in the dark. Not the best feeling to have.

Chastain could not be considered a large place, not by any stretch of the imagination, but it still somehow took nearly four hours for her to cross over every section of it until she arrived near the center of the main square. Of course, her progress was hindered by every villager coming to her and offering help, information, or whatever else they could think of. Sevana waved them away as often as not, occasionally taking readings as some of them had been transported in the past several days. She took notes on them, recording their experiences in the small leather book Pierpoint had given her. Interestingly enough, the range of their travels varied wildly. So far, Clari held the record in distance traveled by a large margin. Sevana couldn't put a finger on why. Perhaps the dreams they had affected the spell? Hmmm.

She finally arrived at the main square. As she walked toward the fountain, she leveled her wand at each building, slowly taking in the reading levels, but these structures didn't differ from anything else in the village. Aish. She really would have to start searching outside the vil—wait.

Sevana froze in place, the wand in her hand nearly vibrating from the force of the magic it detected. Whipping out her notebook, she set the wand to record what it saw, and her hair stood on end. The number was exactly what Pierpoint had recorded on the front page.

Her head whipped up to see what she had pointed the wand at. The courthouse? No, surely not. After all she had gone in and out of that building multiple times since last night. She would have surely felt or seen something before now. But the only other thing in her path was the large stone fountain that dominated the very center of the square.

Double-checking, she lowered the wand a tad to where it pointed directly at the fountain and nothing else. The strength of the magical reading increased significantly. No mistake. This was it.

Her lips peeled back in a feral smile. "Found you."

Sevana plopped down right there on the cobblestones, sitting cross-legged and ignoring the cold that seeped quickly through her pants. Spring it might be, but stone was always cold. Even when she had strong morning light like today, that wouldn't change. She rummaged around a little in her pouch, taking out what she needed for more precise readings by switching to a more sensitive diagnostic wand. She propped open the notebook so that it rested on her knee, letting her easily read the breakdown of the spell as numbers and letters scrawled over the cream colored pages.

The wand first recorded the power level of sixteen, and while that didn't surprise her, it still made her wince. But then it started breaking down the elements forming it: running water (duh, of course, it's a fountain!), reflected light, and artifact.

Artifact.

Sevana swore aloud, thumping a fist against the ground in mixed satisfaction and anger. She'd *known* it had to be an artifact by the way things worked, but at the same time, she truly wished she'd been wrong.

"Sevana?" Decker came and knelt next to her, a worried Krause hovering behind him. Decker himself seemed slightly disturbed by her, either by her expression or the foul language coming out of her mouth.

Gid came around on her other side and sniffed at her curiously. She shoved his nose away and commanded, "Wait," holding up a hand to ward him off. Her eyes went back to scanning the information on the page. It made sense now—far too much sense. Running water had a power level of eight if it came from a pure source (which this apparently did), and reflected light (either sunlight or moonlight) had a power of two, but man-made artifacts, especially those dating back to the days of old magic, could have a power level of up to six. Added together, it came out to an insane power level of sixteen.

The diagnostic wand gave her a few more tidbits of information—most of it useless—and then went still as it had nothing left to report. She put both wand and book down on the cold stone and resisted the urge to start cursing all over again.

Decker kept darting looks between her and the fountain. After a long, uneasy silence, he dared to venture, "Is it the water that's the cause?"

"No," she denied immediately. "Although it certainly isn't helping. No, there's an artifact of very ancient origin buried in the fountain itself. The water and the light around it is simply aiding the artifact and making it more powerful." Alright, sitting here cursing fate and growling wasn't solving the problem. She picked up everything and shoved it back into her pouch before regaining her feet, making Decker stand up with her or be left sitting awkwardly on the cobblestones. "Decker. You mentioned the building of this fountain on your timeline. When exactly did it happen?"

"The final stone was laid in two days before the first sleepwalking incident," Krause answered hollowly. "Sweet mercy above, we never thought the *fountain* would be the cause…."

"It isn't. It's an artifact buried inside of it," she corrected testily. "And the stones? Where did they come from?"

"Oh." Decker pointed northeast. "Remember the ruins I drew on the map? We often pillage stones from there to build things with. Most of the village is built from stones we scavenged."

Scavenged stones from ruins that no one knew anything about. Yes, didn't that sound like a disaster waiting to happen. More wars and scrimmages over land rights had happened in this area of the world than almost any other. Countless civilizations and cities had risen and fallen and most of their records had disappeared along with them. Those ruins could belong to anyone from a saintlike religion to a cult of evil magicians. Who knew what secrets lay buried there!

"Ah…" Decker watched her expression warily. "The artifact came with the stones, didn't it?"

She just glared at him, arms crossed over her chest. "What do you think?"

"Oh." Hunter and ombudsman exchanged glances. "Krause, maybe we'd better stop doing that."

"I think that's for the best," Krause agreed faintly. "Mercy! To think we brought this upon ourselves unknowingly. Artifactor, now what do we do?"

Excellent question. Pity she didn't know the answer.

"I need more information before I can put together a plan. There's someone that I need to confer with, but I can't leave here until the other magicians come and I don't have a way of contacting him without showing up at his doorstep."

Krause's forehead furrowed in confusion. "But you know the cause?"

"I don't," she refuted grouchily. "I know that a man-made artifact is at the root cause of this, but I need to know *what kind* before I can figure out how to disarm or destroy it. Unfortunately, all my wand could tell me was 'origin unknown,' which means that this thing, whatever it is, isn't mentioned in any of the surviving records. At least, none of the records I have access to. Curse the luck."

"And this man you wish to see?" Krause pressed.

"A fellow Artifactor. He specializes in history and artifacts, so if anyone would have an idea of what this thing is, it would be him." Although going to see him would bring about its own set of problems and complications. But she would have to deal with that later. "I'll need to see and examine the ruins before I go. The more information I can bring him, the better."

"I can show you there," Decker offered instantly.

She gave him a nod of agreement. "I'll do that this afternoon."

As ruins went, these failed to impress her. They didn't come close to the size or architectural feats of Nickerchen at least. Of course, the shape of the buildings had been severely impacted by Chastain's occupants stealing rocks for every conceivable purpose over the generations. Who knew what it had looked like five generations ago?

But now, Sevana didn't see anything more than a pile of rocks with moss growing on top.

She stood on the worn path that led to the ruins and got a good long look at it from a distance. None of the walls stood higher than the top of her chin except one tower that stood on the far east side, which leaned badly toward the right. The stones here looked to be granite, matching the composition of most of the village, all of them cut square and about the size of her head. She tried to put an age to them and guessed seven hundred years at least.

In size, it seemed to be as big as Milby, so at one time this was probably a prosperous town. Why, she hadn't the faintest clue, as it didn't reside near any rivers or woods. Perhaps it sat along some ancient trade route?

Shaking her contemplation aside, she asked her guide, "Decker, are there any areas that are known to be dangerous or unstable?"

"No," he answered readily.

"Good. In that case, stay behind me," she ordered both the hunter and his wolf as she drew a wand and crystal out of her bag.

Decker slowly took a step away, eyes on the tools in her hands. "What are those?"

"Scanning and imaging tools."

His mouth formed a silent 'O' of understanding. "To give your consulting Artifactor a clear image of the ruins to study?"

"That and as a bargaining chip." She flashed him a slightly wry smile. "Jacen is a difficult man to deal with even at the best of times, but there's one thing that he can't resist: new knowledge. If I bring him a complete scan of something he's not seen before, he's more likely to talk to me than if I offer a bag of leprechaun gold."

"You're so sure he's not heard of these ruins before?"

"Fairly certain, yes," she responded absently as she slowly

stepped forward, wand held out unwavering in front of her as she tried to copy the image of every nook and cranny.

"How do you know?" Decker persisted, although he thankfully did so from behind as she had requested.

"There's a list of all ruins and ancient sites that have been studied," she answered with growing impatience. "This one isn't listed. I would have remembered it. Why are you asking so many questions?"

"Now how am I supposed to understand what's going on when you don't voluntarily explain anything?" he shot back dryly.

She heaved out an exaggerated sigh but kept her eyes on the task at hand. "You're as bad as Bel."

"Bel?" he repeated blankly. It took a second before it almost audibly clicked. "You call Prince Bellomi, *Bel?!*"

"You know, that's almost his reaction precisely when I said I'd call him that." Although he'd gotten used to it with astonishing speed.

After spluttering for a few seconds, Decker broke down into a low chuckle. "Well, I can see why he was so friendly with you now. It didn't make much sense when I saw him greet you, but you truly do treat him as a friend, don't you?"

"Don't get any strange ideas, Hunter," she retorted acerbically. "I am *not* huggable."

Decker laughed outright at that. "The prince feels otherwise."

"He's brain damaged. He got hit in the head too many times while training."

"If you say so," Decker responded, tone rich with laughter. Clearly, he didn't believe her.

Well, fine, that was his prerogative. But if he thought he could hug her and get away with it, he'd best be prepared to lose an arm or two. She meant what she said. She was *not* huggable. Bel only got by with it because he ambushed her.

She gave him a quick glance over her shoulder. Decker seemed… less strained than when she'd first met him. Probably because the man had actually gotten some sleep last night. With her charms on everyone, he no longer had the fear and worry of their safety hanging over his head. This was the first time she'd seen him truly smile, too.

"Decker, tell me something."

"Hmm?"

"Why are you always hanging around me?"

"Oh. That."

"Yes," she drawled. "That."

"Well, everyone made a unanimous decision and voted that I be available to you while you're here. Sort of like an assistant or a guide. There's a lot that you don't know about this area, after all, and we want to help you in whatever way we can."

So her suspicions were right. He *had* been put in charge of her. Well, this didn't bother her much. Decker reminded her strangely of Sarsen for some reason. Perhaps because the two men were rather similar in personality. She found it easy to get along with him and easy to boss him, so she had no objections to him sticking around.

"Errr, I'm not getting in your way, am I?"

Sevana snorted, amused at the concern in his voice. "I'll tell you when you do."

It was Decker's turn to snort. "Somehow, I didn't doubt that."

They kept up this banter over the next few hours as Sevana scanned every section of the ruins. She found a few symbols carved into the stones, most of them weathered almost beyond recognition, but she took several closer scans of them and hoped for the best. The day had waned into late afternoon before she finished. Fortunately, it didn't take more than a short hike to return to Chastain. No wonder the villagers used this place as a stone quarry of sorts, with it being so conveniently located.

Once they returned, Sevana waved Decker off so he could find dinner and she retreated back to her temporary workroom. But hunger soon drove her out again and she repeated her earlier actions of that morning as she went from one place to another and bought any food that tempted her stomach.

By sunset, she had returned to the evil fountain and sat there on the cobblestones, nursing a tankard of hot mulled cider. What she had told Decker and Krause earlier had been the truth. She couldn't make any plans until she knew exactly what she was dealing with. But that said, she didn't need to know details at this point to know when she had gotten in well over her head.

Letting out a disgruntled sigh, she took a healthy swallow of her cider and let the warmth flow through her. Mmm, good cider. She'd have to remember where she'd bought it and get more tomorrow.

Alright, what to do? She truly couldn't leave the villagers until other magicians arrived that could go out and fetch them home again. But sitting on her hands waiting idly didn't suit her. She couldn't go see Jacen—he lived a full day's travel from here. It put her too far from Chastain. Although the idiot would be plenty reachable if he would just let her put a clock in his area. Why he had to be so stubborn about his privacy, she had no idea.

No matter what Jacen might or might not know, no Artifactor or magician in the known world could defeat a level sixteen spell. They just didn't have enough power to do so on their own, not without creating a spell of a higher level—and such a thing wasn't possible. No matter how she thought about it, basic math and elementology still applied to the situation. It would take two casters, *at least*, to defeat this monstrosity and bring it back under control again.

Sevana shifted slightly to avoid having her whole backend become numb. Sitting cross-legged here on the cobblestones probably didn't count as the brightest of ideas. But she didn't feel like moving yet—despite her tingling legs. She just kept thinking that if she sat here staring long enough, a brilliant solution would just come to her and she wouldn't have to do this the hard way.

Her gut said otherwise.

Decker came to her side and dropped down onto his haunches without saying a word. For several moments they stared at the fountain in companionable silence, neither of them looking at the other. "You're stuck, aren't you?"

"Not exactly," she grumbled. "I can think of three possible solutions."

"But?" he encouraged.

"*But*…none of the solutions can be done alone." She heaved out a resigned sigh. Who was she trying to fool? "Stone the crows, I might as well face it. I'm going to have to split the commission."

"It's going to take two people?"

She propped her chin into both hands, balancing her elbows on her knees so that she hunched over. "I don't have enough power. Even borrowing the power of other elements, the castor of an incantation has to add their power into the mix as well to actually *activate* a spell. I cannot come up with anything that will defeat a sixteen level spell, not on my own. Even with another person it's going to be a mite tricky."

"How so?" Decker's brows were furrowed in a worried frown.

"Blending magic with someone else takes more than power. It takes complete trust in the other person's skills, their instincts, and a certain amount of experience in working with them."

Decker studied her profile for a moment before offering, "You sound as if you already have someone in mind."

"I do. Let's hope he's available." Otherwise she'd call in Master, who was harder to deal with. Shifting to one hip, she dug around in her pouch until she found her miniature Caller. Setting it on the ground in front of her, she enunciated clearly, "Sarsen."

Several seconds ticked by before the Caller lifted its head and assumed Sarsen's rather lanky features. *"Sev! Now this is a surprise. You hardly ever contact me."*

"Got a job I could use an assist on. You free?"

"The last time you called me in for 'help' I was up to my eyebrows in espionage, politics and frozen mobs."

"Is that a complaint I hear?" she demanded wryly.

"Sweet mercy, no! Most fun I've had in ages. So what category does this job fall into? Fun, dangerous, or dangerously fun?"

"Yes," she told him seriously.

"Excellent. I'll be there as soon as I can. Where are you, anyway?"

"Chastain Village."

"Where?" he asked in bewilderment.

"Windamere-Kindin border," she elaborated with forced patience. "A little west of Vanorman."

"Ahh. I know Vanorman. Alright, I should be able to find you

quickly enough. It'll take me three days to get there, though. I'm at Master's right now."

Oh? "In that case, if he has any dragon's breath or a wind element of its same power level, bring it with you." She had a hunch she would need it.

"You want me to filch from Master's stores?" the twenty-nine year old objected in true horror, making a sign with his hands that warded off evil. *"Don't you remember what happened to us the last time we did that?"*

She did. Vividly. With a grim smile she assured him, "Trust me, when he learns what we're up against, he won't mind."

Sarsen paused, his miniature looking up at her in suspicion. *"Sev...just how bad is it?"*

"If this goes wrong, it'll rearrange the landscape of eastern Windamere."

His hand flew in a quick gesture, making a silent prayer of safety. *"I'll raid his storerooms tonight before leaving. Just call Master and explain why. I trust you'll fill me in completely when I get there?"*

"You're not going to be of much help otherwise. And I'm half-hoping that you'll think of a solution that I didn't."

"Me? Out-think the Artifactor prodigy?"

"Hey, miracles happen!"

"Now I know you're desperate. Call Master. I'll pack and get there in two days."

The Caller went still and she picked it up and plopped it back into her pocket. She wanted to get off this cold, hard stone and in a more padded chair before calling Master. He'd keep her talking for at least an hour on the details, knowing him. Rising, she stretched both arms over her chest before bending and retrieving her ceramic tankard from the ground. "I'm going to bed. After all, I'll have to get up early and go to someone's rescue. If the gods are kind, or at least listening, it won't be another squawking child either."

Decker grimaced in sympathy. "From your lips to the gods' ears. In that case, good night, Artifactor."

Master foiled her plan to get to bed early by keeping her awake for three hours talking about the problem. He was worried, justifiably so, and traded information and ideas with her freely on possible solutions. In the end, he gave Sarsen free reign over his storerooms and let them have whatever they thought they would need. She would think him generous if he hadn't looked so obviously shaken by her descriptions.

Of course, Decker woke her up early that morning to play fetch. The dreamer had gone to the island of Ence, of all places (why would anyone dream of that gods-forsaken place?). Ence sat on the very eastern edge of Windamere. In fact, any further, and you fell right into the ocean. It took most of the day to fetch the old woman back, and while grateful for the quick rescue, the matron did *not* appreciate the method. Sevana's mini-skimmer scared the living daylight right out of her and she clung and prayed the entire way home.

By the time they touched down in the main square, two hours or so of daylight were left, and not enough of the day for her to really dig into the problem and do any real work. The skimmer made soft scraping sounds as its full weight came to rest on the cobblestones and the two women became almost swamped with people. Mostly the old woman's family, judging by the hugs, tears, and overlapping inquiries of "are you alright?!"

Sevana quickly unbuckled and wiggled her way through the press of bodies until she could get free. Once there, she took in a deep breath and looked around for Decker. The next time that he sent her harrowing off on a mission to rescue someone, he needed to *warn her* they were afraid of heights!

She spotted him quickly, coming toward her from the Hall's main steps. Following him on either side were two men she didn't recognize with Gid trailing along behind the group. One of them middle-aged, scrawny looking, with a receding hairline and the thickest glasses she had ever seen on a human being. He looked well-dressed, however, and neat as a pin. More interesting, he had a magic pouch resting on his belt. Magician of some sort?

The other man stood a head taller than either of the men he walked with—quite the feat as Decker couldn't be considered 'short' by anyone's standards—but had a very massive and solid build , as if he were a walking barrel. His skin had tanned so dark as to almost make him look Sa Kaoan, but his bright blond hair and blue eyes marked him as Windameran through and through. He also dressed impeccably well and had not one, but two magic pouches riding on his left hip.

Sevana perked up hopefully. The promised magicians, perhaps?

"Sevana," Decker greeted. "Good work."

"You shall pay for not warning me she's afraid of heights," she informed him darkly.

He froze and glanced at the old woman, still buried in relatives, before asking slowly, "What if I didn't know?"

"You'll still pay," she growled, hours of pent-up frustration leaking out.

Decker slumped, muttering, "I reckoned as much," before heaving a great sigh. "What if I buy you dinner?"

After skipping lunch and having a very measly breakfast, food sounded like a sublime plan. "I will magnanimously forgive you if you do so. For now, who are your tagalongs?"

Decker turned and gestured to Glasses with an open palm. "This is Danel Goffin, Wizard and—" Decker turned to indicate the man standing on the other side "—Piotr Roland, Wizard. Gentlemen, Artifactor Sevana Warren."

Goffin took a step forward and offered her a hand, which she reciprocated, and found his grip to be pleasantly firm without being overpowering. "Artifactor Warren, it's a pleasure. Prince Bellomi came to me personally the day you left and asked that I come here immediately."

"I'm glad you did," she answered truthfully. Flying off to the rescue had proven to be a major pain. Sevana would willingly hand that chore over to someone else. She released her grip and offered a hand to Roland. "Wizard Roland."

"Artifactor Warren," he greeted in a surprisingly high voice, grip somewhat flimsy. "Pleasure. Hunter Decker just showed us your tracking board and the charms you put on everyone. It's a wonderfully simplistic system. Thank you for setting it up and making our jobs easier."

"I was trying to make *my* life easier," she responded dryly. "After all, I had no idea how long it would take for anyone to show up and take over. But I assume that I don't need to explain the system to either of you?" That had better be the case, otherwise they weren't magicians of a high enough caliber to be trusted with any job, much less one of this magnitude. But both men just gave her a smile and nod of confirmation, not at all worried. Satisfied, she waved a hand toward her temporary workroom. "Then feel free to move it to wherever you need it to be. I won't miss it."

"We certainly will," Roland assured her. "However, perhaps you can explain just what kind of magic we're up against? Pierpoint gave us some information, but he didn't know much, and I think we need to know what's causing this."

They certainly did. "Over dinner," she said firmly. "I'm famished."

With two other magicians at the village's beck and call, Sevana didn't have a rude pre-dawn awakening and so slept until the sun had properly risen. It made for a much better rising and she didn't feel homicidal upon opening her eyes, just grumpy. Shuffling around, she managed to get dressed, put her hair up into a very messy bun, and find breakfast without knocking anything over or breaking anything. But with a happy belly and some of that amazing hot cider in hand, she felt ready to get to work.

She expected Sarsen to come in at some point tonight or early tomorrow, and when he came, he would have a lot of questions. Right now, she only had answers to some of them. So she took some of her most sensitive tools, her notebook, and a cushion (she did not intend to sit on that hard cobblestone all day) and went to the fountain to work.

The sun slowly climbed high in the sky, moving the shadows around the courtyard and warming her up pleasantly as the sunlight touched her. Sevana blocked out all the distractions—the smells of food being prepared, the sounds of people walking around and talking to each other, the clatter of carts and horses crossing the area, all of it. With single-minded determination, she focused on the task in front of her.

Without warning, a hand landed on her shoulder and she dropped the wand she held, upset the notebook open in her lap, and instinctively reached for the sword at her side before she recognized the man leaning over her. "Decker! For the love of all mercy, *don't do that!*"

"I didn't mean to startle you," he said patiently, "But I called your name three times and you didn't even twitch."

She put a hand to her thumping heart to make sure it would not beat its way out of her chest. "You nearly gave me heart failure."

"It's well past the lunch hour." He sank onto his haunches in front of her, a half-smile on his face. "I was afraid with the way you were focused, you'd work right through it. And Master Krause and I are rather hoping you'd tell us what you found."

Now that he mentioned it…. She peered up at the sky with squinting eyes and discovered the sun had already headed for the western horizon. It had to be two in the afternoon at least. Had she really been sitting here for seven hours? In spite of the thick cushion under her, her whole backend felt numb. Yes, past time to move. With a groan, she put a knee under her and rolled upwards. Decker offered her a hand, but she chose instead to put a hand on his arm and use him as a lever to push her way up. Wincing at the stiffness, she said aloud, "Mental note: bring a proper chair tomorrow."

"Did you discover anything?" he asked her.

"Not much, which in and of itself tells me a great deal."

Decker blinked at her, eyebrows furrowing in confusion as if he didn't quite know how to take that comment.

"Where's Krause?" she asked him, not wanting to repeat the inevitable explanation.

"Oh, he's there." Decker pointed toward the one inn on this side of the village that served lunch. The ombudsman stood on the porch, obviously waiting for them.

"Good." Picking up everything, she shoved it all back into her bag, except the cushion. That she tucked under her arm before walking slowly toward Krause. Her legs, back and buttocks tingled painfully as the blood started flowing again. Oww. Yes, she'd definitely bring a chair tomorrow.

No one said anything as she took a step up into the inn and crossed into the dimmer and cooler room. After baking under a warm sun most of the day, the environment felt pleasant to her overheated body and she unconsciously smiled. The tavern here had a solid plank floor, no sawdust, and highly polished round tables scattered everywhere. The bar that stretched the length of the room held no customers, and its polished surface shone from being recently cleaned. For that matter, the whole room looked as if it hadn't seen a single patron the entire day, but instead stood ready for tonight.

Krause took a table near the bar with all the ease and familiarity of a regular patron (which he might very well be for all she knew) and waved them to join him. Sevana deposited everything in her hands onto the surface of the nearest table before she eased into the chair at his left, not at all sure how her backend would feel about sitting on something solid again, but the angle of it felt fine. She sank back against the wood and relaxed.

A serving girl that could have been Krause's daughter with those looks came out and took their order of "anything hot and easy to dish up" and disappeared back into the kitchen. Krause turned to Sevana with an eager smile and asked, "What have you discovered?"

"Not much," she admitted easily.

"But she said that tells her something," Decker added, still bemused on this point. "Care to explain that?"

Master had trained her from an early age that part of being an Artifactor was explaining things to your clients. After all, they paid your wage, so you owed them explanations on the job you did. She'd gotten better at doing so over the years, but had never changed her opinion that it was troublesome. With a resigned sigh, she started from the beginning.

"I explained to you earlier that an artifact buried in the fountain was the cause of all of this." Both men nodded impatiently. "I also explained that the power level of it is such that I alone can't break it, which is why I called a colleague in, yes? Good, we're on the same page. Today, I wanted to get more information on the origin of the artifact and come up with a few plans of attack on how to defeat it. This is what I discovered.

"First, the age of the artifact and the stone around it dates it at the eighth century, about the time that Windamere was re-taken by Gadon Dragonmanovich and made into the country we know today. This is very, very interesting."

"How?" Krause asked, absolutely riveted.

Just how much magical history did they teach in schools? Probably not enough for him to follow her explanation. Assuming, of course, that he remembered something he learned forty years ago, which might be stretching the bounds of credulity.

"There was a time when magic had very few limits, a time when magicians made their own spells and the class of Artifactors didn't exist. We magicians refer to this as 'the time of great magic' because that's exactly what it is. We have legends, stories, partial histories and such that tell of amazing feats that the magicians of history were able to do. But they were also done in a time of great political upheaval. I'm sure you learned in school about the multitude of nations that began, were conquered, fell to plague or pestilence, or merged with other countries through marriage. Well, all of that shifting about destroyed records or caused them to be lost. And then, at the very end of the eighth century, that great plague swept through all of Mander and wiped out half of the population. I'm afraid the magicians were hit the hardest by it."

"Wait, explain that," Decker requested, just as fascinated as Krause. "I've never heard that the magicians were hit so hard by the plague."

"Of course they were," she said in exasperation. "Think, man. If you suddenly contracted a deadly disease, what would you do?"

"Go see a doctor."

"And when he can't help you?"

"See a magician," he said in sudden understanding.

"They were infected more than anyone else because every single person in their area with the plague came into contact with them. Most magicians didn't have a cure for it either, and so died of it as well." Except the magicians that lived in remote enough regions to not contract the plague or were selfish enough to hide away and let humanity rot. "Many, many techniques and secrets that were passed down from master to student were lost entirely because of this. Worse, some numbskull hit upon the brilliant idea that torching things would keep the sickness from spreading, so whole libraries and record rooms went up in flames."

"Ah," Krause raised a finger hesitantly in the air. "That's not true?"

"Well, it is," she felt forced to admit, "But hot water and strong soap does the job just as well, you know? And if it doesn't come into direct contact with the person, then it's highly likely it's not carrying the disease."

Krause and Decker exchanged a speaking look, their expressions saying *oops*. Which poor blighter's house had they torched in order to keep a disease from spreading? Rolling her eyes, Sevana moved on. "At any rate, we the magical community lost more in sheer knowledge than I can begin to describe. The whole system of magic that our ancestors used became lost almost overnight. The survivors and newly awakened magicians had to experiment and forge their own system of using magic as the old ways no longer made any sense to them."

"So the magic that you use now," Decker summed up quietly, "is entirely different."

"As day is from night," she confirmed grimly. "That artifact dates to the time right before the plague spread, so it was likely used only once or twice before being stored away. For some strange reason, it had been sealed inside of a stone as well. Perhaps to keep it out of the wrong hands? The purpose of doing so died with the creator. At any rate, it's lain dormant until you people moved it and fulfilled the conditions it needed." She could tell from their blank expressions she would have to explain *that* too. "Any magic used, no matter how ancient, has certain conditions that must be met before the magic is activated. This artifact seems to need reflected light—sunlight, in this case—running water, and direction."

"That," Krause said emphatically. "That's the part that I don't understand. What direction?! We haven't given it any!"

"You have," she denied flatly. "This part is half-conjecture on my end, but it makes sense from what I know of ancient artifacts. There are two things you must understand. Magic is not stagnant, like a tool, but is a living thing itself. It's as alive as water or wind. It likes to *move*. It likes to be used. This artifact was lying in the ground for six hundred years and was dying to fulfill its purpose. It leaped at the chance as soon as the conditions had been met. And I'd lay good money that to use the artifact, one would simply picture within their mind's eye the place that they wanted to go in order to direct it."

Decker slumped so that his head hit the table's surface. Against the wood he complained, "Even in *dreams*?"

"As I said, magic likes to be used," she responded tartly. "It might be overreaching its designed bounds, but it's also not unusual for magical things to develop quirks over the years. I have a pair of mud-off boots that now rejects not only mud, but any dirt whatsoever." They were rather fun to wear, too, as it felt like she walked on air. "And those boots are only eight years old! Can you imagine what would happen to something that's several hundred years old?"

"I don't need to imagine," Decker grumbled.

"While all of this is fascinating, does it help in any way?" Krause asked.

"I won't really know until I can consult Jacen, our historian in the Artifactor community." She looked up with a smile as the girl came back with their food, efficiently plopping it down in front of them with a clink of china. Mmmm, it smelled heavenly. Not bothered that she didn't recognize anything on her plate, she picked up a spoon and dug right in.

"Did you find a way to stop it?" Krause pressed, ignoring the plate set in front of him.

She had to swallow the mouthful she had—pleasantly spicy— before she could respond.

"Yes and no. Apparently, the maker gave his toy a shield to erect while it was in use to prevent someone from tampering with it accidentally. Smart, in a way. I imagine that if someone did knock the thing over or hit it with another spell while it was transporting, the result wouldn't be pretty. But that makes our job harder. We have to get around that shield first. Once we do that, we can either work a spell directly against it to counteract its elements and neutralize the artifact's power—"

"Or?" Decker prompted impatiently when she took a long pull from her tankard.

"Or we wear away the power that it's using slowly and remove one of its conditions so that it can no longer work," she finished. Just how they would manage that, she didn't know offhand. She had a few notions to try out, though, assuming Sarsen didn't come up with something better once he got here. "At that point, I'm going to take great delight and pleasure in digging that artifact free and taking it apart. We hardly ever find a still functioning artifact to examine."

"I thought you said the old magic didn't make sense to you anymore," Krause objected, still ignoring his plate of food.

"Well, not all of it," she admitted with a blasé shrug. "But given enough time and experimentation, we're able to figure out a great deal. Those charms you're wearing around your neck are a result of such research."

Krause and Decker both touched the two small metal charms with surprise and looked at them far more carefully than when she'd put them on the first time.

She ate peaceably while they mulled over everything she had said. Eventually, Krause picked up his spoon and started eating as well.

"After lunch, what do you plan to do?" the ombudsman inquired.

"Nothing more I can do at this moment," she denied, seriously considering finding something to satisfy her sweet tooth. Apple tarts sounded good. "Right now, I'm just waiting on Sarsen to arrive."

Sarsen had more or less stolen her idea of using clouds to fuel an airborne vehicle to create his own version of transportation. Instead of designing something he sat on, however, he had made a very long glider that let him hang underneath the wings. He claimed that because his glider didn't weigh as much and had a more streamlined design, it could go faster than either her skimmer or mini-skimmer. She hadn't yet had the chance to race him and prove him wrong.

His glider didn't have the same on-the-spot landing ability as the mini-skimmer, so he came in along the main road, lowering his legs from the back harness and running along, slowly coming to a stop. With such a showy entrance, most of the village came running to see who approached, alerting Sevana as they went.

She had to push through a crowd of spectators, ruthlessly using her elbows to move people bodily aside, and even then she had to squeeze through. With a grunt of effort, she almost exploded out of the crowd and into open air. By that time, Sarsen had unhooked himself from the glider and taken off the goggles he wore while flying, letting them hang around his neck. He waved when he saw her and started jogging forward.

"Sev!"

Decker, from behind her, leaned forward slightly and asked in an undertone, "He's close enough to you to call you by nickname?"

"We trained under the same master."

"Ahhhh."

Sarsen hadn't changed much since she'd last seen him, back

when Bel and company had finally left. He wore black leathers over his lanky frame, probably to protect him from the chilly wind, wiry black hair still cropped razor-short, and dark brown skin looking paler after going through the winter months indoors. His beard was stubbly and his eyes bloodshot, both signs that he hadn't slept well since she'd called him. He slowed to a stop in front of her, looking her over from head to toe, eyes strangely penetrating. "Tell me you didn't try tackling that thing on your own."

"Do I look suicidal to you?" she retorted dryly. "I gathered information and made a rough plan of attack while waiting. Well, that and drank mulled cider. It's quite divine here. You must try it."

Sarsen let out a breath of relief. "Good. Master beat it into my head before I left that we are *not* to try and deal with this alone. In fact, he said if we could borrow the help of other magicians that would be wise."

"There's two more in town," Decker offered.

"Thank mercy." Sarsen belatedly held out a hand in greeting. "Sarsen Vashti, Artifactor."

"Decker," the hunter responded, accepting the offered hand. "I'm one of the hunters of this village."

"He's also our volun-told guide while we're here," Sevana added, still amused by that turn of events. Turning, she spotted Krause headed their way at a quick walk, girth shaking under the force of his pace. "And that is the Ombudsman of Chastain Village, and acting mayor, Krause."

Krause practically beamed up at Sarsen as he held out a hand. "A pleasure, sir. You must be Sevana's colleague that she was expecting."

"Sarsen Vashti, Artifactor," Sarsen introduced himself again patiently. "Pleasure is mine, sir."

"Now that we've made nice, let's get to work," Sevana suggested, wanting to move the pleasantries along. "Get that contraption of yours out of the road first, though."

Sarsen shot her challenging smile. "A contraption that is superior to yours."

"That is a point you have not yet proven, my friend." An

anticipatory tingle went up her spine. After the fountain was properly slayed and defeated, she had every intention of challenging Sarsen to a race.

"Some things are self-evident," Sarsen informed her with mock-gentleness, as if explaining a difficult thing to a child.

"Ha!"

Chuckling, he went back to his glider, shifting it about by the nose and rolling it well free of the road. As he did so, Krause leaned in closer and asked quietly, "How long have you two known each other?"

She opened her mouth, frowned, and mentally added it up. "Thirteen years."

Krause gave her a knowing smile and nod. "That's why you act like siblings."

They were very much like siblings, actually, despite having no blood relation whatsoever. But Master treated all of his apprentices like his own children, so developing such a relationship didn't surprise anyone.

"But you're not actually related…." Decker sounded unsure of that even as he said it.

She gave the man an exasperated look. "I'm short, blond, and fair while he's tall, lanky, and looks Sa Kaon. How can you possibly think we're related?"

Decker raised his hands in surrender, not even daring to comment.

Sarsen came back to them with two large bags slung over his shoulder, one of which Decker stepped forward immediately to help carry. Sarsen handed it over with a thankful nod but didn't slow his pace. "Alright, Sev, tell me some good news."

"I already did," she replied as she turned and started shoving her way back inside the village. Seeing as how the show was over, most people made way for them automatically.

"What, that you didn't start working on your own?" Sarsen's mouth crimped into an unhappy line. "Is that really the only good news you can share?"

She gave a shrug, wishing she actually had something but bad news to report. "I researched extensively yesterday and this morning and analyzed the fountain as much as I could. Here's what I know: the artifact is hidden in one of the stones that make up the central fountain for the courtyard. It's dated at the end of the eighth century—"

Sarsen winced at that.

She caught the expression and paused mid-sentence, clapping in mock-applause. "Oh good boy, you actually remember enough about history to know that's a bad thing!"

He rolled his eyes in a clear bid for patience. "I'm not completely hopeless when it comes to history, Sev."

"Can't prove that by me. Anyway, continuing on—the artifact works on the elements of its own power, reflected light, and running water. Hence the power level of sixteen. There's also a very strong shield up around it at all times."

"Probably to prevent accidents from happening while its magic is active," Sarsen said aloud in a rhetorical tone.

"That was my guess as well. But the shield poses a serious problem. Getting around it will not be an easy task."

Sarsen gave her a long look as they headed toward the main square. "Is this easier or harder than Bel's curse?"

"I'm still debating that."

Krause, following along behind them, piped up. "Was the prince's curse truly so terrible?"

Sarsen looked over his shoulder long enough to answer, "In terms of power, no. Bellomi's curse was somewhere around a ten when Sevana came in. But because it had been attached to him so long, we had to borrow the power of a dragon in order to break it."

"It's not the power levels that make a job easier or harder," Sevana couldn't help but add. "It's the danger level involved. Right now, I don't know which one I would rather deal with: a man-eating dragon with a touchy temper or an equally cantankerous artifact with a high power level."

For some reason, this made Sarsen chuckle. "Well, Sev, you were complaining you were bored."

"Not *that* bored," she grumbled under her breath.

In the next moment, they rounded the building and came into the square, letting Sarsen get his first proper look at the fountain. Unable to resist seeing it for himself, he pulled out a wand from his belt pouch, pointing it at the fountain and activating the spell: "—⌣ ⌔O⌒⌣."

Numbers and words in pure white light traced themselves in the air right in front of his nose. He read them as quickly as the wand could write them, expression becoming grim and set. "You said you had a rough plan, Sev."

"Either find a way to break the shield first, separately, so we can attack the artifact directly, or we attack the elements that are attached to the fountain and slowly wear out its power source."

Sarsen let out a long breath as he put his wand away again. "That's a very rough plan."

"Needs refining," she admitted with an unconcerned shrug. "But I couldn't do much planning until I knew what Master gave you. Let's find a place to sit and spread the goodies out so I know what we have to work with."

They retreated to Sevana's temporary workroom in the Hall, and mysteriously gathered more people along the way. Goffin and Roland came out of thin air, as far as she could tell, but she had no objection to them taking a seat at the long table as they would likely be drawn into this fairly soon. Why Krause and Decker wanted to listen in too she didn't understand at all. Most of their conversation would be in very technical, magical terms that would go straight over both men's heads. If they thought she would stop and explain every little thing to them, they were sorely mistaken.

Sarsen took a look around the room as he stepped in, taking in the size and shape of it, the things Sevana had already brought in and scattered along one end, and the map of the village with all of its magical markers that hadn't been moved yet. He gave an approving smile. "This is quite nice to work in."

Krause seemed relieved. "I'm glad it suits you, Artifactor Vashti."

"Sarsen, please. And yes, better to work here than other jobs I've had. Well." He slung the bag on his shoulder into an out-of-the-way corner before motioning Decker forward. The hunter handed over the bag he carried and Sarsen started to unpack it even as he explained to Sevana, "You told Master some of the elements of the fountain, but you weren't sure then what elements belonged to the shield and what belonged to the fountain."

She nodded sourly. "They're blended very well together. It took me most of the morning to be sure which was which. I take it he threw in a little of everything?"

"All but the kitchen sink." Sarsen listed them off as he sat different glass bottles and jars on the table in a neat row. "Fairy's kiss, acorn from a 1,000-year-old tree, piece of a fallen star, a word from the Book of Truth—"

Sevana had a hard time biting back a gasp at that. Her eyes flew wide as she stared at the miniature leather book on the table. A word from the Book of Truth had a ridiculously high power level, partially because of its rarity (it had been crafted during the time of great magic) and partially because it took considerable skill to lift it from the book's pages. "Master had one of those?!"

"Very well hidden," Sarsen informed her, still looking a little awed. "He said use it only if it's absolutely necessary, and if we don't use it, he *will* come hunting for us if we don't give it back."

She had an impulse to say she had used it and then squirrel it away somewhere.

"Behave, Sev," Sarsen warned her. "You know he'll find out. He always does."

She let out a long, disappointed sigh. "You're right. Alright, what else?"

"Stillness of a moonless night and shiranui."

"Moonless night was used as part of the shield," she informed him absently.

"What, really?" Sarsen let out a wordless growl. "It took considerable digging to find that, too."

"This is Master's storerooms we're talking about. It takes digging to find *anything*." Master could not claim to be organized in any sense of the word. She was the queen of cleanliness in comparison to him. Sevana had a working theory that the man kept accepting multiple apprentices just so he always had a cleaning crew on hand.

Goffin cleared his throat to get their attention. "Sevana, might we know what the shield's elements are?"

"As I said, stillness of a moonless night, dwarven-made mountain stone—"

"Wait, wait," Roland protested, both hands up. "The fountain is made from *dwarven* stone?"

"The ancient ruins lying off to the northeast of here?" she said tartly. "Yes, that's all dwarven stone. It's a minor fortune lying about and not a person in here recognized it for what it was. It's also the reason why the shield around the artifact stayed intact. If they had used any other stone to complete that fountain with, the shield would not have had the energy it needed to activate."

Krause held up a hand. "Ah, ancient tales said that dwarven stone would hold up to any amount of weather without wearing away. Is that really true?"

"You looked at the ruins, didn't you?" Sevana responded, losing patience quickly. "It didn't seem odd to you that all of the stone there still had sharp, prominent edges?"

Krause looked sheepish and couldn't quite meet her eyes. "We didn't think the ruins that old."

Sevana lifted her eyes to the heavens, asking how she ended up working with such ignoramuses.

Sarsen, a kinder and more patient soul than she, said gently, "It's dwarven stone. It's very, very expensive and hard to find in this area of the country. It had to have been shipped all the way from the Shinogee Mountains to get here. If I were you, after all this was over, I'd hire an expert to go through those ruins and dig out anything else that has been buried in them. Then, once you know it's safe to do so, I would take the ruins apart and sell all the stonework before word of this gets out and you have robbers show up to do the work for you."

Goffin, proving to have good business sense, immediately turned to Krause with a professional smile. "I'd be happy to go take a look while I'm here and see if there's anything else dangerous hidden."

"There are at least three things I saw," Sevana told him absently, already focused back on the job at hand. "Anyway, the last element is moonlit water. The stillness of a moonless night and the moonlit water tend to blend together, but I'm fairly certain that they are not directly connected."

Sarsen turned to her with his forehead furrowing. "*Fairly* certain?"

She hesitated before admitting grudgingly, "I'm not entirely sure. I believe that they were meant to blend together to keep the shield attached to the artifact. But there's something about the way it's designed…" she trailed off, still not quite sure what bothered her or why. "I feel like I'm missing something."

"I'll take a look," he promised. "Maybe I'll see it. Alright, so, with those elements and the ones of the artifact, what does that leave us? The acorn we can toss out."

Seeing the two villager's confusion, Goffin explained in an aside, "It clashes with the water elements. It wouldn't work well."

Both men made silent "ah" sounds as Sevana and Sarsen sorted out what was on the table into *useful* and *not useful* piles. "Fairy's kiss will blend well, as will the word from the Book of Truth—"

"—although I'd rather not use that if we don't absolutely have to," Sarsen put in.

"—which leaves us with the shiranui from Master," Sevana finished. "Plus the captured sunlight and flask of sulfur mud from the Mudlands that I have."

Roland leaned over the table to peer at the bottled mud. "Now when did you have a chance to get that? It's ridiculously hard to buy on the market."

"When I was still working on the solution to Bel's curse, I took him there to test something and stocked up while I could." She said this as if it didn't mean anything, but she could tell from the gleam in Roland's eyes that she had caught his interest. "I have a few other flasks in my storerooms, if you're interested?"

"We'll talk prices after this," he promised firmly.

Sarsen poked her in the ribs, making her jump. "Will you focus?"

Ignoring her dark scowl, he pointed at the useable pile. "Now, if we're aiming on taking down that shield first, I suggest we use some sort of combination of shiranui, mud from the Mudlands, and captured sunlight."

Sevana held up a hand in a staying motion. "Wait, Sarsen. Don't get ahead of things. We don't know what will happen if we break the shield."

He opened his mouth, paused, and subsided into a thoughtful hum as he stared blankly at the ceiling.

Decker cleared his throat. "You said there was another Artifactor you wanted to speak with, a historian that specializes in these things. Why? I mean, you sound as if you know what to do."

She shook her head in denial. "There are too many unquantified facets to this problem. How strongly is the shield tied to the artifact? By destroying it, do we destroy the artifact as well? Does it have some sort of fail-safe where attacking one part will make it transport, or burn, or do something else entirely? Can we use a spell that is only slightly stronger to attack with? Or will it be too weak to take down the shield? If not, will it cause a magical backlash that will destroy half the village?"

"You see our hesitation," Sarsen added, taking pity on their unease at Sevana's words. "We don't want to do anything, or try something when we only have half the information and we're guessing at the other half. Jacen—the other Artifactor—might or might not know anything, but we still need to discuss this with him. He might know something, or he might be able to help us figure out more. We reckon it's worth the aggravation to research as much as we can before we tackle your fountain."

"By all means," Krause choked out, face ashen, visions of destroyed villages dancing in his head.

"Until then, I take it we're counting on you two to keep track of everyone and rescue them when they need it?" Sarsen asked the magicians sitting at the table.

"That we will," Roland assured him.

"Good. Well, it's too late to leave tonight, so why don't we go to

Jacen's tomorrow?"

Sevana smiled at him sweetly. "We can even take our own vehicles. How about I race you there?"

A feral smile lit up Sarsen's face at the open challenge. "Mixing business with pleasure, Sev?"

"Always."

They flew directly north toward Denniston Forest and the Belen-Kindin border. Sevana pushed *Putter* to its absolute limits, flying far faster than prudence dictated, and she stayed neck and neck with Sarsen the entire way. The way the air whipped around her felt exhilarating like she had never experienced before. She caught herself laughing aloud several times just from the adrenaline rush.

They reached Jacen's place in about half the time it should have taken. Sevana navigated *Putter* to land on a slight knoll outside the front door in a small circular motion, settling down with an easy bump and short skid on the slick grass. Sarsen, of course, had to come in even easier and used up much more ground in order to land. He came to a stop about five feet ahead of her, on the road that led up to the gated door, unbuckling the harness as he completely rolled to a stop.

"I won!" she called to him as she climbed off the mini-skimmer.

Sarsen stopped with his hands on the last set of buckles and frowned up at her. "What are you talking about? We got here the same time!"

"I landed a good fifteen seconds before you did," she pointed out victoriously.

"The landing doesn't count!"

"Who says? If you wanted to only count airtime, you should have said so from the beginning!"

He lowered his goggles to give her a dark glower. "We're racing on the way back. No way I'm letting this cheap victory of yours slide."

She gave him a cheeky grin. "Fine by me." As she waited for

him to get completely free, she grabbed the bag with her notes and the scans she'd taken, slinging it casually over one shoulder. Then she took a long look around the area.

Place looked as she'd remembered, with the ridiculous gates guarding his front door. Jacen, like most Artifactors, chose to live near virgin forest and have access to a variety of natural elements. The four story brick building—which had all the size of a warehouse—sat right on the edge of the woods, the main door facing open grassland. He must have had quite the challenge shipping *that* much red brick here to build his house with, especially since it sat far removed from the nearest village.

The 'gates' were actually tall columns of white sculptures that resembled two fearsome warriors in battle armor with a sword clutched in front of them. They stood as tall as the building. Jacen had put them there to discourage visitors, and most of the time, it worked like a charm.

Sarsen joined her on the knoll and she fell in step with him, crossing to the narrow stone walkway that led straight to the front door.

"Which personality do you think we'll meet today?"

Her companion grimaced. "He's got four of them. It's anyone's guess."

Jacen had been cursed as a small child, and while the curse had been broken, it had done unexpected damage to his mind. His personality had split into four different types, each radically different than the next, and no one knew why he switched between one personality and the next. Most people found him unsettling to be around, hence why he chose to live in relative isolation, but to those that knew him, he was a good man and an excellent Artifactor. Sevana had only encountered three of his personalities so far and she usually found her visits with him to be entertaining, in one way or another.

They stopped right in front of the two statues and looked up. A warding spell had been put around the property, and aside from breaking through it (which Sevana would do if necessary), the only way to get past it was to answer the questions the statues put to them.

When they came close enough, the statues came alive and their eyes opened with a grating sound as stone moved against stone, heads turning in jerky intervals to see the visitors standing below them. In a deep voice that vibrated the air, they asked in unison, "You who have traveled far to reach this gate, do you seek passage to the Artifactor's realm?"

Sevana blinked. "Did he change the greeting? They didn't say that last time."

Sarsen shrugged, unconcerned by this, and answered them. "We do."

"How may we know thee as friends?"

Huh. They hadn't said that last time either. Sevana no longer knew if she had the right answer to get past these louts or not. She glanced at Sarsen who looked just as confused and unsure of what to say.

Thinking quickly, she offered, "We bring him knowledge he seeks and secrets that he can reveal."

Either her imagination was playing tricks on her, or did she see a hint of a smile behind those sculpted beards? "You may pass."

Well, they'd apparently liked that answer. Sevana passed through with an uncertain look overhead, not quite sure what Jacen had been thinking when he'd made those things. "Melodramatic, much?"

"He's always had a certain flare for that," Sarsen observed, sounding resigned.

"Well, sure, but isn't this over the top?" Shaking it off, she lengthened her stride. The walkway wound around a few large plots of cultivated beds, none of which held flowers, but all sorts of different herbs. It'd still been arranged in an appealing way, inviting the eye to stop and look a little longer. Considerable care had been taken to make this closed-in yard clean and neat. Come to think of it, one of his personalities was the overly helpful sort…it would be just like him to obsess over appearances like this.

They reached the front door of the house—a normal wooden one painted white this time—and Sarsen reached out to bang the brass knocker. It clanged in loud peals, leaving no doubt that anyone inside could hear it. For several seconds, they stood there with no sign of being heard, but then the sound of locks being undone came faintly through the wood. In the next instant, the door was jerked roughly open.

Jacen stood in the doorway, black hair tied up in a high ponytail as usual, skin pale from lack of sunlight, his usual white coat smeared with all sorts of colors and metal filings from whatever he had been working on. The outright glare on his face didn't match his usual expression though.

Sevana tensed up. One could not, of course, tell by looking at a person from the outside which personality was in control. At least, not at first. But their expressions and mannerisms would give it away soon enough. This expression hinted strongly that Jacen didn't inhabit his mind just now.

"Ah, hello?" Sarsen ventured uncertainly, obviously picking up that they were being faced with one of the other personalities. "We're here to speak with Jacen about—"

"No," Not-Jacen said vehemently before he slammed the door shut in their faces.

She'd encountered this personality before. "Jaston," she said in recognition.

"Jaston," Sarsen agreed in exasperation. "Why did we have to meet his grumpy personality straight off?"

"He tends to switch between one and the other fairly quickly," Sevana muttered to herself, trying to be hopeful about the situation. "Maybe if we give it a few minutes and try again, we'll get Jacen."

"You know that's wishful thinking."

"Shut it. I'm trying to think positive. Otherwise we've come all this way for nothing and we'll have to try again tomorrow."

They waited impatiently in front of the door, not speaking for several long minutes before Sarsen blew out a breath and raised his hand, knocking again.

It took a minute, as it had before, as if Jacen had retreated to some other section of the house and had to come back to the door. He even had to undo the same locks again. This time, however, he greeted them in an entirely different way. Jaston had obviously switched with another personality as instead of a growl and a slamming door, Not-Jacen lounged up against the doorframe, hip canted, arm braced so that he *leaned* toward them, eyes sultry, and gave his guests a head-to-toe scan. "Well, hello Sexy—" he purred.

Sarsen grabbed the door handle and roughly slammed it shut.

Sevana spluttered, staring up at him incredulously. "Ah, why did you do that?"

"I am absolutely not dealing with Jocelin," Sarsen said firmly, still gripping the door handle to prevent it from being opened.

Jocelin? The personality that she'd never met before? "Wait, his fourth personality is a flirt?"

"You don't want to be around him, trust me. Of all of his personalities, *that* one is the most challenging to handle."

Sevana stared up at him, studying his expression. Why did he look slightly…panicky? "And you know this because?"

"Prior experience."

Oh, did she ever want the full story on *that*. From the way Sarsen had clamped his jaw shut, it would take serious trickery to get it out of him, though. And likely, Jacen wouldn't remember a thing about it because it was Jocelin that was in control and not him. Curse the luck.

Several taut minutes ticked by before Sarsen carefully undid his grip on the door handle. Almost gingerly this time he knocked again. The process repeated of someone on the other side unlocking the bolts and opening the portal, but this time, it was a normal smile that greeted them. "Well, hello!"

Sevana looked at him suspiciously. Two of the personalities she had a hard time differentiating between because on the surface, they were similar. Jensen reacted like Jacen in many ways, but where Jacen was a competent Artifactor, Jensen was a walking disaster. She didn't know which man she had in front of her. "Hello," she greeted. "It's been a while."

"It has," Jacen (?) agreed, smile widening. "Come in, come in. It's unexpected to see you here together. Is this business, or…?"

"We have come here for help," Sarsen admitted. (Sevana noted

the omission of 'your help' with interest. Sarsen didn't know who
they spoke with either, eh?) "We've come across a very troublesome
artifact that dates from the eighth century."

"Ohhh," he responded, eyes lighting up. "Do tell. Still active and
functioning?"

"Unfortunately," Sevana grumbled.

Their host glanced at her, frown passing quickly over his face. "I
sense a long story coming. Here, come in, let's sit while you explain."

He waved them through the foyer and into another room, this one
pleasantly decorated with landscapes on the walls and comfortable
furniture arrayed around the room. Sevana took an armchair and sank
into it with a sigh of leather, Sarsen taking the armchair next to hers.
Their host sat across from them, taking an aging armchair that had
seen better days and propping his feet up on a mismatched ottoman.

"So, tell me what's going on."

Sevana dutifully explained, not skipping any of the particulars,
and started from when Decker had first come to her with a request for
help. She went through everything until yesterday when Sarsen had
arrived, ending with, "I have detailed diagnostics and scans for you to
look at, since I can't bring the artifact itself."

Jacen (?) had listened intently to all of this, hands clasped in front
of his chin, eyes trained on her. "Fascinating. You know, I do believe
I read about something like this. Hold on a moment, would you? Let
me fetch it. I believe I remember which book it was in." Without
waiting for a response, he leaped lightly out of the chair and scurried
off, heading for the back of the building.

In a low tone, Sevana asked, "Is it Jacen or Jensen we're dealing
with?"

"I can't tell," Sarsen growled. "They're so alike in some ways.
And he hasn't moved around enough, or said enough, for me to spot
any differences."

"And if it is Jensen?" She hated to think about that, but had
to. "He's already switched personalities three times in the past
fifteen minutes, which has to be a new record for him. Typically his
personalities stay for several hours at a time."

"Which means we'd need to stay and wait here for several hours before he could possibly switch to Jacen."

"Or Jocelin," she said in resignation. "Or Jaston."

"I normally don't mind all of this, but it sure makes matters difficult when it's *Jacen* we need to speak with." Sarsen rubbed at his eyes with the pads of his fingers. "And we're facing a dangerous situation, to boot. I surely do wish Master could find a way to regulate Jacen's mind."

She shook her head. "The mind is a strange thing, stranger than anything else, and no one understands it. We still don't know why Jacen's mind broke in the first place. Besides, most of the time I find his other personalities entertaining."

"That's because you have a twisted sense of humor."

Sevana laughed and didn't even try to deny it.

From somewhere deep within the building, a roar of flame burst out, flashing down the hallway with blue-green light. Tremors rocked through the house, shaking everything so that the glass windows rattled, and the very frame of the building moaned under the force of it.

Sevana jerked to her feet and tore down the hallway, scrambling in her pouch for a shielding charm and a wand with her free hand even as she ran. Sarsen followed closely at her heels, yelling, "Jacen?! Are you alright? Answer me!"

The flames still licked along the floor in little puddles at the very end of the hallway, silently indicating where they needed to go. Sevana skidded to a stop in front of the open doorway, avoiding the larger chunks of wood that used to be the door. She took in the sight with wide eyes and a whistle.

Pre-explosion, this had probably been Jacen's potions lab or something along those lines. Three tables sat in a large "I" shape, with the remains of vials, mortars, bottles and the like spread out along the surfaces. She couldn't begin to guess what he had been working on judging from what little had survived the explosion, but the blue-green fire indicated that the highly volatile substance of captured shiranui had been involved somehow.

The brunet Artifactor huddled underneath the tables in the fetal position, hands around his head, eyes screwed shut. He didn't even looked singed, so the explosion must have gone up and outward, the tables protecting him.

She and Sarsen sighed at the same time, "Jensen."

The man on the floor tentatively lowered his hands and opened his eyes. "Yes?"

Sarsen waved his wand over the room, snuffing out what remained of the flames, before sinking down onto his haunches so he could meet the other man's eyes. "Jensen, how did this happen?"

"Ah, well, the book I wanted to show you was in this room on the back shelf—"

A shelf under very heavy shields and wards, Sevana noted in amusement, likely to prevent Jensen from touching them or inadvertently destroying them.

"—but I knocked into the corner of the table accidentally, and when I did, something fell over. I lost my balance and went straight to the floor, so I can't tell you what it was, as I didn't see it, but flames immediately went *WHOOSH!*" his hands spread out in demonstration. "What was that?"

"Shiranui fire and something else," Sevana supplied, a grin slowly spreading over her face. Oh, Jacen would be livid when he saw *this* mess. And he had no one to blame but himself, in a way.

Jensen slowly climbed out from under the table and gained his feet. He looked around the room from one corner to the other, taking in the destroyed tables, the scorch marks on the wooden floor and (previously) white walls, the way the wards on the bookshelves still flickered in defense, and his face fell in open dismay. "Jacen's not going to be happy about this."

"Understatement," Sevana assured him, finding great pleasure in all of this. Visiting this place never got old.

Sarsen sighed, and having pity on Jensen, offered, "We'll help you clean this up, as much as we can."

"Oh, would you? Thank you ever so much." Jensen went toward the main table with outstretched hands. "What should we do with all of this, do you—oops."

Several remains of glass bottles and vials fell from the table and crashed to the floor in a loud spray, sending glass shards in every direction. Jensen froze, hands poised over the table, and gave them a sheepish look.

Sarsen looked at Sevana and muttered, "Do you think that if I shake him really hard, he'll switch over to Jacen?"

"Not a chance," she denied pleasantly. "But I'd pay good money to watch you do it."

Jacen was indeed not happy when he came back to himself. Jensen switched out after the worst of the mess had been cleared away. Sevana knew almost instantly when the switch had been made because the other Artifactor stopped mid-motion, blinking as if coming to himself, and he took a good look around the room as if he hadn't seen it before. Then his head fell back and he groaned, "*What* did Jensen do this time?"

"Welcome back, Jacen," Sevana greeted with an evil smile.

He shot her a dark look. "What, you couldn't prevent him from doing this?"

"We weren't actually sure it wasn't you," Sarsen apologized, putting the last of the remains of the door into a trash bag. He actually did regret it, unlike Sevana, who found the whole thing funny. "It's hard for us to tell the difference between you and Jensen right off."

Jacen waved this away, as he'd heard similar things many times before, and turned to brace his back against the wall with a soft thud. "So what did he do?"

"He knocked whatever potion you had brewing with shiranui fire over," Sevana told him benignly. "Or so I assume, judging from the spectacular fireworks we saw of blue-green fire."

If it were possible for one personality to strangle another one, Jacen would have done it at that moment. He looked ready to commit murder, anyway. But he blew out a deep breath, letting go of his anger, and asked instead, "How long have you two been here?"

"About three hours," Sarsen answered, finally setting the cleanup work aside. "We actually came for your expertise."

"Oh?" Jacen's eyes stopped roving over the half-destroyed room and finally settled on his two guests. "That sounds intriguing. You came across something from the old magicks?"

"Something that is still active and causing trouble," Sarsen confirmed with an unhappy stretch of the mouth. One couldn't really describe it as a smile.

Jacen, conversely, perked up with true interest. "It's rare that anything from that time is still functional, much less capable of activating itself. What is it doing? And where is it?"

Sevana mentally resigned herself to explaining all of this *again* (since Jacen hadn't heard it the first time) and started from the top. As she explained the situation, Jacen interrupted her with questions now and again and even dove for his protected bookshelf at one point and grabbed an empty notebook to take quick notes in. She catalogued that reaction for future reference. If this situation ever came up again, the surefire way of knowing the difference between Jacen and Jensen would be that *Jacen* would ask questions.

By the time she finished, Jacen worried at his bottom lip with his teeth, staring at the notebook in his hands with unfocused eyes. "Sevana…I don't like this picture you're painting."

"What, you think I do?"

"I can see why you're worried. In fact, *I'm* worried." He finally put the notebook aside so he could look at her directly, expression and voice intense. "I have never seen an artifact from that time rated so high in power. For that matter, I've never seen one that will use magic constantly like this, unchecked. They will occasionally activate themselves, certainly, but it usually only happens once. Mayhap twice. And you say this has been going on for *months?*"

"About five, I believe."

He scrubbed at the back of his neck with an open hand, turning so that he could pace the width of the room in an agitated stride. "Are you sure that the shield's power rating isn't skewing the overall reading?"

"Positive. The shield itself is an eight in power."

He stopped abruptly, facing his bookshelf, and stayed like that for several taut seconds, thinking so hard that it seemed he barely breathed for a moment. "I think I know what this is."

Sevana let out a pent-up breath. Best news she'd had all week. "Go on."

"Magicians of that time often made tools and such for people that had either no magical ability or were still in the learning process. Gadget magic is what they were called, or gadgicks for short. " He shot them both a crooked smile. "Rather like we do today with our charms and bottled potions. But their inventions were on a much more powerful scale, and with a more…hmmm…how to say this? A more intuitive approach. The devices were designed to pick up the *intent* of the user more than any spoken command."

Sevana's stomach started twisting in sick understanding. So she'd only been half-right. The artifact worked because it was actively searching for destinations to send people to, and it chose anyone that pictured a different place, even in sleep.

"Some of the gadgicks that they used for transportation are like yours. Or so I've read in some of the more ancient texts. I found a description once in a catalogue, or what looked like one, of a merchant's wares that claimed it could transport any cargo or body of people any distance."

Sarsen leaned against a table's edge, bracing his hands on the top of the surface, and let out a long sigh. "Couldn't describe it any better than that."

"With so many people around it, thinking of different locations and images in their minds, even subconsciously, the gadgick must feel that it needs to be constantly on." Jacen stared at the floor and muttered, "Or it's developed some pretty interesting quirks over the past few hundred years."

"I'm betting on the latter," Sevana grumbled. "Alright, so you recognize this thing. How do we turn it off?"

"Have you tried taking everyone out of the village?"

"It doesn't work for any length of time, or so I'm told," she answered with a resigned shrug. "One of the magicians they hired suggested they do that, but the device brought them all back again the next night. It must have some sort of 'return home' clause in it?" When Jacen nodded wryly, she grimaced. Stone the crows, she hated being right sometimes. "Did those long dead magicians think of every fail-safe?"

"It was their job to do so."

"Shut it, Sarsen, I don't want to hear that right now. Jacen, the only thing we could think to do was to destroy the shield first and then tackle the artifact—gadgick, whatever—next. Can we do that without creating a dangerous backlash in power?"

Jacen held a hand in front of him and tipped it back and forth in an uncertain gesture. "Perhaps? I'd like to look at those scans you took before giving you a firm answer. But that'll take me at least a few hours and some research. What time is it?"

Sarsen pulled out a pocket watch from his jacket before answering, "Nearly four in the afternoon."

"Then I should probably get dinner started first."

Who knew how many meals Jacen had accidentally skipped today because his other personalities hadn't bothered to eat, or assumed a different personality would take care of it? "Why don't *I* cook while you and Sarsen research?"

Jacen shot her a hopeful smile. "Would you? I'm thoroughly sick of my cooking at this point."

"It sounds like a fair trade to me."

Jacen, mercy be praised, had a fully stocked kitchen so she had a good selection of ingredients to cook from. The place reminded her oddly of a potions lab in its setup, though. Aside from the main table, she only had one long stretch of counter space, a sink with some very interesting stains, and a single cold box. Did the man only cook to survive?

She ended up making a thick stew and biscuits, as it looked like several of his vegetables wouldn't survive another day. The men came in like hungry wolves, their noses in the air, sniffing their way into the kitchen with comments of the smell alone killing them.

Everyone pitched in to get bowls and dinner on the table, and then they ate with gusto and a distinct lack of conversation until half the pot of stew had been consumed, and only then did the spoons stay in the bowls.

"Alright," Sevana turned to Jacen. "How goes it?"

"Your scans are exquisitely detailed, as always," he praised her, sitting back with a contented sigh. "It almost feels like I'm standing in that village square when I look at them. I'd like to run a few more calculations, double-check a fact or two, but my initial impression is: no. Destroying the shield shouldn't cause any backlashes and you will be able to attack it directly. Note that I do not mean *safely* attack it directly. I think that there will be another fail-safe once you get past that shield. What that might be is anyone's guess. So if you're going to attack that shield, you must be ready to instantly attack the gadgick itself, otherwise I can't predict what will happen."

A fact she'd already thought of, but she nodded to show her understanding. He, after all, was the expert on this.

"Why don't the two of you stay the night?" he offered. "I'll stay up and do some more research, get you some more facts to work off of. It's rather too late to leave anyway unless you want to try flying about in the dark."

"I'm not a bat, so I'll pass on that idea," Sevana snarked. "But you understand that if you switch over to Jocelin again, we'll lock you in a room somewhere."

He blinked at her. "Jocelin came out today?"

"We met *everyone* today," Sarsen assured him dryly.

"Oh. So that's how I lost half the day…" Jacen trailed off and shrugged. After twenty years of this, he'd grown accustomed to holes in his memory or whole hours of time passing without his knowing. "Fine, if Jocelin causes you problems, lock us in a room somewhere. Just make sure it's a room that I have idiot-proofed. I never know what the others will try."

Sevana personally felt no need to sleep so she offered, "Why don't I stay up and research with you? I usually work late at night anyway."

"Oh." Jacen lit up in a delighted smile. "That sounds fun. In that case, dishes can wait. Let's go up to my library."

They spent the entire night reviewing things in more depth, cross-referencing it with other gadgicks that Jacen had previously researched that came from the same era, and double-checking math and theories. They sketched out designs, elements, and possibilities until their eyes crossed and their heads felt fit to explode. Without their notice, the night fell way to day, and the sun crept in through the library window, making the lamps they'd lit unnecessary.

Sarsen ambled into the room, stifling a yawn behind one hand, looking bleary-eyed but unfairly rested. "Oh? You two are still at it?"

Sevana gave him a sleep-deprived glower.

"Right. Obviously a stupid question."

They'd slowly emptied the shelves during the course of the night, stacking them up on the large table and the two armchairs, which was how Sevana and Jacen eventually ended up on the floor. Easing past her, Sarsen sank into the only other available seat—a half-cluttered loveseat that had seen better days. As he did so, he looked at Jacen who lay flat on the floor, his hands propped behind his head, and ventured, "Good morning, Jacen?"

"Morning," Jacen responded, a tired smile etched into his face. "Not sure if it's a good one yet."

"Oh?"

Sevana slouched further into herself, back braced against a chair, nearly folded in half. She made grumbling, inarticulate noises, not about to explain what they had deduced. She didn't even want to think about it, much less say it aloud.

Sarsen pointed a finger at her and said, "Judging from that expression, I'm not going to like this, am I?"

"We sure don't." Jacen heaved a heavy sigh and sat upright, crossing his legs comfortably before he started to explain. "I can run you through the numbers, logic, and such later if you wish, but here's the gist of it: first and foremost, I do not believe that this device was meant to transport just people."

"Uhh?" Sarsen said in confusion, as if Jacen was suddenly speaking in a foreign language.

"Yes, I realize that it has only been transporting people," Jacen responded patiently. "But the only time I have seen a design like this was for a transport that would handle caravans and the like. So, not just people, but objects of all sorts. Also, it was made to use for very long distances. So it's recent habit of transporting people a very long way is actually a fundamentally sound feature and not some erratic behavior."

Sarsen scratched at the back of his head for a moment, weighing that in his mind before offering, "I can't say that makes me feel any better. If it was supposed to transport things as well, how'd they manage it?"

"They had a way of marking things that needed to be transported. Because no one is doing that, only people are going." Jacen shrugged, grimacing. "Yes, I'm aware that you're not sure how the people are marked either. These are logical deductions, you understand, I don't have a great deal of concrete evidence to support my theories. I'm simply making educated guesses depending on what you and Sevana are telling me."

"Noted." Sarsen blew out a long breath. "Alright, anything else?"

"Now, this next part isn't so much guesswork as it is basic math. Yes, you can tackle the shield around the gadgick separately. No, it won't cause any kind of magic backlash that will destroy your surroundings. However, we do not believe that the shield is so separate that the gadgick isn't feeding it power somehow."

Brows furrowing deeply, he said slowly, "Sevana, you said that the elements of the shield were blended so well with some of the elements of the artifact that it took you some time to unravel them."

"After taking a thorough look at her scans and notes, I saw why." Jacen made a face. "Do you remember the shield that your master put around Ence? The one that prevents it from being flooded during storms and such?"

"Yes?" Sarsen was clearly a little fuzzy on the details.

Heaving a resigned sigh, Sevana finally started to participate in the conversation. "The shield didn't need to be active at all times, not really, so he designed it so that it would be in a sort of standby mode during the fair seasons, but if water ever started to encroach past a certain point, it would activate. And if, for whatever reason, the water rose past a certain level, it would activate a second line of defense that would cover the town completely."

"It did so by drawing upon the power of the sea as an added element, thereby making it stronger," Jacen added. "I think this shield works off the same general principle. Right now, it's in a rather standby mode. It'll warn people off, or prevent accidental tampering, but it won't really hurt someone nor do anything drastic. But if you tamper with it too much, or attack it directly, it'll activate the shield so that it's much stronger."

Sarsen pressed his fingers against his eyes and rubbed. "You don't think we're dealing with a level eight spell."

"I will bet you a year's salary that as soon as you attack that thing, it'll rise to a level ten. Possibly a level twelve." Jacen glanced at both their faces, taking in the pained expressions and offered meekly, "Good luck?"

"I don't *want* to break an ancient shield with a twelve power level!" Sevana whined to no one in particular.

Sarsen kept rubbing at his eyes. "I clearly should have asked after breakfast."

"First good idea anyone's had in the past twelve hours." Sevana rolled to her feet and headed out of the room. "Jacen, you got eggs?"

He perked up. "You're making breakfast?"

She backtracked to the door to put her head around it and give him an exasperated look. "No, I'm going to throw eggs at you."

"I've got ham too," he offered with an ingenious smile.

"Come find it for me."

Jacen popped up immediately and followed her out, tired but happy at the thought of food he wouldn't have to make himself.

Sarsen followed at a slower pace, still yawning and thinking, judging from the mumbling.

Sevana stifled a yawn herself, trying to walk straight and not stumble into the walls as she moved. She probably shouldn't try to leave after breakfast—she might very well crash considering how tired she was. Alright, breakfast, then nap. As much as she now knew, she didn't have a solid plan on how to attack that shield right now anyway. Even if she and Sarsen left right this minute for Chastain, it wouldn't do the village any good.

They'd come up with a plan tomorrow.

Even after a four-hour nap, Sevana failed to feel either refreshed or revived. In fact, the whole idea of sleeping backfired on her terribly. She awoke grouchy, irritable, and even more aware of the fact that she'd been up all night doing some very complex thinking.

Jacen—wise man—made them a late lunch, after which they bade him farewell and promised that they would keep him updated. (Actually, Sevana more or less threatened that she would contact him again if none of their ideas worked. Jacen, true professional that he was, looked pleased by this instead of worried.) But after the past two days, neither she nor Sarsen felt particularly in the mood to race back to Chastain and instead climbed back into the sky at a moderately fast clip.

As tired as she felt physically, Sevana felt oddly alert. Even as she flew through the clouds, feeling the moist air slide pleasantly along her skin, her mind whirled at high speed. How to beat that shield? Jacen thought it possible to attack it with something that was slightly lower, somewhere around a level nine in power, as long as they hit the shield hard and fast enough that it couldn't engage its higher strength. This plan sounded slightly risky, but Sevana had dealt with riskier things—calling on a water dragon to help break a ten-year-old curse, for example. Trying to break a shield so fast that it couldn't react properly sounded like a lark in comparison.

Hmmm…she and Jacen had come up with the idea of using fairy's kiss and shiranui as a combined attack. Shiranui was volatile and capricious, but because of that it was an excellent element to use for quick casting. Fairy's kiss would combine well with it because it also came from a mystical source, but best yet—the elements combined would have a rating of ten in power. More than powerful enough to deal with that shield in a quick, decisive blow.

Or so she hoped, anyway.

She ran figures and calculations in her head as she flew, wishing that she had the ability to write things down and fly at the same time, but in truth, she didn't really need to. Sevana had developed the pattern of writing her ideas out as a young apprentice and had never outgrown the habit. But after so many years of doing this, she could do it all in her head now and retain what worked and what didn't.

By the time she had more or less worked out the answer, they had reached Chastain. The sun set in a pretty display of deep purples and mauves and oranges, casting the whole land in cool shadow, which also made it semi-tricky to land properly. Sevana had a devil of a time finding a good spot to land in that wouldn't put her in a muddy patch. Sarsen had it easier as he came in using the road, the clearest path in the area. She finally chose a place just outside the main road and settled there, absently casting a steal-me-not charm on it as she climbed off. (Not that she thought anyone would try for that, but one never knew.)

Sarsen did the same to his glider before he sauntered to where she stood waiting on him. "Sev. I think I have a solution to the shield."

"So do I," she responded, mouth quirked up. "Fairy's kiss and shiranui?"

"That's the answer I reached too. Jacen's suggestion just makes too much sense. Let's try this tomorrow morning, after we've both gotten a good night's sleep."

She blinked at him, not following. "Tomorrow? Isn't that a little too quick? We haven't worked out a real solution to the gadgick, artifact, whateveryouwanttocallit yet."

Sarsen held up a finger. "Our solution for the gadgick will in some part depend on if the shield can be broken. I want to test breaking the shield first before we plan any further. If the fairy's kiss and shiranui doesn't work, we'll have to find something else, and those elements—"

"—must blend well with whatever we use to break the gadgick," she finished with an understanding groan. "It's official. I'm tired. I should have realized that."

"The other reason why I want to sleep first," he agreed sympathetically. "I'm not at my best at the moment either. Besides, I want to cue up the other two magicians and have them on standby, just in case Jacen's predictions are wrong."

Probably not a bad idea at that. "I'm getting dinner before bed, then. Since you unfairly got more sleep than I did, *you* go talk to them."

"Unfairly?" he objected mildly, dark eyes laughing. "As I recall, you volunteered to stay up all night researching."

"I did *not*." Or at least, she hadn't intended to stay up *all* night when she'd offered to help Jacen out. She wrinkled her nose at him as Sarsen just laughed, refusing to argue the point. Turning on her heel, she headed into the village, stifling a yawn as she went. Bed. She definitely wanted a bed. Maybe with a proper eight hours of sleep, her mind wouldn't feel like mush.

Sevana, in fact, slept ten hours, waking leisurely and without any prompting from the outside world. She stretched, feeling well rested, and rolled out of her bed at the inn that had been set aside for her. After washing her face, she dressed in her usual clothes of pants, shirt and vest, pulled on her favorite boots, and ambled down the stairs.

The main room of the inn looked oddly vacant for this time of the morning. Only Sarsen sat at a table, the remains of a breakfast in front of him and a cup of something steaming in his hands. He saluted her with it as she came into view.

"Morning, Sev."

"Good morning," she returned, looking around the room in growing confusion. Even the view through the large windows showed very little life. Strange—the inn faced the courtyard of the main square; she should be seeing tons of traffic. "Where is everyone?"

"Out," Sarsen supplied after swallowing a mouthful from his

mug. "While you slept, I have been working."

"I don't see how that has anything to do with missing people," she informed him as she sauntered over to the chair. Halfway into it, she froze as a disturbing thought occurred. "Unless…unless that thing has suddenly started transporting more than one person at a time?" she asked in sudden alarm.

He waved a hand in negation. "No, no. Nothing like that. I actually had everyone clear out after breakfast this morning. They're waiting outside the village just in case something goes wrong today."

She let out a breath of relief as she slid the rest of the way into the chair. "So you're saying that we're ready to go?"

"Waiting on you," he confirmed with a quirk of the brows.

She looked at the appetizing spread of food in front of her, obviously ordered for her as Sarsen hadn't touched the plate at all, and informed him firmly, "I'm eating first."

"Figured you would."

Tucking in, she ate the food with considerable pleasure. Half the fun of eating food that she didn't make came from the fact that she wouldn't have to clean up after the meal either.

"Here's my idea for the casted spell." Sarsen slid a piece of paper across the table to rest in front of her.

She chewed as she leaned forward slightly, reading the diagram with ease (in spite of the abominable handwriting). "Why have both of us attack simultaneously? You think we can overwhelm the shield easier that way?"

"I'm not as optimistic as either you or Jacen," he responded with a minute shake of the head. "This thing has given every sign of having an almost individual awareness. Either the person who made it designed it very, *very* well so that it can react on its own in most circumstances, or…or it's developed some very interesting quirks over the past few hundred years. Regardless, I don't think that it's going to react well when we hit it. In fact, I predict that by the time we get through that shield, we're going to feel half-dead afterwards."

"Pessimist."

Sarsen shrugged, not insulted. "Perhaps."

She looked at his design again, not seeing any flaws in it, but not really expecting any. They did, after all, train under the same master. She mentally reviewed everything she knew of that gadgick as well, different scenarios and simulations flashing through her mind, and she had to grudgingly admit that perhaps Sarsen would prove right in the end. She hoped Jacen would be right—that a fast, fierce attack would be able to break through that shield. But she wouldn't bet on it either.

Even Jacen hadn't been willing to bet that it would work.

With a scrape of the spoon against her plate, she popped the last bite into her mouth. "Alright, let's be about it."

Sarsen stood with her, leading the way out the front door and into the mellow morning sun. Even if she hadn't known that the villagers had left this morning and waited outside, she would have been able to tell just from the smell alone. She couldn't detect any scents of food, baking bread, spices, or anything else that she had come to associate with the usual morning of this village. Their footsteps across the cobblestones rang in an eerily hollow way. She'd never heard silence quite this loud before.

In silent camaraderie, she and Sarsen stopped a few feet from the fountain and started their preparations. Sarsen pulled out two vials from his pouch, one which contained fairy's kiss, the other the flickering blue light of shiranui fire. He unstopped both with a slight *pop* as the corks left the bottles. Wands in hand, they coaxed both elements out, winding them around the wands so that they could draw the casted insignia into the air itself in blazing white lines. The spell hummed as Sevana wrote the incantation within a small circle, enclosed it with a circular line, and began the second line of script. She felt and saw the difference when the last line completed the incantation. It warmed the air considerably and flickered with shiranui power.

The incantation wouldn't hold long. The shiranui already wanted free, to be released, and it would be fighting her control in a few moments. That's why it worked so well for casted spells—but also why it didn't work at all for charms. It was too unstable for that.

Sarsen completed his written incantation as well and put the vials back in his pouch. He took a half step to the side, putting more distance between them, and glanced at her. "Ready?"

"Ready," she confirmed.

"Alright. On three. One, two, three!"

In perfect unison they said strongly, "// ⌐⌐ // ⎯⌐⊙⌐⌐"

For a split second, she thought it worked. The shield flinched, concaving inward as if a log had just been swung at it, forcing it to bend backward or break. In the next heartbeat, it flared upwards in a surge of power so strong it sent a thrill straight up her spine. It raged like a blue and white bonfire, beautiful and dangerous all at once. She knew instantly that Sarsen's pessimism had been dead-on—nothing a human could do could match the reflexes of a magical device.

She had just enough time to half-swear in her head before the shield threw back their attack, making the incantations splinter in a thousand pieces and scatter like broken glass. In sheer instinct, she threw her arms up to protect her face, curling slightly inwards to keep her head from smacking first into the hard stone under her. But that was all she could do. The force of it robbed her of breath, of reason, as the backlash hit her with all the force of a giant's hand.

Sevana lay there gasping, lungs on fire with the need for oxygen, head swirling, every nerve in her body screaming with a sensitivity that just bordered on pain. Her back and head protested at the abuse from slamming into solid ground. It took several seconds for her to draw enough air into her lungs to be able to breathe properly. Then it took a few more before her vision cleared instead of looking dark, as if she were going to pass out any moment.

"Sev?" a hand touched her lightly on the shoulder. "Sev?"

Sarsen. She swallowed—a useless gesture that made her throat burn—and managed, "Alive."

"I can see that. You're breathing and your eyes are open." Even though the words were half-joking, Sarsen sounded relieved.

"I thought—" an errant cough cut off the rest of the sentence and she had to clear her lungs and throat before she could try again. Owww. Coughing bad. She had to remember not to do that for the next few days. "I thought you said we'd feel half-dead after we were through with this."

"I did." Sarsen let go of her and rolled back so that he could lie flat again. Now that she could pay better attention, he looked like she felt—deprived of air, eyes whirling, a fine tremor shaking him from head to toe. She could hear it in his voice, too, as he spoke. "I feel more three-quarters dead. You?"

"Same," she groaned. "*Ugh*. Never trust an evil spell to measure properly."

"Since when was it evil?"

"It's thwarting me. Anything that thwarts me is evil."

Sarsen started to laugh and then groaned when it made already unhappy muscles twinge. "That sounds suspiciously like Sevana-logic."

"Is there any other kind?" This back-and-forth levity oddly helped. She didn't feel like death warmed over anymore. Her status could now be updated to 'ineligible for burial within the next twenty-four hours.' "More importantly, did we succeed?"

They both timidly raised their heads to look forward.

The fountain looked completely unharmed, not even singed, as water flowed out of it unimpeded. It looked, actually, as if they hadn't done a single thing.

Sevana let her head fall back. "It's official. It's evil."

Sarsen at her side groaned. "Pure evil. Now what?"

"I wish I knew."

Decker found them ten minutes later, still flat on their backs in front of the fountain, neither of them anxious to move and test the limits of throbbing muscles. He called for help, picked Sevana up bodily and took her straight to the small doctor's clinic a block away.

She informed him that just because her eyes were spinning around in her head, that didn't mean she couldn't walk.

He ignored her.

It took two men to carry in Sarsen. Sevana sat propped up on one of the two beds in the room, watching blearily as they carried her friend in. In this small of a room, they found the walkway too cramped for three men to really move around in, but they managed to shuffle about and gently set Sarsen down on the edge of the bed. He collapsed in a controlled fall so that his head hit the pillow, not bothering to go through the extra effort of bringing his legs up, which made him look like a deflated balloon.

The doctor, a rather thin man with a beak of a nose and wispy hair, leaned in front of her, blocking her view of the room completely. He came so close she could smell his breath, a not entirely pleasant sensation. "What are you doing?" she grouched.

"Checking for signs of concussion," he responded without batting an eyelash. "Your eyes are reacting normally. Good. How do you feel?"

"Like a building fell on top of me." She knew exactly how that felt, too. "Will you move?"

"Nothing broken, tender, bleeding?" he persisted, trying to lift her arms so that he could get a look at her from every angle.

"No, no, and no," she responded in exasperation. "Decker, did you have to bring me here? This is pointless, we're not injured."

Decker put his shoulders against the wall in a clear sign of determination to keep her from leaving. In an arch voice he drawled, "Do you remember what you said to me when I got to you? I asked what happened and you said, 'Death to all evil!'"

Alright, out of context, that probably did sound…less than lucid.

Sarsen let out a pained chuckle. "We're not injured, Decker. We were just talking about how the fountain is now officially evil because it's thwarting us before you showed up. That's why she said that."

He blinked in sudden understanding. "Oh."

Krause shouldered his way through—no mean feat, considering how jam-packed the room had become—and demanded, "Then what happened?"

"Our hopeful plan was more hopeful than we'd imagined," Sarsen answered wearily. He finally dragged both legs up onto the bed so that people had more room to walk, although judging from that wince, it hurt to do it. "The shield slammed up almost before we could get the spell fully released and it reflected our own attack back at us."

If not for their personal protection charms, they'd be seriously burned by now. Not to mention the cracked skulls, bruises and broken bones the doctor had obviously expected.

Krause's forehead furrowed into a deep line. "So what now?"

"We don't know," Sarsen admitted.

"I want to put gunpowder around the base of the fountain and blow it up," Sevana suggested in black humor.

"No, Sev," Sarsen told her again, patiently. To the room of alarmed adults he added, "You're right to look scared, as she's only half-kidding. I admit, if we break the fountain free of the square, we could lift it out entirely and take the problem to a remote region so that we can slowly figure out a solution elsewhere. It would give the village some peace again."

"I'd rather not have a gigantic hole in the middle of town," Krause said weakly.

"I reckoned as much." Sarsen dredged up a half smile.

She'd let Sarsen have his way—for now. But if they didn't find another solution within the next week, she'd sneak out in the dead of night and blow it sky high.

From Sarsen's pouch came a small, tiny voice calling out, "*Sarsen! Sarsen! Pick up your Caller!*"

They both looked at the bag in dread. "Master," she sighed.

"Of course he'd call, just to see if it worked or not," Sarsen said rhetorically.

"Wait, what are you doing!" she protested as he reached for his bag.

"Answering him, of course."

"What do you mean, of course?" she spluttered. "If you do that, he'll rush over here in a bout of his parental concern, and then we'll never be rid of him!"

Sarsen paused and gave her an odd look. "You sound as if you don't want him here."

"Of course I don't want him here! He's insanely expensive!"

He gave her quite the look for that. "Sev, we can obviously use some experienced help on this one. We tried everything we could think of and the thing threw us around like a pair of wet dolls. I, for one, want the man's devious mind. Not to mention his power. Three Artifactors might well be able to crack the gadgick."

He might well be right, and she wouldn't really be opposed to another opinion, but she hadn't been kidding—Master's fees were no laughing matter. She'd already invested a lot of time into this problem and she *deserved* the reward that came with it. "If you answer him and he comes, his share is coming out of yours," she warned him.

Sarsen didn't quite roll his eyes as he brought the Caller out of the bag, letting it rest in his open palm. "Master."

"*There you are!*" She couldn't see the face of the tiny Caller from here, as its back was to her, but the tone conveyed enough to guess at the expression. "*Sarsen, you look like five miles of bad road during a summer storm. What happened?!*"

"Our plan didn't work. The shield reacted faster than we could and our own attack was reflected back on us."

"*Tell me you were wearing a shield charm.*"

"We both were," Sevana assured him, feeling like shaking her head. What did he take his former students for, anyway? Idiots? "We're fine, Master. Just a mite sore."

He spun about in Sarsen's hand to look at her. "*Oh no, sweetling, don't tell me you got hit by this too!*"

"Did you forget the part where this is my contracted job? Why in sweet mercy would I make Sarsen do all the work?"

"Because you're devious and conniving," Master and Sarsen said in unison.

She gave them a lethal glare. "You're both going to pay for that later."

Master waved a hand, dismissing her threat altogether. "*I don't want either of you to move or try anything else until I get there.*"

"Don't you dare come!" she objected. "You're insanely expensive. I do *not* want to pay you."

Master gave her his patented, parental, I can't believe she just said something so stupid look. "*Sweetling, do you honestly think that I am just going to sit over here and watch this play out? It's defeated two of my best students and is still kicking. Of course I'm coming!"*

Decker, still planted near the doorway, cleared his throat. When he caught her eye, he said mildly, "Didn't you get permission from the king to commandeer help as you needed it? And a seal to act as a purse to pay for it?"

Sevana snapped her fingers as she abruptly remembered. Actually, in the face of this nearly insurmountable problem, she *had* forgotten that. "Bless your memory, Decker. I can make *Aren* pay for him! Alright, Master, in that case you can come."

"Like I was waiting for your permission." Master shook his head in amusement. *"I'll be there tomorrow. Now, I mean it, you two. Do. Not. Move."*

"Not a problem," Sevana assured him sourly.

"Neither of us feel like it at the moment," Sarsen chimed in, equally sour.

"Good. Sleep. It's the best medicine for you at the moment." With that said, the Caller went still and quiet again.

Sevana would absolutely never, ever admit this aloud, but she felt vastly reassured that her Master was coming. He had never once met a problem that he couldn't defeat. Lips curved at the corners, she settled down a little more into the bed, closed her eyes, and drifted off into a sound sleep.

Sevana had a foot halfway into her boot when a knock sounded in a loud rap on the door. Through the wood, a very familiar voice called, "Sweetling!"

Master? She blinked, more than a little taken aback. The village clock had barely chimed out the eighth hour! Most people had barely eaten breakfast at this point. For that matter, she'd been awake just barely long enough to get dressed. How in sweet mercy's sake had he made it all the way from the Standor Mountains in a little over sixteen hours?!

"Enter!" she called after several seconds of dumbfounded surprise.

The door swung sharply open, revealing the form of her aging master. Joles Tashjian looked as he always did—white hair in a knot on the top of his head, skin wrinkled and the color of aged bronze, his customary jacket bulging with multiple pockets filled to the brim. Despite the fact that he ate like a starving horse, he always looked a tad too thin. He didn't appear to be at all tired from travelling throughout the night. In fact, he seemed unfairly spry and alert, a feeling that Sevana did not share in the least. After yesterday's events, her body felt sore and misused, and she had not had the best night's sleep because of it.

Hinun padded in behind him, and came directly to her to greet her with a nose in her ribs. Used to this treatment, she gave him a good scratch behind the ears in welcome, making his tail wag happily.

Master leaned down in front of her, looking her over with a

paternal/clinical eye. "Sweetling, you look roughed over."

"I feel it, too," she responded churlishly. "I think what really rankles is that even after all that, the fountain doesn't even look singed. Have you seen Sarsen yet?"

"He said he'd meet us for breakfast."

Food sounded like a splendid idea. "How in the world did you get here so fast?"

"Oh, that?" Master lit up in a smug smile. "It works."

She regarded him blankly, beyond confused by what he meant. It works? What did? He pointed toward the window and she finished shoving her foot into her boot, tied it, and went to see what he seemed so pleased about. Through the small window, she could see a contraption sitting just outside the building's main door. It looked like nothing more than a wooden box with four ordinary wooden wheels. But she recognized it instantly. "You finally got that contraption to work?!"

"I did," he responded, smile growing, chest puffing out a little with pride.

"But you swore you wouldn't use it at all until it became self-navigating!" she protested. Master had built it a good three years ago, intending to make a vehicle that would travel without conscious direction from its owner and could go anywhere on land. Travelling on land had been the easiest part of the design. It was the *without human control* that had stumped him for the past three years.

"I had a breakthrough last fall," Master admitted. "All I had to do was create a trainable map that would be inscribed into the vehicle itself. So I drove to every major city in Kindin and Windamere, letting the route record itself, and then all I had to do was add some necessary safety precautions to the design." He rubbed at his chin and grimaced. "Incantation is still hideously complex, though."

She didn't even want to try and imagine it. It hurt her head just thinking about it. "There's no way that Chastain was on your map, though!"

"Well, no, but Winfield is. And it's only a few hours from Winfield to here. I slept on the way to Winfield, and when I got to the city, I drove it myself from there on. Worked beautifully." Blinking at her, he offered ingeniously, "Want one?"

"Master, don't ask stupid questions. Of course I want a vehicle I don't have to drive!"

He patted her on the shoulder and laughed, the sound rich and deep. "I'll teach you how to make your own after this job is finished, then."

"Yes, please, let's not handle two impossible jobs at once," she responded, only half-joking. "For now, breakfast? And we'll try and catch you up as we eat."

He nodded in agreement and gestured for her to take the lead, which she did. As she made her way through the hallway, something moved in the bag at her waist and a distant sounding male voice said something that was so muffled she couldn't make it out. Eyebrow quirked—who would try to contact her at this hour of the morning?— she reached in and pulled her Caller free. "Yes?"

The Caller formed into the features of Pierpoint, arms crossed over his chest in a clear gesture of forced patience. "*Sevana. Did it occur to you at any point that we would like an update?*"

Actually…no, it hadn't.

Master leaned around her shoulder and greeted Pierpoint with a cordial, "Hello, Pierpoint."

"*Well hello, Tashjian!*" Pierpoint seemed both surprised and pleased. "*I'm glad to see you in Chastain, but is the problem truly that serious that she had to call for your help?*"

"Serious isn't the word I'd use," Master refuted with a slight shake of the head. "It's more complicated than anything."

"*How so?*"

Sevana, in the interest of getting food into her stomach, decided to sum it up in short sentences. "The artifact is annoying, upsetting, and downright evil, but it's not destructive. It is, in fact, doing what it was designed to do—transport people. So there's no need to be worried about it destroying half the countryside." Pierpoint let out a breath of relief over that, looking as if a hundred-pound weight had just fallen from his shoulders. "It is, however, thwarting our best efforts in shutting it off. We tried getting past its basic shield yesterday and have the bruises to show for our efforts."

"Hence why it's now considered evil and you called in your master for help," Pierpoint summed up wryly. *"I think I see the full picture. Is there anything that you need? Any help that we can send your way?"*

"You can warn Aren that he's going to pay for Master's fees," Sevana said with a heartless smile.

"That I'll do. Anything else?"

"At this point, we don't know," Master admitted. "I only just arrived and neither Sevana nor Sarsen has been able to fill me in yet. We'll get back to you once we have a better idea of how to approach the problem."

"Well enough. I'll pass along what you've told me for now. Oh, and Sevana—Morgan is very upset with you about that note you left behind. He said it was depressingly short on details and that he's quite cross with you right now."

"He'll live." She shoved the Caller back into her bag and continued toward the dining room.

"Sevana," Master scolded.

Without turning to see his expression, she responded calmly, "I told him what he needed to know. He's just being a worrywart."

From behind her there came a long, drawn-out sigh.

Sarsen, obviously anticipating them, had already ordered breakfast and it sat on the table like a lure, tempting the hungry with enticing smells. He'd even ordered a plate for Hinun, which sat on the floor at his feet. The wolf went directly there and started inhaling food. Sevana gave nothing more than a hello grunt to Sarsen before sitting down at the table and eating everything in sight.

Master had more manners, exchanging cordial words as he and Sarsen tucked in. Or he tried to, at least. She and Sarsen had both taken potions and applied poultices yesterday that helped them to heal faster—they wouldn't be moving at all today if they hadn't. But the side effect of accelerated healing was extreme hunger. Master spoke of things that didn't require a response and let them consume to their heart's content.

After two plates, Sevana felt deliciously stuffed to the gills and finally relaxed back into the wooden chair with a sigh of satisfaction. Looking about, she belatedly noticed that the room had the usual hustle and bustle of the morning with people coming and going for breakfast as they started their day. Something about the way they kept glancing at her table, and the lower pitch in conversation, caught her attention. Oh? "Are they talking about us?"

"All sorts of rumors are flying about what happened yesterday," Sarsen informed her, still eating although at a much slower rate. He actually seemed to chew now instead of just inhaling. "I've had several people come by and ask if it was safe to go near the fountain."

After seeing what happened yesterday, she supposed she didn't blame their caution. "What did you tell them?"

"To avoid it for now. I don't think it'll cause anyone injury—after all, they interacted with it for months without ill effect—but we're going to be working in that area for the next few days. We'll need plenty of space around us as we try things."

Master nodded in satisfaction. "Good. You're right, we don't want to be tripping over anyone while working. Now, sweetling, you've more or less told me the basics but I need more than that. Start from the beginning and leave nothing out."

She did just that, the routine of explaining the complexity of the problem and the solutions she had tried so ingrained in her that it felt like an odd sort of homecoming. She'd been reporting and explaining to this man for nearly a decade. To see his patience, his sharp attention trained on her, felt wonderfully familiar and reassuring.

When she'd finished, he sat there for several seconds, just pondering, before he spoke slowly. "There are several questions I have that are in want of answers. You said Jacen believed that this gadgick was in fact designed to transport not just people, but objects? Then why hasn't it been doing so?"

"There's some other feature, some piece of the gadgick's design that we're missing," she admitted frankly. "They must have had a way of signaling what inanimate objects needed to be transported. I'm just not sure of how they did it."

"I'd like to get an answer to this riddle. I have a feeling it would help us if we knew more of how this thing worked." Master sat back and looked up blindly at the ceiling, mind clearly whirling at high speeds. "I'd also like to know what the original site looked like. You said they've been harvesting stones from the ruins for generations, correct? But all of this trouble only started up in the past several months. So it had to have been recent that the right stone, or element, was moved. Surely there's someone here that would be able to describe to us what the ruins originally looked like six months ago."

A good thought that she hadn't tracked down. She'd been so busy trying to find a magical solution to the problem that she hadn't thought to ask some of the more obvious solutions. "I'll ask Decker. He might not know, but I'm sure he can tell us who would."

"Please do so." He rubbed at his chin, making a rasping sound against the stubble. "After what happened to the two of you yesterday, I don't believe that doing another frontal attack against the gadgick is the right approach. Trying to overwhelm power with more power would no doubt work, but it would take considerable manpower and some rather dangerous elemental combinations to pull it off. Not that I blame either of you for trying it—I certainly would have in your shoes."

"It would, after all, be the easiest solution," Sarsen sighed. "If it had worked, that is. So, you think we should do an indirect approach. How?"

"Robbing it of its power source." Master finally dropped his eyes to give them a wry smile and shrug of the shoulders. "But that begs the question, which one? There are several elements powering the gadgick right now. Which one would be the safest to remove from the equation? Or the easiest? Is there an easy one to choose? I can't know at this point without a better grasp of how exactly the gadgick works."

Sevana frowned as she followed along with his train of thought. "I would think the water element would be the easiest to remove."

"I'm inclined to agree," Master admitted. "But how to do so is the question. Is this something we can achieve by dismantling the water fountain itself? Or do we need to go even farther away from it so as to not set the shield off?"

All very good questions. She wished she had an answer. "Let me track down Decker and get some answers as to where this thing was. Surely that will help us figure at least part of it out."

"I certainly hope so," Sarsen muttered under his breath.

"I also want something else explained." Master braced his forearms against the table and leaned forward slightly. "You said that Jacen believed this gadgick was made for non-magical people to use to transport themselves long distance. Correct? And that he also said it was made to transport luggage and things of that sort as well."

She had a feeling he was leading up to something but simply nodded confirmation and let him continue.

"Now, your working theory at the moment is that the reason why it is transporting people in their sleep is because that is the only time they picture an image in their head of where to go. Is that right? But there's something that doesn't connect with this idea."

Sevana's brows drew together. He'd lost her. "What doesn't?"

"The rules of travel magic." He raised a hand to stop them from objecting. "Hear me out. No matter how amazing the old magic is, and how incomprehensible most of it is to us, there are certain fundamental rules that are inescapable. One is that in order to transport both people *and* objects, it would take more than just a mental picture of where to go. It would take a command, an insignia, *something* to move a group of people and their luggage all at once. Also, it troubles me that this only happens in sleep. People wish aloud to go to different places all the time. Why wait until the user is sleeping? Why the delay? I can't imagine that this was an intended feature."

"It didn't make a lot of sense to me either," Sarsen admitted. "No offense to Jacen."

"Even he admitted that he wasn't sure why it worked that way," Sevana added thoughtfully. "It was just the only theory that made any kind of sense that we could think of. So you think something else is at play here?"

"I think the original design has been badly knocked askew somehow." Master's tone grew more ruminative. "Although I'm not sure how. But I'm very hesitant to do anything else until we have more information. Just knowing where the gadgick originally rested and what the area looked like around it will tell us a great deal, I think. If I can just answer one of the questions I've posed, it'll allow us to make some logical deductions from there and perhaps we can think of a different line of attack."

Since she had spent the whole of yesterday with her thoughts circling each other like a dog chasing its tail, she didn't have any objections to more information. Pushing back from the table with a slight scrape of her chair, she waved for the other two to follow her. "In that case, let's go find Decker."

Decker hadn't the faintest idea, as he never hunted in that area, but he took them to Krause, who in turn took them to Hube. Hube, as it happened, was the village carpenter. He sat in his cluttered, dusty shop, carving on a long beam of wood, and listened to their request. Then he sat back on a nearby barstool, absently brushing wood shavings from his shirt and beard, dark eyes crinkled up at the corners in silent amusement.

"Do I 'member how the stones were laid out? I took it apart brick by brick and then rebuilt it meself. Of course I 'member!"

Sevana felt like raising her eyes to the heavens in a heartfelt prayer of thanks. "Then can you describe it to us?"

"I'll do you one better." He stood and twisted about, reaching for a slightly dingy pad of paper lying nearby, and grabbed a pencil that had seen sharper days. With rough, steady strokes, he sketched out in bold lines the layout. "This here, this is where the fountain's topper was," he explained even as he kept drawing, his eyes never leaving the paper.

"Wait, the topper?" Master pointed out the narrow window of the shop to where the fountain sat, several blocks away. "Do you mean to tell me that a part of that fountain was carried *intact* from the ruins?"

"Sure was." Hube nodded in confirmation, pausing long enough to respond directly. "That decorative lookin' piece on top is straight from the ruins. All I did was clean it up a bit and cart it over. Now, all the stones that make up the fountain are from the platform."

"Platform?" Sevana prompted impatiently.

Hube went back to his drawing. "Don't know what else to call it. Never could figure out what it was for. A large stretch of stones made up a raised platform, stretching about the length and breadth of the courtyard, I'd say. Most of the stones have been picked up and carted off, they being the easiest ones to get to, see. And they were pretty. I used 'em to build quite a few things in the village—houses, streets, walls, and the like." He tapped the center of the platform area he had marked off. "But the top of the fountain, it sat right smack in the middle. Had a canal of sorts running toward it from either end, splitting the area straight through. Probably carried water to it at one point, but the spring that fed it was well dried up by the time we came along."

"Pretty?" Sarsen asked with a slightly baffled frown.

Sevana shared the confusion. The stones looked to be of excellent cut, no mistake, but she hadn't seen much of a difference between the ones used for the fountain and the ones used everywhere else.

Hube nodded. "Used 'em to tile the inside of the fountain with, and you have to know what you're lookin' for 'cause of the water distorting things, but the stones had a really pretty design carved into 'em. Most people have at least one in their homes, above the fireplace or the doorway or some such. A decorative piece, you could call it."

Sevana's eyes closed in fatalistic understanding as the pieces started to click. "I don't even have to look to know."

"Neither do I," Master agreed, blowing out a breath.

Hube blinked at them, head cocked in question, obviously not following.

"The pretty designs on those stones weren't designs at all," Sarsen explained patiently. Although from the expression on his face, it looked like he wanted to find some hard surface and start banging his head against it. "They were, in fact, magical incantations that gave the artifact power and direction."

Hube's eyes bulged, nearly falling out of his head.

"I'd bet direction more than power," Master added. "Finally, *finally* this is starting to make sense. How did the gadgick know who and what to transport? Everything on top of that platform, of course.

The canal that connected to the fountain supplied it with water so that it had all the power it needed. By removing the stones, and using it to build all over this village, it has turned this entire place into a platform. Putting the fountain *back* in the center and supplying it with water was the final piece. It had everything it needed to function again."

"It also explains why the destinations are so random, and why it's transporting only a person at a time and no objects." Sevana felt torn between elation at getting some true answers and frustration that the answer had been right in front of her this whole time. She just hadn't known enough to know what questions to ask. "I'd bet that part of the incantation inscribed in those stones also gave it *instructions*. With the stones literally scattered everywhere, with no rhyme or reason to it, the gadgick must be getting some very confusing and mixed-up signals."

"I'm amazed it's actually working as well as it is," Sarsen agreed. "Although we're still missing something—I mean, it's only transporting people. If the stones are throughout the village, shouldn't things be disappearing as well? Or—" he cut himself off as all three of them exchanged understanding looks. "The water."

"The water," Master agreed. "I'd lay good odds that the water plays into this somehow. I'm just not quite sure how. Direct contact?"

"It would have to be." Sevana chewed at a thumbnail before adding, almost to herself, "Or it could be the reflected light...no, I suppose not. It wouldn't explain why the stones outside haven't had some sort of effect."

Hube looked between them with a wildly panicked expression. "W-wait, did I cause all this?"

Master laid a comforting hand on his shoulder, expression and voice gentle. "Master Hube, you could *not* have known what those stones were. Or what they were intended to do. Indeed, it's taken *four Artifactors* to figure it out! And even now there are parts of this puzzle we haven't worked through completely."

"Unfortunately true," Sevana grimaced. Oh, to have some sort of device that would let her go back in time. It would make solving the current problem so much easier.

"Indeed, by telling us what you have and giving us this wonderful drawing to look at, you've given us valuable information that we were in sore need of." Master gave him a particularly charming, sincere smile known to make puppies whine and children giggle. "For that, you have my heartfelt thanks."

Hube nodded in acknowledgement, but he clearly felt rattled by the notion that he'd directly played a part in the current disastrous state of affairs.

Sevana turned to the other two men. "As I see it, we have two options at the moment. Either we focus on the fountain and try to dismantle it, *or* we first go throughout the village and hunt up those inscribed stones and remove them. The second option won't fix the problem, not really, but it'll give us more leisure to work with."

Sarsen grimaced. "Although it would be very tedious."

"It would be just like a scavenger hunt," Master disagreed, face lighting up with childish enthusiasm. "It sounds fun!"

She and Sarsen both gave him a weary look. Why did he have to be so cheerful at the worst times? "I say we try dismantling the fountain first," she said firmly.

Master actually *pouted* at her, although his dancing eyes suggested that he was only half-serious. "You never want to play with me, sweetling."

She rolled her eyes. "Why do I always have to be the adult? Fountain first."

"I'm not sure if that will work well, Sev," Sarsen warned. "I mean, look at what happened yesterday."

"Well, I'm half-inclined to agree with you," she admitted with a wince. "But I'm still trying to be hopeful. Yesterday, we attacked the fountain *magically*. And we actually targeted the gadgick more than the fountain. If we can just remove one or two stones from the very base of the fountain, draining most of the water, we *might* be able to weaken the gadgick enough to turn if off completely."

"That's a very large *if,* sweetling." Master frowned and rubbed at his chin as he thought. "But I suppose it bears trying. We'll need to approach this cautiously, though. Say, one of us tries to remove the stone, the other two have shields and protective charms at the ready."

If it meant avoiding the disastrous scene from yesterday, Sevana was all for it. "Then I'll handle removing the stone."

Both men let out a squawk of protest, words overlapping.

"Sev, you can't take on the most dangerous part of the job—"

"Sweetling, you're still sore and aching from yesterday—"

She held up both hands to forestall the rest of their objections. "This isn't up for debate, gentlemen. This is a task that *I* took on. I will be the one that bears the brunt of the dangers. I would rather have the two of you protecting me in case this does go wrong."

"But sweetling—" Master started again, stubborn and worried.

"No," she said in a tone that brooked no disagreement. "If you're so worried about what might happen, then you'd best focus on casting strong shields around me."

Master stared at her for a long moment, eyes searching for any sign of hesitation on her part. He didn't find any. With a long groan, his shoulders slumped and he complained to Sarsen, "She's impossible to deal with when she gets like this."

"I know." Sarsen grimaced, passing a hand wearily over his face. "Alright, Sev, we'll try it your way."

"Good." Turning on her heel, she headed for the door. "Let's go try it, then."

"Wait, now?!" Sarsen objected, scrambling after her. "Oh, my thanks, Master Hube."

She paused and nodded thanks to the man as well—he had been very helpful—before asking Sarsen dryly, "What, you have something else to do on your schedule?"

"Well, no, but—"

"This isn't going to take any elaborate preparations," she pointed out, not slowing her pace as she started up the street and toward the main square.

"She does have a point." Master kept up with her quick pace easily, not seeming to be at all fazed by her snap decision. "And if this doesn't work, we need to know it now so that we can go on to the next idea. We have plenty of time, as it's still relatively early in the morning. We might as well try it now rather than later."

"Well, I suppose you're both right...."

Finally, they both saw the sense of trying it now. It wouldn't take more than a few minutes to see if it would work or not. Either the shield would not react or it would. It was as simple as that. Hmmm. But how to approach this problem specifically? They'd tried magic yesterday. Would it be better to go with a completely non-magical approach this time? Perhaps the shield had only been designed to react to magical interference. Perhaps taking a stonemason's tools to it wouldn't trigger the shield at all.

Even inside of her head that sounded like wishful thinking.

During the course of her career, Sevana had found it handy to carry a wide range of tools on her. Most of the time, all she really needed were her wands, crystals, potions, and the protective charms. But occasionally, she found it necessary to carve an incantation into rock and she didn't like having to go all the way back to her workroom just to fetch the right tools. Because of that, her pouch always had a cross pein hammer and a bull point chisel, both tools of the trade for stonemasons. These two tools alone had the right weight and precision to let her carve fine details into stone. They might not be right for the job of working a stone out of a fountain, but for the purpose of testing a theory, they'd do just fine.

Sevana crossed the square, not oblivious to the onlookers that paused and watched the three Artifactors make a beeline for the fountain. If they wanted to look, she'd let them. They had proven yesterday, after all, that the shield really would only react to whoever attacked it and no one else.

She stopped right at the basin's edge and took a look at the fountain with new eyes. The 'decorative piece' as Hube called it sat in the very center, on the third and upmost level of the fountain, and didn't look at all extraordinary. Oh, it looked interesting, granted. Some ancient and long dead stonemason had carved it to be a fairy maiden with a jug on her shoulder and flowers all around her feet. The jug let out a constant stream of water that flowed from the basin at her feet and into the second level, and from there to the third. The water didn't have a strong flow to it, compared to other fountains she'd seen, but it kept the water moving at a strong enough clip that some of it sprayed her face lightly with errant drops as she knelt at the fountain's edge.

She took out her bull point chisel and hammer from her leather pouch, shifting to try and find a more comfortable angle for her knees. "Are you two ready?"

Master and Sarsen stood near either shoulder, their wands out in one hand, a protective charm clutched in the other. Hinun stood directly behind her, not only looking on with great interest, but keeping other people from getting too close. In fact, he stood so close that she could feel his breath against her back. Now, just where had he come from? He'd been napping on the inn's front porch during breakfast and they'd left him there when they went to speak with Hube.

"Ready, sweetling," Master assured her calmly.

Taking a breath, and casting a fervent prayer up toward the heavens that this would work, she leaned forward and placed the chisel in the mortar between two stones. Raising her hammer, she hit the chisel squarely.

In the next second, a strong force threw her backward, knocking her directly into the wolf. Her breath escaped her lungs in a *whoosh* but she didn't go far. Hinun had braced himself and caught her body weight, preventing her from doing anything more than losing her balance.

She blinked, shaking her head slightly to clear it, and looked up. Master and Sarsen's faces were strained with clenched jaws and brows furrowed, the charms in their hands flaring and burning in white light as they activated. Clearly, the fountain's shield tested both of their magical strength. But it didn't last for more than a few moments. As quickly as it had flared up, it died back down again, leaving no sign that anything had occurred. Even her attempt to chisel at the mortar hadn't left a single scratch behind.

Curse it.

With a pat of thanks to Hinun's back, she pushed herself to her feet. "That was a spectacular failure."

Master let his arms relax to his sides. "But it does answer our question. The shield protects from *all* interference, magical and otherwise. We are going to have to do this the hard way."

"Master," Sarsen requested in weary resignation, "Why do you grin like a delighted child when you say that?"

"I like scavenger hunts!" Master protested, smile becoming outright impish.

Sevana looked at that expression and groaned. This would turn out to be a long, long day.

Sevana landed roughly on her right side and skidded slightly on the ground, sharp pointy things pricking her and scratching even through the clothes. With a hiss of pain she finally fetched to a stop against a very wide tree trunk that slammed into her back. It knocked the air right out of her lungs and she gasped, eyes going dark for a moment.

For several long moments she just lay there gasping for breath. Alive? She must be. She was in too much pain to be dead. As she got her breath back, she took mental stock. Her skin sent up pain signals from the scratches—for purely superficial wounds, they were putting up quite the fuss—back aching right down to the bones from the trunk digging into her, her whole right side complaining in general. But none of it seemed serious enough to prevent her getting up and moving.

She'd been transported. *She'd been TRANSPORTED.* In the dead of night, just like all the other villagers! Sweet mercy, even though she'd taken precautions against something like this happening, she wasn't remotely happy about being dumped outside in the middle of the night!

Something wet and slightly smelly touched her face. Flinching back from it instinctively, she looked up, forcing her eyes to focus. Black. Black and…gold eyes. Eh?

"Hinun, did you come with me?" Granted, he'd been sleeping with her, but—

Hinun let out a soft huff and nosed her again, this time getting her cheek nice and wet with slobber.

"UGH, off!" Pushing him away, she wiped at her face and struggled to sit up. It hurt more than expected, but not enough for it to be from broken bones. She'd probably have quite the pattern of black and blue bruises to show though. Sitting upright, she leaned her back against the trunk and took a good look around.

Her heart abruptly sank. Not a single thing looked remotely familiar.

Sevana traveled a great deal because of her profession and she had been in and around the world more often than she could count. That said, there were still areas that she'd never been to and this appeared to be one of them. (She couldn't see how the evil fountain would know that, but she just knew it had somehow done this on purpose.) In every direction all she could see were trees—large, thick, ancient trees that rose so high into the sky that they obscured all sight of the sun. It felt like twilight in here because of the dimness. Most of the ground had nothing but moss and boulders with a few errant saplings here and there struggling to survive.

Where in the world had that thing sent her?

For that matter, why had she also been affected?

She turned back to the wolf that sat patiently next to her. He didn't seem injured in any way, as he just sat there and panted, not at all distressed. "And how in sweet mercy's name did you manage to follow me here?"

He leaned forward and bit her sleeve in a demonstrative manner before pulling back.

"You grabbed me?" she repeated in shock. "Why? Trying to prevent me from going?"

Hinun let out a soft huff.

Incredible. Just how sensitive was he to magic that he could feel the spell building and react *that* quickly? Maybe she should look into getting a wolf of her own—oh wait. She couldn't. She had a cat. A useless one at that.

She used the trunk behind her as a support as she pushed her way to her feet. Her body sent signals of *don't do that!* She ignored them and kept moving. "Hinun, can you smell people anywhere nearby?

Fire or food being cooked, anything like that?" It would at least give them a destination for now, and once she knew where they were, she could call for help. Useless to do so now—the first question they'd ask would be "Where are you?" and Sevana hated the words *I don't know* with a passion.

Hinun lifted his nose in the air and started sniffing, his head swiveling this way and that as he sought a scent. He did this for a good minute before he stepped forward a few feet, sniffing harder.

"That way? You don't look too sure of that. Too faint for you to be certain, eh? Well, it's as good a direction as any. Lead on." She fell into step behind him and they weaved their way around the massive trees. Sevana felt about as tall and significant as an ant in this place. This primitive, untouched forest must be at least two thousand years old. Very few forests in Mander could boast such an age and it gave her some sort of clue on their whereabouts.

Unfortunately, most of the forests that fit these surroundings were in far western Kindin. It would be quite the task of fetching her home again if she really was where she thought she was.

She couldn't make it more than two steps before the bad lighting forced her to light her wand with a quick spell. It hovered in front of her forehead, lighting her path, letting her see her surroundings a bit better. At least, it let her see where she put her feet down. The massive trunks of the trees blocked her light from penetrating more than a short distance in any direction. Sevana judged it to be pre-dawn, but she couldn't see anything more than smatterings of the sky above her and it didn't give her any solid clue to the time. The grayish-blue color could belong to twilight or just before sunrise.

In a village with a transportation artifact acting up, she had never dared to get completely undressed, and that was to her aid right now. She did not have shoes on, so the odd sticks and pebbles on the ground dug into her feet, making her wince and curse. But at least she had warm trousers and a sweater instead of a flimsy nightgown. Although she firmly intended to buy shoes the minute she reached a town. Or village. Or a random trading post, for that matter.

With no clock, and the sky blocked overhead, Sevana had no way of keeping track of the time. It felt like an endless eternity before she stepped around the last massive tree and entered what seemed to be a more normal forest. At least here, the trees didn't loom overhead and she could climb one if she felt inclined to do so. The lighting also improved, mellow sunlight filtering in through the leaves. Alright, so it looked like dawn had arrived while she wandered aimlessly through a pitch-black forest. First good news she'd had all night.

"Hinun? Any signs of people?"

He huffed in agreement, his pace picking up slightly. Obviously, he had a firmer line on a scent this time.

"Good." She followed him on aching, cold feet, trying to avoid the obvious sticks that waited to trip her up. She missed a few of the ones buried under a thick carpet of dry leaves, unfortunately, and got scratched for her efforts. "From now on," she promised herself between clenched teeth, "I will go to sleep with my boots tied to my wrist."

They abruptly left the forest, stepping into a wide expanse of rolling grassland. In the near distance, she saw a thriving port town that sat right on the edge of the water, the docks busy with ships coming and going. Blinking to let her eyes adjust to the brighter light, she lifted one hand to her forehead and did a slow turn, taking in everything in front of her. The coastline turned and twisted like a snake, making a rough crescent shape until it faded off into the far distance. To her left, she had another shoreline with the same sort of massive trees and primitive forest like the one she had just left.

Her heart sank. She had never been in this part of the world, but the way the land was shaped and the landmarks she saw were unmistakable. That thrice-cursed, gormless artifact had transported her completely across the world! She was on the far west coast of Kindin, near Ocean Woods. It would, in fact, take the better part of four days to fetch her back to Chastain.

Letting her head fall back, she let out a groan. "If it wasn't a priceless artifact, I'd take great delight in smashing it into little tiny pieces for this."

Hinun let out an inquiring whine.

"It's alright," she assured him with a long sigh. "I know where we are." Digging through her pouch, she lifted her Caller out and let it rest on her open palm. "Master."

It didn't even take a full second before the Caller came abruptly alive. "*Sevana! Where are you? You're not doing anything reckless, are you?*"

What, did he think she got out of bed at some forsaken hour of the morning to test out a theory? "Master, I'm not in Windamere."

The Caller went abruptly still, Master's expression on the white porcelain becoming set, as if he had just braced himself for the worst. "*Then where are you?*"

"Just outside of Boscareno, near Ocean Woods," she responded sourly. "That thrice-cursed gadgick transported me in my sleep."

"*IT DID WHAT?!*"

"We obviously didn't find enough stones yesterday to make any real difference." She made a face. "Unfortunately. It would make our lives simpler if we had."

"*Never mind that right now. Are you alright, sweetling?*"

"I've had better nights, but I'm fine. So's Hinun."

Master rubbed at the bridge of his nose. "*My wolf is with you?*"

"Well, he was sleeping with me." She shrugged. "He said he grabbed me when he felt me abruptly shift. So he tagged along on this adventure."

"*I suppose I am relieved to hear that, in a way. Wait, how are you able to call me?*"

"Fortunately for all, I've been wrapping the strap of my magic pouch around my wrist and sleeping with it every night since I came to Chastain. Just in case something like this happened." And to think last night she had nearly not done so because she thought the danger mostly passed. Who said that paranoia didn't pay off?

"*Good thinking on your part. Alright. I shall come to get you.*"

After the night she just had, she had absolutely no desire to come up with some way of transporting herself back. Her farsee glasses were back in Chastain, laying on the table. The nearest clock she had was in Tavaris, far south of here, and it would take the better part of two days to get to it by conventional means of travel. (In other words, the foul beasts known as horses.) And she didn't even want to think about how troubling it would be to go into a major city with a wolf in tow. "Fine. I'll be here."

The Caller went still in her hands. Blowing out a breath, she looked down at Hinun and said, "Shoes first. And then let's find breakfast, shall we?"

They actually ended up eating breakfast first, as neither she nor Hinun had the desire to shop on an empty stomach. Fortunately, food stalls didn't care if their patrons were shoed or not. But after that, they went on a shopping spree of sorts based upon the funds in her wallet. Something else she had prepared for, in the (un)likely event of her being transported, was having the means necessary to return. She'd placed a goodly amount of money, a spare wand, and a few charms into her magical pouch. From there, she could finance her stay in the town and buy some necessary clothes. Her own were rather wrecked after last night's events.

She could always work a small, local job or fulfill some task posted on the town's job request board if she ran low on money, but it proved unnecessary to worry. Boscareno didn't have much size to it, as it primarily served as a stop for sailors and traders after sailing around Kitra Isle. The docks, in fact, made up most of the town, and taverns, bars, restaurants and a few tradesmen shops made up the rest. In the course of walking down the main street and finding a clothing store, she saw three bar fights that tumbled out into the open road, one robbery, and one attempted murder. To label this place as 'lawless' would be putting it mildly. Thank mercy Hinun had come along with her. With a gigantic wolf trotting along at her side, no one quite dared to mess with her.

Because of the town's makeup, and its rough clientele, none of the rooms at the inns proved to be very expensive. In fact, it only took her three tries to find a decent inn with clean bedding and a good price. She could stay here, eat well, and be comfortable while waiting on Master without even being in danger of running through all her money. If she had to be transported willy-nilly to some foreign place, Sevana guessed Boscareno wasn't half-bad all in all.

She took a quick bath and changed into her new clothes. By that time, her stomach started rumbling for lunch, so she and Hinun went out again. The inn might have decent beds, but judging from the slightly repulsive smell emanating from the kitchen, she would need to find her meals elsewhere.

Hmm, now, where to eat? Another street vendor? That had proven to be surprisingly good food this morning. She wouldn't be averse to the idea. She'd already explored down this street, so perhaps she should go up instead. Sevana made it all of three feet.

"What the—?!"

Sevana couldn't believe her eyes. She knew Kindin had a harsh reaction to thievery, but…no rationalization could explain this. In front of her, right in the middle of the street, a bear of a man gripped a child's arm and raged at him, the other hand a balled fist ready to strike. The boy couldn't have been more than eight, with an emasculate frame, rags passing for clothes, and hair that hung into his face. He looked terrified but oddly resigned at the same time, as if he had been in this position before and knew exactly what to expect.

Sevana's Kindish couldn't be described as completely perfect, and the way the merchant—she assumed him to be one from his dress— screamed at the boy didn't help her understanding, so she didn't catch all of what he said. But it boiled down to this being the second time the boy had stolen food from him, and *this* time he wouldn't get another chance to roam free.

If someone applied the proper amount of thumb screws, lye, and hot irons, Sevana might reluctantly admit that she had a soft spot for children. She blamed this mushy tendency on her little brother, Shion. Being a big sister to him had conditioned her to be more protective and patient with children than she was naturally inclined to be. In fact, she'd often wondered if her easy willingness to help a certain child prince had been because he'd been in the body of a young child.

Seeing a child being threatened with violence made her protective instincts raise its head like a coiled snake preparing to strike. The more she watched, the more intense her anger grew until red seemed to cloud her vision. Anyone with a trace of compassion would have let the kid off at the very least, seeing how desperate he was for food. But this merchant was clearly one of the few individuals in the world that had *less* compassion than she, because he didn't seem the least bit moved by the boy's plight, and was instead threatening him with punishments that made her hair stand on end.

The whole scene made her blood boil.

Making a snap decision, she stalked forward, raising her voice to a booming pitch.

"Hold it, you walking bear rug!"

The merchant didn't notice her. He kept shaking the boy and screaming. Sevana's hand started twitching, itching for a wand so she could hex the blighter. It would be just desserts, in her opinion. Perhaps fortunately for the merchant, she didn't have a good wand handy in her pouch for hexing people. Although…she did have that one crystal that might be encouraged to react *like* a hex….

Before she could properly develop this idea, one of the assistants hovering nearby noticed her and said something to the man while tugging insistently on one sleeve, and finally the merchant paused and snapped his head around to glare at her. "Vat you vant, voman?!"

"That boy in your grasp," she snapped back. "If you had any pity in you, you'd see he's starved and on death's doorstep and you wouldn't be shaking him, but feeding him! But if you're so blind with greed you can't see it, I'll take him from you and see to him myself."

"This boy stole from me *two* times!" the merchant bellowed like a wounded bear.

"And you should have gotten the hint the first time!" she growled back, stopping directly in front of him. She had to crane her neck to look up at him, as he towered over her, but the difference in height didn't faze her. "Aish, forget it! You merchants only really speak in one language. How much?"

He frowned down at her, eyebrows forming a straight line. "Vhat?"

"How much did he steal from you?" she elaborated, toe tapping an impatient rhythm. "I'll reimburse you for it if you'll give him to me."

"*Vou* pay for him?" he parroted in stunned surprise. "Vhat for? He belong to vou?"

The boy looked at her askance, clearly wondering the same thing. She glanced at him before answering them both, "He doesn't. But that doesn't matter to you. All you need to know is that I'll reimburse you for what he stole and take him off your hands so you won't have to deal with him again."

A greedy light sparked in the merchant's eyes. "He stole bread, cheeze, fruit vine—it cost three silver."

"It cost one silver," she corrected immediately, knowing good and well the game he played. "And you're trying to get the value of what he stole *last* time out of me. That's not the deal. I'll pay you one silver for what he stole *this* time."

"Two," he riposted immediately.

"One," she maintained firmly. "It's a good bargain, merchant. If you sent him off to prison, or cut off his hands for thieving as you were threatening earlier, it won't reimburse you for what he's already eaten. It might salve your anger, but it won't put money back in your pocket. The silver I offer will."

He hesitated, weighing scales in his eyes as he calculated at high speeds.

"Plus, I'll take him out of this area, out of the country entirely," she added, sweetening the deal. "There's *no* possibility of him returning to steal from you again."

He looked at her under lowered brows, eyes probing. Didn't entirely buy that last statement, eh? "Two," he repeated.

Stubborn, greedy, gormless twit…urgh. "Fine." She dug into her pouch without breaking eye contact with him, pulled two silver free and slammed them into his open hand. "But don't you dare report him to the authorities or anything else like that. He's mine now."

For the first time, a hint of curiosity came over the man's face. "Vhat you vant with him?"

"My business."

The merchant just shrugged before letting go and putting a hand on the boy's back, pushing him forward. Sevana, knowing good and well that the kid would probably try to bolt as soon as he thought he could, caught hold of his wrist in a firm grip. "Good. Come along, kiddo."

He fought her grasp for a second, making a sound of fear in the back of his throat. Huh? Oh, right. "The wolf is a friend, he won't hurt you."

The boy didn't look at her, his eyes fixed on Hinun, but when Hinun didn't do anything more than stare back, the child cautiously started to follow her.

He stumbled along in her wake as she headed back up the street. When they were a good distance away, she studied her new charge. Still couldn't see his face, not with the hair hanging so badly over his eyes, but what she could see made her stomach twist. Blond hair matted and filthy to where it almost looked brunet, pale skin mottled with bruises and small cuts, no sign of extra flesh on him anywhere. She wanted to ask a lot of questions, but had a feeling he wouldn't say a word. Not now. He didn't trust her now. She had to prove some goodwill first, otherwise they wouldn't make any progress.

Groaning, she looked toward the heavens. She already had enough trouble on her hands. Just what was she doing, picking up a stray?

Alright, done deal now. She'd manage somehow.

A food stall caught her eye. It didn't offer much, just a booth with two tables out front and a sign with the menu scrawled in chalk. But a good smell wafted from it and she didn't think the kid would care what he ate at this point. She made a beeline for it.

For a split second, her grip loosened. The boy ripped his hand free and took off like a shot.

Sevana was so startled by this abrupt movement that she just stood there and gaped for a second. For a boy in such a poor condition, he moved like lightning! Then she let out a growl. Oh for the love of all—

"Hinun?"

The wolf looked up at her curiously.

She pointed to the fleeing boy. "Fetch."

His tongue lolled out to one side in amusement before he took off in a quick lope.

While she waited for the two to return, she went to the vendor, calling out as she approached, "Three meat pies, two ciders, and a fruit tart."

By the time that she had situated herself comfortably at the table and taken a bite, the duo had returned. Hinun had the boy's arm in his mouth, the grip clearly firm without being painful. At least, she didn't see any blood trailing out of his mouth.

The white of the boy's eyes showed. Sevana thought about explaining how Hinun would never in a million years harm a child. Then she thought better of it. Naw, if the kid was scared of Hinun, he'd think twice about running off again.

"Good job," she praised the wolf, lowering a meat pie to the ground. "Here. Kid, sit and eat."

He peeked up at her from under his bangs but slowly moved, doing as she said. As soon as he sat at the table, he started gobbling it down. Sevana shifted on the wooden bench, the wood cold against her thighs and arms, and ate at a much slower rate. She mostly watched him, trying to think of a solution to this problem she'd just adopted.

He ate the meat pie in seconds, drained the cider, and almost reached for the food in front of her before he froze and withdrew his hands reluctantly. Silently, she pushed the tart at him and he snatched it up, devouring that in three quick bites as well, nearly choking in the process.

"Slow down," she advised. "Too much food at once will make you sick. Besides, after this, you won't need to worry about meals anymore."

He froze again, looking at her anxiously. "A-are you a slaver?"

Oh? That wasn't a Kindin accent at all. He sounded Windameran. Just how in the wide green world had the kid come all the way out here? She snorted at his question, amused. "No. I'm an Artifactor. Name's Sevana Warran."

He blinked at her several times, his expression blank. "Artifactor?"

"Do you know what that is?"

"A…er, type of magician?"

"Sort of. We make all the spells, potions, and tools that magicians use," she explained. "We're magical experts, I suppose you can say. The wolf is Hinun, a friend."

He looked rather impressed by this. "So, why'd you help me?"

"Can't ignore a person in trouble," she shrugged. "It's a bad habit I picked up from my Master."

For some reason, he looked disappointed at this. "So…it's not 'cause you sensed magic in me?"

What, he thought she picked him up because she thought he might make a good apprentice? That only happened in fairy tales. "Sorry kid. You don't have a shred of magical ability in you."

He slumped in on himself, eyes falling to the table. In a smaller, world-weary voice he asked, "Then what? Whatcha plan to do with me?"

"Now that," she admitted ruefully, "Is an excellent question."

They started with a bath, haircut, and a change of clothes.

Sevana mistakenly tried just sending him into the bathroom with directions to wash thoroughly first. When he came out wet, but still mostly dirty, she mentally kicked herself. Why did she think that a little boy with no raising would know how to properly wash?

Grabbing him by the arm, she towed him back into the bathroom and this time, she scrubbed him down herself. There was a lot of splashing and protests from her wet captive, but she didn't let up until he actually looked and smelled clean. When he finally escaped, the bath water was muddy and filthy.

Wrapping him in a towel, she sat him on a stool and started in on his hair next. It was so matted, getting a comb through it was nigh impossible. She started cutting out the worst chunks, working through the rest carefully to avoid scalping him completely.

He started squirming, head jerking from side to side.

"If you don't stop that, you're going to lose an ear," she casually threatened.

The fidgeting abruptly ceased.

"What's your name, anyway?" Sevana hadn't thought to ask before.

He muttered something she couldn't hear.

"What? And speak up properly."

"Sky," he repeated, exhaling noisily.

Sky? What an odd name.

"Don't know what my real name is," he admitted. "I been working ships ever since I was little, till the last one sank near the coast and stranded me here. But people call me Sky 'cause it's the color of my eyes."

True, he did have the most amazing sky-blue eyes. She could see where the nickname came from. But if he didn't even know what his real name was, then odds of him having any family to return to were extremely low.

"You…" he paused, visibly searching for the best words. "You told Bristly earlier that I wouldn't stay here."

"Bristly? Oh, you mean that bear of a merchant?" Accurate nickname, considering the way his beard had bristled out as he talked. She grinned, liking the creativity. "Yes, I did."

"So where you going?"

"*We* are going to Windamere," she corrected. "That's where I live. Although right now I have a job on the Windamere border that I'm in the middle of. I need to get back to it."

"Oh."

What, no more questions? Sevana had this lurking suspicion that he didn't trust her completely yet. Ah well, time would sort that out.

"Oww!"

She stopped attacking that particular tangle with the comb and shifted to the scissors instead. "Sky," she asked in exasperation and no little amount of irritation, "When was the last time that you cut your hair?"

He thought about that for a second before offering, "Don't remember?"

She believed that answer. "Kid, I've seen bird nests that weren't as tangled as this. I'm going to have to cut this very short to get it decent looking again."

He shrugged, obviously not caring.

Well, if he didn't care, she certainly didn't. Sevana went back to work with intense concentration. It had been a while since she'd cut anyone's hair and she would admit, to herself at least, that it wasn't one of the things she was particularly talented in. It took her two tries to get the cut even on all sides, and he ended up with hair that was barely more than a finger's length. A bit short and choppy looking, but the knots and tangles were gone, you could run a comb through it without problem, and it actually looked blond now. Sevana considered it a win and dusted him free of hair. "Alright, you're done. Pull some clothes on. My stomach is rumbling for dinner."

He went for the new clothes folded on the bed with commendable alacrity. Sevana just focused on brushing herself free of hair before folding her rolled up sleeves down. She couldn't believe it had taken three hours to buy him new clothes, bathe him, and get his hair cut.

Well, at least it had occupied her time, right?

Shaking her head, she waited for him to pull on his boots before shooing him out the door.

Sevana woke up slowly, stretching her arms out as she did so. Mmmm, so comfortable. It was nice, once in a while, to not wake up because you had a cat on your chest cutting off all air, or because a mountain rumbled at you, or because someone had an emergency that needed attention *right this minute*. As rude as her trip here had been, Sevana admitted that it rather felt like a vacation now.

A wet nose poked her in the ribs.

I take it back. There's still someone here to wake me up, she grumbled internally. Cracking open one eye, she glared at Hinun. "What?"

He gave an anxious whine and did a half-step toward the door, clearly wanting her to follow him.

For a moment, she didn't follow. If Hinun wanted out, he could do that himself. He knew how to open doors. So why…? She sat up, and as she did, her gaze fell on the narrow bed on the opposite end of the room.

The empty bed.

Oh sweet mercy…really? Had Sky really taken off sometime during the night?

Groaning, she flopped back onto the bed, making the springs squeak. This was ridiculous. She'd been nice to the kid, hadn't she?

Or at least, she'd fed him, and bought him good clothes, and hadn't yelled at him. Considering the treatment he was used to, that surely qualified as 'nice.' So why had he taken off?

But she knew the answer to that question before she even asked it.

Street rats like Sky learned very early on that no one offered a free meal. The cold, merciless world they inhabited took more than it gave, and if they weren't quick or careful enough, then someone would eventually take advantage of them. Better to take what they could and run rather than trust anyone or anything. Really, she should have known that not giving him a definite reason why she helped him would make him wary of her. Well, war*ier*.

Now that he had taken off, what was she supposed to do? Most would probably shrug, thinking he had made his choice, and let him go. But Sevana knew good and well that if she let the kid be, he'd be right back in the same situation she'd found him in tomorrow. It wasn't enough to save him for just one day.

Hinun let out another whine, impatient at her stillness.

"Wait," she told him without taking her eyes off the ceiling. "I'm thinking."

He let out a disgusted huff.

"Unless you want the kid to run off again, let me think."

That got her nothing but silence.

What could she possibly do with a nonmagical child? If he'd had any sort of magical talent, she would have taken him straight to a master of some sort and bought him an apprenticeship. But as he didn't, that couldn't happen. So what else...hmm.

Her own thoughts sparked something, a memory of a promise that she had made months ago. A nonmagical child.

A young child that no one wanted? Check.

A child with a certain attractiveness to them? With all that dirt and grime gone, he had proven to be fairly cute. So, check.

A child under no magical influence whatsoever? Check.

Sevana grinned in feral satisfaction. Perfect. She could kill two birds with one stone this way.

Throwing back the covers, she came quickly to her feet, reaching for her clothes as she did so. "Hinun, you got his scent?"

The wolf looked at her as if she had asked a particularly dumb question.

Which, granted, it had been. "Sorry I asked. Alright, let me get together a basket of food and then we'll go after him."

By the time she finished buying breakfast, Hinun was dancing with impatience. He'd apparently attached himself to the kid. But then, he thought of all children as little creatures he had to protect, so she should have expected this reaction. When she signaled that she was ready, he promptly led her straight out of the 'nicer' section of town and into the slums.

Sevana had been in a variety of places in her life, everywhere from dragon's lairs to castle dungeons, with sometimes very hostile creatures to keep her company. She and danger were more than nodding acquaintances. But this place unnerved her. The buildings were in such sorry shape that only the fact they leaned against each other kept them upright. Nothing had window panes, rotting boards were nailed over the window frames and most of the doorways. The place had litter and refuse of all sorts strewn in the streets and stacked up in the alleyways. It stank like rotting fish and horse piss. Her nose curled up at the smell and it took considerable effort to not gag.

How Hinun could bear to put his nose against the ground was beyond her.

After several minutes of wading through trash, her nose shut down completely, which actually gave her some relief. Hinun lifted his nose, sneezed, then bounded off in a fast sprint.

Sevana felt absolutely no need to try and follow. Anyone that tried to keep up with a wolf was foolhardy. Besides, it would have been unnecessary. Hinun showed up a few minutes later with the boy in tow, tail wagging happily.

Sky, having experienced this before, didn't look terrified this time. He did look bewildered and somewhat angry, though, if that narrow-eyed look at her was anything to judge by.

Hinun dragged him straight to her and then dropped the arm, tongue lolling in amusement.

Crossing his arms in front of his chest, Sky demanded of her, "You keep sending him after me! But you don't know what to do with me, right? Then why hunt me down?"

"For the fun of it?"

Sky's eyes crossed as if he couldn't even comprehend this answer.

"But I do have a plan," she admitted cheerfully.

"…You do?"

"Sure. Master's the reason why I have this bad habit. So he gets to deal with you."

Sky gave her a weary look.

"Not a plan, eh?" Sevana chuckled, enjoying the teasing. "Well, I've got another one but first you need to answer a few questions for me, verify some things." She looked around and found a pair of stone steps that were relatively clear of refuse. She put a hand between his shoulder blades—thereby encouraging him to not run—and more or less forced him to go that direction. "Why don't we sit, have breakfast, and talk."

His eyes fell to the covered basket in her free hand and his tongue darted out to wet his lips. Sevana actually didn't have the habit of eating breakfast regularly, but she figured if she fed him, Sky would be more willing to hear her out. If she approached this right, she might even convince him to trust her, and then she wouldn't have to send Hinun after him again.

(Of course, she still intended to spell the door and window shut tonight.)

They sat on the cold and uninviting stone steps without a word passing between them, Hinun sitting at her feet. She passed bread and cheese around, then carved the hunk of cured ham into three equal slices. Hinun gulped his down, as usual, and Sky seemed intent on imitating him.

With him chewing, she started asking what she needed to know.

"Alright, Sky. Do you have family of any sort? Anyone that would miss you?"

He shook his head in short, jerky motions.

She hummed to herself again thoughtfully. This just might work. "Sky, what do you know about the Fae?"

"The who?"

"The Fae are a magical race that live deep within enchanted woods. They are beautiful, talented, and very strong people. Their magic is some of the most elegant and the most deadly ever seen by man. They are known to be wonderful allies and terrible enemies."

"Have you met them?" he interrupted, fascinated.

"I have," she answered, glad to see his interest. "The rumors don't do them justice. In fact, I made a promise to one and I think you can help me fulfill it."

His eyes crossed and he pointed at himself incredulously. "ME? But you said I don't have magic!"

"It's a good thing, too." Smirking, she paused for a second and bit into the ham. Hmm, not bad.

"You see, the Fae, for whatever reason, are unable to have children of their own. So they adopt them—they take human children, and over the years of living with them, the child slowly becomes a Fae like their adopted parents. By the time they reach adulthood, they are fully Fae, as if they had never been human in the first place."

It started to connect with him. She could see in his eyes that he suspected why she'd told him all of this. "W-what kind of children?" he asked in a trembling voice.

She ticked the points off on her fingers. "Any child that is unwanted by humans, is physically appealing, and is not under any magical influence. You fit the requirements perfectly."

He looked down at himself. "Appealing?" he asked doubtfully.

"It's just a matter of feeding you," she assured him, not unsympathetic. "Trust me. You're not ugly, just neglected. That said, I made a promise to one of the Fae months ago that if I ever saw a human child that didn't have a family and met the requirements, I would bring that child to him." Well, actually she'd promised to bring

Bel back, but close enough. "He and his wife are desperate for a child of their own, you see. Now, the question is this: do you want to go and meet them?"

He looked up at her with eyes wide. He looked…terrified. And hopeful. And anxious, all at once. "W-what if I don't?"

"I take you with me, find you a master that you can apprentice under, and you can make your own way in life," she answered steadily. "No matter what you choose, I'm not leaving you here. My master would come down on me like a hammer if I did."

He hesitated, mouth opening and closing without making a sound. She could see the thoughts flashing over his face, everything she had told him about the Fae conflicting with the view he had of himself. "I-I can't become like that."

"Sure you can," she denied easily. "Their magic will take care of that. Question is, do you want to? I warn you, if you go to them, they won't ever let you go. The Fae are a very tightknit community. They are very loyal to each other and they never, ever leave home."

She might as well have described a utopia to the boy. He looked so wistful that it was nearly painful to see. "You…you sure they'd take me?"

"In a heartbeat. And they'd be quite cross if I tried to take you back." Actually, they'd probably string her up by her toes and leave her for the wolves if she tried.

That settled it. He might not fully believe her, but he wanted to at least try. He nodded slowly. "T-then I want to meet 'em."

"Good enough for me." She took another bite of her breakfast. "Now, I should tell you, I can't take you to them immediately. I'm in the middle of a very important job at the moment. So you'll need to tag along with me for a few days, perhaps longer, before I can take you to the Fae."

He seemed oddly relieved, as if he wanted a delay to let all of this settle in his mind. "What kind of a job?"

"There's a village in trouble on the Windamere-Kindin border. I got transported out here accidentally, so I'm just waiting on my friend to come fetch me back again." In fact, while they were waiting, she might as well put the time to use and buy the kid some more changes of clothes. Right after she dumped him into another tub of hot water. "We'll work on getting some meat on you and some decent clothes before I take you to Noppers Woods. That's where the Fae live."

Food, at least, he could understand and he nodded happily.

Definitely needed those locking spells tonight, huh. She gave an internal sigh of resignation and kept eating. Well, if he did escape again, Hinun would find him.

Sevana actually felt glad after a certain point that she'd picked Sky up. Not just because it got her out of potential hot water with the Fae, but because it gave her something constructive to do while waiting for her ride.

In the time it took for Master to come fetch her, she made sure that Sky had multiple baths, ate at every opportunity, and bought two sets of clothes. He really needed more than that, but that's all her limited purse could afford. He looked better after two days of care. Still far too scrawny, and with traces of bruises and cuts here and there, but overall much healthier. She didn't worry about him putting some meat on, not with the way he ate. He could put Kip at his most hungry to shame.

To her surprise, now that she had given him a definite reason for his rescue, he seemed willing to trust her. If she had known that an excuse would work this kind of miracle, she'd have made something up on the spot when he'd asked her the first time. He still didn't trust the idea of becoming some fantastic, mythical creature, but he did trust that she had a plan in mind for him. Really, that was all she needed him to understand at this point.

By displaying consistent kindness in feeding him, Sky opened up to her bit by bit until he hung about and pestered her with questions. That was, until she hit upon the bright idea of sending him out with Hinun to "get some exercise." In spite of Hinun tracking him down twice and towing him back like a wanted criminal, the two of them had become friends. Sky liked the idea of having the responsibility of seeing to his wolf friend. Hinun, of course, could see to himself perfectly well without a human's interference. But he'd also spent the last twenty years with Master and a string of apprentices young and old. He knew how to look out for Sky.

Really, watching them interact, she couldn't figure out who was protecting who.

But they went out of the city for several hours at a time, romping and playing with each other, only coming back for dinner. It worked out perfectly as it got Sky out of her hair and let her have some peace to think.

She needed to think.

Master's hypothesis of how the gadgick worked made sense, but until this point, half of it had been deduction and guesswork. But now, experiencing things as she had firsthand, she knew exactly how it worked. And knowing that, she knew precisely what to do once she returned to Chastain.

Three days after her distress call, Master showed up early morning in his self-navigating box-on-wheels. He looked (and smelled) as if he had travelled straight there. Clothes beyond wrinkled, hair wispy and standing on end, beard fully started, and dark circles under his eyes. He looked like some sort of half-formed ghoul, really.

She met him at the inn door, smile wry. "Master."

"Sweetling." He wrapped her up in a strong bear hug that lifted her off her feet and made breathing a tad difficult.

"What is wrong with everyone?" she protested, trying to shove her way out of the embrace. "I'm not huggable!"

He ignored her, as he usually did during such protests, and sighed against the top of her head. "I'm glad to see you safe."

"I told you I was, didn't I?"

"*Your* definition of safe and *mine* are worlds apart," he countered dryly, finally letting her feet touch the floor again. "Oh? Who's this?"

Oh, right. She hadn't told him about Sky yet. Turning, she found the boy standing at the foot of the stairs. Hinun went directly to Master and pressed against his leg in greeting, which Master returned with a scratch behind one ear, but he didn't take his eyes off the nervous former street rat.

"This is Sky," Sevana introduced, not quite sure how to explain the semi-complicated relationship forged between them. "Sky, my Master, Tashjian Joles. He's come to take us to Chastain."

Sky relaxed a hair and gave the older Artifactor a deep bow. "Sir. It's an honor."

Master, putting on that charming smile of his, crossed to Sky so that he could sink to one knee, putting them on eye level. "The pleasure is mine, young sir. Tell me, how are you and Sevana acquainted?"

"She, uh, rescued me. Sir." Sky couldn't quite meet those penetrating eyes and he kept dropping his own gaze toward the floor. "I was…ah…in a bit of a pickle. She picked me up and promised to find me a home."

"I see." Master half-turned to beam at her. "Sweetling, I'm proud of you. You *did* learn to help people after all."

Sevana rolled her eyes expressively, putting one hand on her hip. "With you drumming it into my head day and night, did I have a choice? At any rate, I think Sky can smooth some ruffled feathers for me."

Master cocked an eyebrow. "Oh?"

"The Fae."

"Ohhh. Right, they're quite cross with you since you took Bel from them." Seeing Sky's confusion, Master patted him on the shoulder and said in a confidential tone, "You see, last fall, Sevana was helping to break a young man's curse. But the Fae picked him up and tried to adopt him. Sevana had to go and retrieve him, which upset the Fae. The only reason they let him go was because of the curse warping his body. Fae don't understand human magic, so they couldn't do anything about it. Still, it left bad relations between them. Sevana had to promise that if she found a child who was in need of a family, one without magic already on him, that she'd bring that child to them."

"Yes, sir," Sky managed neutrally. "So she told me. I don't think these Fae will take me, though."

Master cocked his head in question. "Why not?"

"'Cause I—" Sky bit his lip, cutting himself off.

"Child, you seem to have suffered through hard times, but all of the Fae are people who had a rough childhood." Master gave him a nod of reassurance. "I have no doubt they'll take you in and consider themselves blessed for it. But you'll see that for yourself soon, no doubt."

Sevana had already issued these assurances several times and had frankly gotten tired of the repetition. Hoping to cut it short, she cleared her throat. "Master, why don't you get a bath and a hot meal? I think we can leave after that."

"Are you suggesting I stink, sweetling?"

"You do," she responded promptly. "Hinun, back me up on this."

The wolf let out a whine of agreement.

Master put a hand to his heart in mock-hurt. "I go without sleep or comfort to get here and this is the thanks I get?"

"This and that are separate matters. Bath." After being cooped up in the carriage for three days, he'd probably enjoy one, so she knew he didn't really mind the order.

Chuckling, he pushed himself back to his feet. "It seems I've been outvoted on the matter. Then I shall. But let's leave soon. I want to hear about your experience. I trust it gave you some valuable insight?"

"Yes, because tromping around in primitive woods in the dead of night always pays off in the end," she snarked, only to smile when he laughed out loud. Waving him away, she headed for the door. Time enough to explain her findings later, when they were all cooped up in that carriage on the way back toward Windamere. For now, they both had preparations to see to.

The space on the inside of the carriage did not, of course, match the outside. Master had crafted the written incantation so that on the inside, it seemed as if they had a spacious room to lounge about in. It reminded her strongly of the tales of the genie's lamp, especially since Master had decorated it in rich greens and blues and golds with comfortable pillows strewn about on long benches. It even had large windows so that they could watch the passing scenery if they so wished.

Because Master had driven directly to her from Chastain, the vehicle had "learned" the path and so he didn't need to do anything to control its return trip. He simply turned it around and ordered, "To Chastain."

Sevana nearly went green with envy once she saw how easy operating the vehicle was. Oh yes. She would have one of these. She would also figure out how to duplicate his "learned" routes so that she wouldn't have to repeat his work.

They lounged about at their ease, eating some of the food Sevana had bought, without a care in the world. For the first hour, Sky went from one bench to the other, looking out every window, thrilled to be riding in a *magic vehicle*. But the excitement wore off and he eventually curled up with Hinun to take a nap.

Sevana watched him peacefully snooze, one hand wrapped around the wolf's leg. He probably hadn't been able to sleep well during his few short years in this world. It had probably never been completely safe for him to fall deeply asleep. It said a great deal that he felt he could do so now. But then, with a wolf guarding your bedside, what did anyone need to worry about?

With Sky fully asleep, the adults turned the conversation to more serious matters.

"Alright, sweetling." Master shifted a little so that he faced her more directly, a pillow propping up one arm. "What happened exactly?"

"I think your theory is wrong and right at the same time." She grabbed a pillow and hugged it to her, getting comfortable for what would no doubt be a long discussion. "The incantation in the stones provided direction, I agree with you there. But I don't think it signified what was meant to be transported and what wasn't. If you think about it, it makes no sense. You can't tell the gadgick *everything on this platform of stones needs to go* because the fountain and gadgick are also on the platform. They'd be transported right along with everything else."

"Ah." Master blinked, then looked a little sheepish. "I hadn't thought of that. But you're right."

"Now, you were right in that the water is the key. I will bet you anything you care to name that the way the gadgick recognized what needed to be transported was through the water. With anything living, they ingested some of it or somehow absorbed it into their body. With the inanimate objects, the water was painted on with an insignia of some sort. I'm guessing something very similar to what's on the stones."

"A water-painted insignia so that the gadgick would think that it should be transported as well?" Master's head canted to the side as he thought it through. "That sounds...complex."

"We're talking about a device that could carry a small caravan to the other side of Kindin," she retorted bluntly. "What part of this is *simplistic*?

"...You have a very good point, sweetling. Your theory might not be perfectly accurate but I would say it's very close. We won't know for sure, of course, until we can actually examine the gadgick."

"I detest guesswork," she groaned.

"I hear you. Still, the ingestion of the water by people makes a great deal of sense." Master rubbed at his chin thoughtfully with one hand. "It would explain why most of the village was transported at one point or another. Every person there uses that fountain as a water source. They all drink it or come into direct contact with it somehow or other."

"Except the few hunters that live well outside the village," she confirmed. "That bothered me for days. Why the exception? But of course, they never went near the fountain. They never needed to. They had their own water sources near their homes. They only came into the village to do business."

"Finally, the mystery is solved. Or would be, but you and Hinun didn't drink any of the water...ah...you did?"

Sevana grimaced. "Because I was sitting so close to the fountain trying to pry a stone loose, some of it splashed on me. And of course,

Hinun was pressed up against me most of the time and it splashed on him, too. That, apparently, was enough water to count."

Master blew out a breath. "It's a good thing we told everyone to steer well clear of the fountain, then. At least we can easily contain the situation now."

"That is a blessing," she agreed. "It gives us some breathing room in dealing with the problem. While I was gone, did Sarsen find all the stones and remove them?"

"He and most of the village promised to do so by the time we returned," Master assured her. "Which will help as well, of course. Although I do think we should call him soon and explain everything you just told me to make *sure* no one goes near that fountain."

"Agreed." The more ways they could safeguard the villagers, the better. "But before you call him, let's come up with a plan. I think the only way to deal with the gadgick now is to cut off its water source. Do you think it's possible to find the spring that feeds it and dam it up?"

"I would hope so. How easy or difficult the job turns out to be I can't begin to guess. But surely the man that installed the fountain— what was his name again?"

"Hube."

"Right, right. I would think Hube would be able to tell us where the spring is being piped in since he built the fountain. It should be a relatively simple matter to dam it up and let the water out of the fountain."

Sevana quirked a brow at him. "I notice you didn't say *easy*."

"In my experience, removing a power element from an ancient artifact is *never* easy," Master grumbled.

Sevana perked up with interest. She'd been vaguely aware that Master had dealt with ancient artifacts before, but this was the first time he had mentioned them himself. "How many have you come across?"

"This will be the fifth, I think." For some reason his eyes crinkled up in a small smile. "The first one was early in my career. In fact, I think I'd only been an Artifactor as long as you have been when I took the job on. I quickly realized I had gotten in over my head and had to call my master for help."

She glared at him. "Is that supposed to make me feel better?"

"Just a fact, sweetling."

"Humph."

Chuckling, Master reached for the bag sitting at his feet. "Alright, let's call Sarsen and tell him we're adding an item to his scavenger list, shall we?"

The return trip to Chastain would have taken three days, but Sevana insisted they stop the night before they were due and stay at an inn. If it were just she and Master, they'd likely have pressed on, but a young boy and a wolf couldn't put up with a confined space for three days straight. Sevana absolutely refused to share space with a stir-crazy eight year old and a whiny wolf.

So they stopped at a decent inn, all of them taking great delight in soaking in a hot tub and having a hot meal. Sevana felt secretly glad that she'd had an excuse to clean up before they arrived at the village again. She hardly wanted to arrive smelly and mussed from the long trip.

They arrived at Chastain midmorning to the relief of the entire village. Sarsen ran to meet them, looking far more relieved than the whole village combined, if that were possible. Sevana managed to get one foot out of the carriage before he grabbed her around the waist and hugged her. "Sev," he said against her temple.

Sevana just sighed and put up with it. First Bel, then Hana, then Master and now Sarsen. Clearly, a hugging disease of some sort was going around and most of her inner circle had become infected. She'd go looking for the cure later since saying *I'm not huggable!* clearly had no effect whatsoever.

"I'm so glad you're back," he told her, finally setting her gently to earth.

"You're only glad I'm back because you feel overwhelmed by everything," she responded dryly, cocking a challenging brow at him.

"Do you realize how many stones make up this village?" he whined. He looked wide-eyed and a little frenzied, as if he hadn't been getting enough sleep and became dry-drunk because of it.

"It's alright, we'll take over from here," she soothed. She made silent plans to get him drugged with a sleeping potion and in a quiet room as soon as she could manage it. He *clearly* needed to sleep for a few hours.

"Sarsen, this is Sky," Master introduced, a hand on the boy's shoulder. "He'll be in our care for a while until we can take him to his new home."

Sarsen managed a smile. "Hello, Sky."

Sky gave a shy nod back, but he clearly felt wary of Sarsen. (Sevana didn't blame the kid. At the moment, *she* felt wary of Sarsen.)

"New home?" Sarsen asked him, making an attempt to put the boy more at ease. "Where is that?"

"Um…Sevana said she'd take me to meet the Fae."

Sarsen's eyes flew wide and his mouth moved for several seconds, visibly searching for a response. "W-well. I'm impressed. Sky, how did you manage to talk her into that?"

She smacked him lightly on the back of the head. "I volunteered, you dolt."

Sarsen gave her a look askance. "Did you hit your head somehow when you were transported?"

"Now, now, Sarsen," Master scolded good-naturedly. "Don't spoil the moment. I *like* it when Sevana tries to help people."

Since not one person had expected such behavior from her, Sevana was beginning to wonder why she even bothered. Abruptly changing the subject, she asked, "Sarsen, are all the stones found?"

"No, not yet. I think we're close though."

"And the spring?" Master prompted.

"Hube wasn't sure where it came from, exactly. But he knows two people with dowsing rods that will help us look for it."

Good enough progress, to her mind. "In that case, go sleep. We'll take matters over from here."

Chastain Village had two men that were widely known as the "Dowsing Experts" and Hube called them in to help before Sevana had even arrived. They stood in the courtyard waiting on instructions, which Sevana would have loved to issue, but she had two problems that needed to be sorted first:

1) Sky

2) Sarsen

Sarsen had been up far too long and stressed because of her disappearance. Catching Master's eye, she inclined her head toward the dry-drunk Artifactor, silently asking what he intended to do about him. If he didn't take charge, she'd drug the man right here and cart him to a bed somewhere.

Master shrugged, half-amused, and gave her a casual salute. Then he grabbed Sarsen from behind, hands clamped on both elbows, and frog-marched the man straight for the inn. "Sarsen, I think you need rest."

"Eh?" Sarsen struggled a little on instinct, but he had no choice but to move where Master directed. "No, I'm fine. Perhaps a little tired, but I can still work."

"No, no, we're here now. We'll handle things while you take a nice nap."

The conversation faded as they disappeared into the inn. Sevana blew out a breath. Alright, one problem sorted. Now, what to do with the other? She looked down at Sky, who stood as close as he dared to her without actually wrapping his arms around her leg. He had formed a strange attachment to her, like a duckling imprinting on the first thing it saw. Really, if the kid had any sense, he'd choose *Master* to follow around. She could hardly be described as the motherly sort with her sharp tongue. But he'd spent the past seven days with her without showing any signs of wanting to distance himself.

He felt her eyes on him and looked up hesitantly. "You have to work now?"

"I do," she admitted frankly.

He chewed on his bottom lip for a moment before venturing tentatively, "Can I come with you?"

Now that was the question. Could he? Sevana didn't think that any part of this new plan would have any danger to it. They were not going to go anywhere *near* that fountain or the shields around the gadgick, so the odds of them being in danger or getting transported again later were low. "Well, why not?"

He lit up in a bright smile.

"It's going to be boring, though," she felt like warning him. "We're just going to be walking around in circles until we figure out where the underground water spring is, and then we'll be digging up a hole to actually get to it." How they would manage to dam it up was a problem she did not yet have a solution for, as it would take seeing the area to come up with a good plan. "Wouldn't you rather do something else?"

"I'll be good," he promised faithfully.

Well, granted, this child didn't have anything in common with the typical brat. He'd been working for his living for years now, although she found it hard to remember that sometimes. He had the maturity of a young teen instead of a normal child. He knew exactly how to behave at work and likely wouldn't get in her way. Besides, Gid was standing right next to Decker. If Sky did start to become an irritant, she could always send him off to play with the wolf.

If he wanted to go along, she wouldn't stop him. She wouldn't know where to put him anyway, in this village of strangers. So she shrugged and waved him on. "Come along, then."

Decker, seeing that she had more or less sorted things out, took a step away from the waiting men, calling to her, "Ready to start?"

"Yes!"

He paused and gave the boy trailing along at her heels an odd look. "Ah, and who's the boy?"

"My love child," she answered without batting an eye.

For a split second, he almost believed her. She could see it in those wide eyes. Then he blinked, his common sense kicking in, and gave Sky a dubious look. "Unless you had a child at ten years old, I highly doubt that."

Sevana just laughed. "I almost had you going for a moment."

"You almost did," he admitted. Sinking to one knee, he offered a hand toward Sky. "I'm Decker, a huntsman in this village."

Sky accepted the hand in a warrior's clasp, as well as he could with his smaller build, and gave Decker a game smile. "I'm Sky. I'm not really her child. She's just helping me."

"Oh?" Decker gave Sevana a quick glance upwards. "Well, lucky you. Did you know that this is the woman that broke the curse on Prince Bellomi?"

Sky froze before whirling, craning his neck so that he could stare up at her. "Really?!"

"Really," she assured him, both amused and flattered by his reaction. "Have you heard this story?"

He nodded vigorously. "*Everybody* was talkin' 'bout it for *months*. They said it's how he got back his throne, too."

"That was certainly the main reason," she agreed. That and her freezing a room full of people. "But I'll regale you with the full tale later, on our way back to Big. For now, we have work to do."

"Ah," Decker regained his feet and pointed down at Sky's head. "Shouldn't we find him a place to stay while we work first?"

"It's not necessary," she assured him. "We're not doing anything dangerous today, and he wants to go along."

From the look on Decker's face, he didn't quite agree with her, but he shrugged it off and half-turned, gesturing to the other men. "This is Denis and Bernard. Goodmen, this is Sevana Warran and Sky."

"Artifactor Warran," Denis greeted with a respectful nod of the head. He looked like a liveryman—smelled like one too—with a stocky build and a short mustache. His compatriot, Bernard, just gave a nod. She guessed his profession to be farmer, based on the rough condition of his hands, the worn-out knees, and dark tan.

"Gentlemen," she greeted in turn. "I trust you have a plan?"

"Yes ma'am," Bernard assured her. "We got different methods, me and Denis. He does it all in straight lines, and I follow my instincts. So we figure, we'll divide up the area that Hube thinks the spring is in and just go at it. This don't usually take more than a few hours."

"It's going to have to be outside the village," she warned them. "Anything closer than that might set off the artifact."

"Yes, ma'am," Denis guaranteed her with a patient smile. "We've been told so by Sarsen."

Good enough. "Then I'll just follow along behind you. Feel free to start."

They left the village at a walk, no one in a particular hurry to get this over with, not with the immediate threat of being transported removed. Sarsen had done his job well—with almost all of the incantation stones now accounted for, the last person to have been transported was Sevana herself.

She found the irony of that painfully funny, in a twisted sort of way.

Once out of the village proper, they led off to the north, heading in the direction of the ruins although they stopped well shy of them. This made sense to Sevana—of course they knew a spring of some sort was in this area. It's where the artifact had originally been, after all. The spring's source at the platform had disappeared, but it had likely only moved, not dried up altogether.

Different people used different types of tools for dowsing. The only one that Sevana had any personal experience with was a pendant, which would swing from one hand freely. She had used it before as a student, still training under Master, to find minerals although she had never used it since. But these men used other tools. Denis pulled out a weathered stick from the pack on his back, the end of it shaped in a

"Y." It looked like any other branch taken from a tree that had been sanded down and shaped by human hands.

Bernard instead had two rods in his hands, both of them in an "L" shape that he obviously intended to use. He lifted the rods to where they were perpendicular to each other and the ground. Denis also lifted his so that the stick stayed perpendicular to the ground. Then, with only a glance to each other, they started off, both of them going opposite ways.

Seeing that she couldn't follow both men at once, she decided to follow Denis. Really, they were fortunate the weather had held so fair so that they weren't doing this in a pre-summer heat wave or a lingering winter chill. If she had to tramp around in aimless circles in and around trees, this was the perfect weather to do it in.

Sky had been quiet while they'd talked, but with none of the adults saying anything, he dared to ask, "What are they doing?"

Decker cocked his head slightly. "Didn't Sevana explain? No? Alright, well, the fountain that you saw in the middle of the square? It's got a rather troublesome magic device in it that we're trying to shut off. But the only way to do that, or so I'm told, is to take the water out of the fountain."

"Why?" Sky asked with intensity, as if truly trying to understand.

"The water gives the magic…what did Sarsen call it? A gadgick?" he asked Sevana. At her nod, he continued, "The gadgick, then. Anyway, the water gives it power. So they think if they can find the source of the water, and divert it so the gadgick doesn't receive any, then the gadgick will stop working. After that, they can remove it without any problem."

"Oh." Sky looked at the two grown men playing with sticks and his face screwed up in a doubtful frown. "So how do you find water with sticks?"

Sevana laughed outright, finding this question hilarious. "It does look odd, doesn't it?"

Decker shook his head in resignation. "I can see you're not going to explain. Sky, what you're seeing is an ancient art called *dowsing*. The sticks in those men's hands will react to water, you see. So even though they're above ground like this, the sticks will dip forward, pointing toward the water under the earth."

"Well, actually, the two rods will swing," she corrected. "They'll either cross each other, or swing away from each other. But he's right in that the y-stick will dip forward."

"Oh." He chewed on this information for a while before asking, "Is this how you broke the prince's curse?"

"No, not at all," she denied easily, striding slowly behind Denis as the man crossed through a shady grove of trees. "I borrowed the strength of a water dragon to do it."

"EHHHH?" All four males stopped dead and snapped their heads around to stare at her incredulously. Even though Bernard walked a good twenty feet away at this point, he could apparently still hear her.

"You're, ah, exaggerating?" Decker asked.

"Not in the slightest."

When she didn't elaborate, he gave her a long look. "What will it take for me to hear the story?"

"Dinner," she responded sweetly. "With dessert, of course."

"Of course." Mouth quirked in a dry smile, he flipped a hand, palm up, in acknowledgement. "Fine. Dinner's on me. What happened?"

Mouth quirked up in a wry smile, she mentally shrugged and prepared to tell the story. Really, there was no reason why she shouldn't. And what did they have to do out here, anyway, while waiting for the rods to react?

So she started from the beginning, from when she kidnapped the prince from his palace bedroom, and went all the way to the end when she walked out while leaving a frozen room of people behind. During the course of her career, she rarely told stories like this to anyone except Master or Sarsen, so it came as a surprise to her that she found the retelling…enjoyable. Seeing their reactions, their intense interest, felt flattering.

She had the full tale out and was fielding questions when Bernard's rods abruptly crossed. "Found it!" he called.

Everyone went directly to his side. "How far down, can you tell?" Sevana asked, staring at the rods with interest. Did she imagine that they vibrated slightly in his hands?

"I'd say maybe ten feet down?" Bernard's brows furrowed as he considered this. "Maybe less than that. It's a good, strong reaction."

"Alright, map it," she ordered. "See if it traces back to the village or not. If it does, we know we have the right source."

"Sure thing." He turned on his heels, reversing direction, and started for the village, paying close attention to the rods in his hands.

Sevana held her breath as they walked. They all did. If this didn't turn out to be the right one, they'd have to map it regardless before starting again, just so they didn't mistake it for a new line. But she truly hoped that this would be the correct one. She'd already been at this job longer than she'd anticipated, and at the rate things were going, it'd take another week at least to wrap it up.

Bernard went in a beeline—literally. He went in this direction for a while, then twisted a little the opposite way, stopped over a particularly large body of water (he assumed it to be a pond or something along those lines), but he always moved forward. He came to the village outskirts an hour after finding the source, and they all breathed a sigh of relief.

"I think it's safe to call it, ma'am," Bernard announced, letting the rods relax at his sides.

"I agree." Of course, this line directly crossed the road. She highly doubted anyone would let her dig in the middle of it. "Trace back a good ten feet, away from the road, and mark it for me. I'll go get the shovels."

"Ah, ma'am?" Denis scratched at the back of his head, giving her a funny look. "If it's shovels you want, we've got plenty."

"I don't doubt that," she assured him dryly. "But which would *you* rather dig with? Ordinary, plain old shovels? Or an Artifactor's shovel, able to cut through anything like it was soft butter?"

"Ahhh…"

"I thought as much." Smirking, she told Decker, "Round up a crew of volunteers for me. I'm going through my clock to get the shovels, but it'll be a quick trip. We'll need plenty of space to work in, so carve out a five-foot by five-foot hole."

"I'll have people together by the time you get back," he promised.

Of course, that left her with the question once again of what to do with Sky. Or no, perhaps it didn't. With children, it all depended on how she phrased the question. *I'm going to fetch a dozen shovels* would not be the right way to say it. She looked down at him and asked, "So, how would you like to take a trip through a magic portal and be inside a talking mountain?"

His eyes lit up. "YES!"

"That's what I thought." The three men—all apparently experienced with children—bit back laughter. Smug, she took Sky by the hand and led him toward her makeshift workroom, where the clock sat. "Be back in a few minutes!"

I need a dam expert.

Sevana sat staring at the map Bernard and Denis had drawn for her, showing where the river was, as well as two other bodies of water. When Master had first proposed the idea of diverting or somehow stopping the water source that fed into the fountain, it had sounded so easy, so simplistic. All they needed to do was find the water source, trace it, and block it. Right?

Wrong.

She hadn't thought about it until she'd gone back to Big with a wide-eyed Sky in tow, but as she went to retrieve the shovels, it occurred to her that none of the magicians knew much about constructing dams. Why should they? They were hardly ever called to do such a thing. So she went to her research room and spent a few minutes finding a promising book that would explain such a method and perhaps give her a pointer or two on designing it. She'd tucked it under one arm, and with Decker and Sky's help, dragged a dozen shovels back through. Then she'd carried them to the site that Bernard had marked for digging, finding five men already on standby, waiting on her.

Letting the men do the heavy work, she sat nearby on a portable chair, book and map propped up in her lap, and read. Or she had been reading. Now she just stared at the map in frustration.

Water, by nature, doesn't disappear just because one wants it to. It does not stop flowing or stay stationary because a powerful, important and beautiful Artifactor wants it to. Water, being water, would flow, and if something tried to impede it, it would find a different route to flow in, but it wouldn't just *stop*. The book had mentioned oh-so-casually that if one was to build a dam, especially an underground dam as she wished to do, that one would *of course* need to extract the excess water with wells, through a dam body made of sand or through means of a drainage pipe. It had, in fact, mentioned it so casually that she'd nearly skimmed over it entirely.

Curse Master's hide, but he had hit the nail precisely on the head earlier. Extracting the gadgick from the fountain would indeed be a simple matter but it would *not* be easy. She couldn't just block the underground stream and not expect repercussions. She would have to come up with some sort of outlet for the pent-up water or she would create a flood plain right here near the road.

She sat there, absently listening to the men talk about how nice the weather was, and how the wind took the edge of heat off, all of it washing over her without really interrupting her thoughts.

"I'm an Artifactor," she complained aloud to no one in particular. "Not an architect!"

Decker, of course, heard her and trotted over. "Problem?"

"What am I supposed to do with the pent-up water?" she asked him, tired of thinking of solutions. It seemed on this job that's all she'd done—run into increasingly frustrating problems she had to devise solutions to. "We can't just dam up the underground stream and not expect flooding to happen."

"Ah." He snapped his fingers, an obvious light going off in his head. "I hadn't thought of that."

"You and me both," she grumbled under her breath.

"But is it really necessary?" He turned to look back at the hole the men were digging, looking thoughtful. "I mean, you said the fountain would dry out in about three days on its own. This is only temporary, right?"

"Do you want the road and all the streets in the village flooded?" she asked mock-sweetly.

"Errr…"

"Then that rather answers the question, doesn't it?"

Decker frowned, thought another moment, and then suggested, "Hube would probably have an idea of how to go about this."

True, the man seemed capable of building anything. And he knew the lay of the land and what building materials were available as well. "Get him."

With a sloppy salute, he put his shovel down and jogged toward the village at an easy lope.

Turning to the little boy sitting so patiently at her side, she requested, "Go get Master for me as well. He might have solutions to this problem that I don't know about."

He copied Decker's gesture exactly before hopping to his feet and sprinting for the village in that universal speed that all children seemed to move in. Sevana smiled as she watched him. Having a gopher on hand at all times had its perks. Maybe she should think about taking on an apprentice after all.

Then she remembered the trouble Bel used to get into and rethought that idea.

The men came surprisingly quickly, too quickly for her to get much further into the book and see if there were specific directions on how to build one of those sand dams. (Not that she had any idea of where she'd get *that* much sand.)

She closed the book with a thump and stood as they reached her. "Alright, gentlemen, here's the problem. When we dam up that water, it's going to build up and create a flood right here near the road."

"Sure will," Hube agreed casually, almost cheerfully. "So what's the plan for that?"

She flicked her eyes to him in a glare. "Why don't you tell me? I have never built a dam before and have no experience in this."

"Well, from what ya folks are tellin' me, this dam of yours is temporary." He waited for a confirming nod before continuing. "So it won't need anything real fancy to fix it. I'm thinking a draining pipe and a timber dam would likely do us fine."

"Timber dam?" Her book hadn't mentioned anything like that.

"They don't build 'em often these days, as they don't last more than a handful of years," Hube explained, warming up to his subject. "They have to be wet to maintain the water retention, see, and they rot fast like a barrel would. But for what we're doing, we don't need anything that'll last more than a week. They're usually built across rivers and streams, that sort of thing, but we can make a square one to hold water with."

"Like a pool," Master suggested.

Hube grinned. "That's a better way of puttin' it, yes. Now, trick is, to hold that much water, it's gonna need to be more than one layer. See, way you do it is, build one level with the logs crisscrossing, for strength. Then build another layer a foot away. The gap between 'em you fill with dirt and rock. Gives it the strength it needs to hold the water's weight."

Sevana didn't underestimate the weight water could have. If Hube thought it would take two levels of wood and another of stone, he was likely right.

"Instead of constructing a large pool, let's try to make two smaller ones," Master suggested. "After all, we have no idea how much water is going to spill over because of our dam. We might not need a particularly large pool."

She stared at the hole, which looked impressively deep from here, and tried to calculate something she couldn't see. As one would expect, it was nearly impossible. "I suppose if two small pools don't do the job, we can always build more."

"We'll need to keep an eye on 'em, make sure we got time to build another," Hube concurred.

Sevana patted him on the shoulder, a wide smile on her face. "Go for it, Hube."

He blinked at her several times before raising a hand and pointing at himself. "What, me do it?"

"You want two complete amateurs to build a dam off that

description? This close to the village?" she countered.

He blinked again, mentally picturing the outcome of that, then chuckled. "Sounds like a bad idea. Alrighty, let's get on with it then. You two gonna leave it all up to me?"

"We'll help," Master promised just as Sevana opened her mouth to say, *I certainly am*. "Tell us what materials you need and we'll get them for you."

"Mighty good of you, Master Joles," Hube said sincerely and with no small measure of relief. "If you would then start getting me the timber. Long trees, at least twenty feet tall, and a good foot in diameter. They won't have the strength they need otherwise. Strip 'em of the branches, if you would. I'll go back and draw up plans today, figure out how much we'll need. But you'd best get a dozen trees felled."

"We'll see to it," Master promised.

"Then I'll get on those plans." Hube headed back for his shop at a quick stride, the walk of a man set about on important business.

Sevana looked at the forest around her, seeing plenty of trees that fit Hube's criteria, but most of them looked dangerously close to the workers. She liked people volunteering to help her. They were less likely to do so if it got around that she dropped trees on them. "We're going to need to move away from this area a little before we go around chopping things down."

"Not too far," Decker cautioned. "As it is, it'll take several teams of horses to drag the lumber over."

Sevana waved that away. "Don't worry about that. We can lift them."

Decker looked at the pouch on her waist in bemusement. "You have a spell for that?"

"Certainly. Magic is handy that way."

"We have a spell that will let us cut the trees down as well," Master assured him, seeming amused at Decker's reaction.

The huntsman pondered that for a moment before jerking a thumb to indicate the hole the men were still digging. "And you don't have a spell that will do that?"

"We do, actually." Master grinned at Decker's expression. "We're not making them dig for the fun of it, Decker. In truth, the spell we would use for this situation doesn't dig anything out, but it *banishes* the dirt. It's a permanent thing, and on living soil like this, it would have a detrimental effect. It would prevent anything from growing in this area for years. It's far better that it's dug out instead of magicked out."

"That said, we'll spare you the extra labor involved with the dams as much as we can." Sevana spun in a slow circle as she said this, taking a good look around the landscape. She didn't want to cut anything too close to the road, as that would obviously cause problems, and this area had odd patches with copses of trees and grass. The nearest section of tall trees that didn't endanger anything would be... "There. Let's start there and see how many we can get."

Master quirked a brow at her. "I bet tonight's dinner that I can get six trees over here faster than you can."

She stared at him from the corner of her eye. Oh? Someone felt feisty. "With or without branches?"

"Without."

"You're on, old goat."

Master laughed out loud in delight. "You haven't called me that in ages."

Actually, she couldn't immediately remember the last time she had called him that. He always liked it when she did, though, for some strange reason.

Wanting to keep Sky out of harm's way but still nearby, she turned to him and said, "Sky, this man is a notorious brat. I don't trust him. I need you to be the judge."

Sky perked up, happy to be included. "Sure!"

"Stand near the workmen," she directed, "and keep an eye on things. Also keep an eye on them. If they hit water, tell me but don't get too close to where we're logging. It's likely to get dangerous over there."

"I'll stay over here," he promised.

Sevana, glad to have that sorted, gave her Master a challenging look. "Well? Shall we start?"

"Don't pout later when I win, sweetling."

She snorted, already heading for the tree line. "I return those words right back to you."

No one could dig a hole, build a dam, and construct two timber pools in a single afternoon, of course. In fact, they still had a little digging left to do by the time the sun started to sink over the horizon. Sevana sent Master and Sky on ahead to the inn for dinner, making a detour by Hube's to see how the plans were coming along. She spent several minutes looking over his design, but really, he knew what to do better than she did, so she didn't give him more than a nod of approval. By the time she made it back to the inn, the three boys had claimed a back corner table, plates of half-consumed food in front of them. Hinun lay at Master's feet, an empty bowl beside him. It was sad when the wolf got dinner before she did. Sarsen, the only one facing the door, saw her approach and waved at her. "Sev!" he called over the din of overlapping conversations, "I heard you lost!"

She rolled her eyes. Only Sarsen would dare to tease her in a room full of people. Several patrons at nearby tables stopped abruptly and looked around with interest, no doubt curious about what she had to say to *that*. "I did not lose," she retorted with a sardonic look at the grinning Master. "I have a witness to prove that, too."

"Your witness is bribable," Master informed her. "For the sake of two helpings of blueberry cobbler, he confessed that I did beat you. By a good five feet, too."

"That's because you *threw* the log five feet!" she riposted, slinging herself into the only empty chair at the table.

Master, not at all ashamed of such reckless behavior, chuckled and shrugged.

Sarsen, glancing between them, dared to ask, "Threw?"

"I ask you, what kind of an idiot throws a twenty-foot log? Any kind of distance?" Just remembering it made her heart thump harder. "I mean, he was about ten feet away from the workers, granted, but it's still nearly six thousand pounds, you know? It left a huge dent in the ground and made a sound loud enough to shave off five years of everyone's life."

"No one came even close to being hurt," Master defended himself. "And I still won."

Sevana felt justified in her reaction when Sarsen raised both hands to his temples and rubbed, trying to stave off a headache just mentally picturing this scene. "Clearly, the next time I enter a competition with this old goat, I'm going to have to put some safety rules down first. Is it just me, or is he getting more reckless in his old age?"

"Right here at the table," Master said mildly, pointing at himself.

Sarsen ignored him. "No, he was always reckless. He was just more careful in front of you because *you* tended to be reckless and he was trying to set a good example."

"Really? Why do you suppose he's abruptly stopped doing that?"

"Maybe because he's old and he doesn't care what people think anymore? Or maybe he's figured he's set the example already and you know to follow it?"

"Surely he's not so naïve as to believe that," Sevana disagreed.

Master cleared his throat meaningfully. "Still right here."

Their banter got interrupted by Sky, who'd fallen into a helpless case of giggles.

Her eyes crinkling at the corners in a silent smile, she inquired dryly, "Are we entertaining you, Sky?"

He nodded, unable to say anything because he was laughing too much. "D-do you al-always do this?"

"When you live with people for ten years, you get warped by their twisted sense of humor," she explained mock-dolefully.

"Don't believe her," Master warned Sky. "She came to me twisted. If anything, she warped *us*."

Sevana made a scoffing sound, which for some reason made

Sky burst into a whole new round of giggles. Kid must have his own warped sense of humor to find all this so funny. "Changing the subject—I'm no expert but Hube's plans looked fine. I think we can start building the timber doohickey tomorrow while the men finish digging the hole."

"Doohickey?" Master objected mildly.

"Well, what do you want me to call it?" Sevana countered half-absently, twisting in her chair to try and find a server. The place was busy, heaven knew, but she'd been sitting here a while without anyone coming to the table. "It's not a timber dam, although Hube calls it that half the time."

"It's a pool," Master informed her patiently.

"Oh? Every pool I know of is either decorative or intended for swimming. You going to hop into it, Master?"

Far from discouraged, he perked up, eyes shining with interest. "Oooh. Now there's a thought."

Sarsen let out a groan and slumped. "You just had to suggest that, didn't you?"

Sevana spared him a glance. "I guarantee that it would have taken the children in this village a whole minute to have the same thought after they saw two standing bodies of clean water."

"Point," he acknowledged ruefully. "Judging from that longing expression…Sky, you want to join in, don't you?"

Sky looked away from the table, toward the floor, and said in a small voice, "I can't swim."

Every adult at the table snapped around, staring at him incredulously. Although really, this shouldn't have surprised any of them. As ridiculous as it seemed, most sailors didn't know how to swim. Sevana had always thought it stupid in the extreme to have a career in water when you didn't have the faintest idea how to stay afloat in it, but that seemed to be the norm. Rubbing her hands together, she stared at that bowed head thoughtfully. The Fae no doubt had their own ways to deal with water, and they would teach him, but in the meantime it seemed foolish to leave him exposed to a possible danger without teaching him anything.

"Right." Turning to Master and Sarsen, she asked, "Who's going to drown-proof the kid?"

"Since I fully intend to go swimming in it anyway, why don't I do it?" Master volunteered with a selfless smile that didn't fool anyone at the table. "Besides, it's dangerous if you two do it. Your teaching methods are something else."

"No one has ever died on me," Sevana defended herself with a wounded hand over her heart.

"Or me!" Sarsen objected good-naturedly.

"*Yet*," Master grumbled under his breath. "Don't worry, Sky, I'll make sure you can swim well. You can leave it to me. I taught these two, and they do just fine in water."

Sky's grin stretched from ear to ear. "Thanks, Master!"

"Not at all, not at all."

Sevana went back to trying to catch a server's eye, and finally managed it a few moments later. She put in an order for anything that was ready to dish up right this moment before she sat back in her chair and properly faced the table again. "Alright, let's come up with a timeline for this. Hube isn't sure how long it will take to build the two timber pools, since we're capable of lifting all the logs in place, which apparently is the most time-consuming part of the job. But he said if we can lift them so easily, he thinks we can put a pool together in a day."

"So two days for two pools?" Master cocked his head, eyes on the ceiling as he started calculating things. "Alright. With a fountain of this size, it will take about three days for the water to evaporate, especially in this heat. I think this might work out to where everything will be done about the same time. We can finish digging by lunch tomorrow, or thereabouts. The first pool will be put together by evening. So the day after tomorrow, we can put the dam into place, and while the pool fills, we'll build another one."

"While that pool is being built, the fountain will be draining dry," Sarsen picked up the topic as Master slowed, becoming distracted by his own thoughts so much that he forgot to speak. "So, we'll have a two-day wait or so until we can do anything."

"During that two-day wait we need to keep an eye on the pools to make sure they won't overflow," Sevana reminded. "Which I suppose Master can do, since he'll be swimming in them anyway."

He gave her a benign smile. "It's best to combine work with pleasure."

Sevana, not disagreeing with this philosophy, said seriously, "It is."

Sarsen, well used to this silliness, kept going without trouble. "So what are we going to do for two days while waiting on the fountain to dry?"

"I vote we make preparations." Sevana braced her forearms on the table and leaned against it, tone and manner completely serious. "I do not want this thing in the village any longer than it needs to be. I don't want to run the risk of activating some other feature to it that we don't know about yet. I want to seal this thing up in a metal box and send it immediately to Jacen for study."

"He would be the best choice," Sarsen admitted.

"One of us, at least, has to stay here and put everything back in order once the gadgick is out," she continued. "Since I originally took this job, I think that should be me. So it's up to the two of you—which one wants to leave immediately for Jacen's once the gadgick is out?"

Master and Sarsen shared a speaking look for several seconds. Then Master's mouth quirked up in a slight smile. "I wouldn't mind going," he admitted frankly. "I haven't seen Jacen for quite some time. Also, I'd like to stay a few days and help him research the gadgick. I want a better understanding of how it works."

She nodded in satisfaction. "Then that's settled. Sarsen, you're stuck with me doing the cleanup."

"Fine, fine. Should be the easier job, leastways." He rubbed at his chin for a moment before asking, "What about Goffin and Roland? Should we send them home tomorrow? I don't think they can help us much from here on."

Sevana blinked. "Wait, they're still here?"

"They weren't sure if taking all those stones out would actually do the trick," Sarsen confessed. "We decided to wait a day or two and see how things went."

Ah. Well, true, none of their previous theories had proven to be exactly correct. It made sense to play it safe for a day or so. "They can go home tomorrow as far as I'm concerned."

"Then I'll tell 'em. You were the last to go, anyway. I don't think we have to worry about people disappearing in their sleep anymore."

She should hope not, for pity's sake.

By the time that Sevana had rolled out of bed the next morning, dressed, eaten breakfast, and gone back to the worksite, three men had already beaten her there and resumed digging. Sky chose to follow along again and stayed faithfully at her heels like some sort of hunting dog. The metaphor became more accurate than she intended when she realized he had a wolf on *his* heels.

Hube arrived on scene shortly after she did, along with Master and Sarsen, so they went to work.

Making a timber pool, as it turned out, didn't differ much from making a log cabin. The ends of the logs had to be notched out in a particular way so that the logs would fit together tightly. For every two logs saddled and stacked together, Hube would use either small trees or saplings to bind everything, preventing anything from slipping or slowly spreading apart under the force of the water. She found it interesting that he didn't strip the branches off before he used them. He said it would add strength and a little "filler," whatever that meant. He did this routinely, binding layer upon layer together. After watching him do this once, Sevana and the rest felt they could do the same and started helping him. It wasn't as easy as it looked—nothing ever was—but Hube patiently taught them the finer tricks, and within the course of an hour, they had the hang of it.

With all four adults working well together, and a judicious amount of magic, they had the first level of the pool built by noon. Sevana had never worked physically harder in her life. She felt drenched with sweat, her clothes sticking to her back and waist, tendrils of hair clinging to her temples. She had a whole new level of respect for anyone that built dams for a living. After all, they did this *without* magic.

Maybe she should come up with some sort of product to sell to them…hmm.

They took a break for lunch at noon, which Sky had eagerly gone and fetched from the inn's kitchen in the form of a picnic. Sevana didn't want to do anything more than take a nap after eating, but unfortunately, the rest of the work beckoned. With a groan, she forced herself back to her feet and went back to it.

For some strange reason, building the second level of the pool went faster than building the first. Perhaps because they all knew what they were doing at this point and weren't waiting on Hube's directions? Because they were now used to how the others worked? Or more likely a combination of the two. Regardless, they had the second level up in a matter of three hours.

Using their carrying and lifting spells, the three Artifactors gathered up the stripped branches from yesterday and the dirt that had been dug up to get to the underground stream, and used all of that to fill the space in between the two layers. Sevana hadn't been sure that it would be enough to fill the space, but it turned out to be fine. Barely. She had no idea what they would do about the fill-in for the second pool, though.

Now came the fun part.

According to Hube, there were several possible ways to construct a sub dam. But because they weren't in the dry season—far from it— they were limited on what they could build with. He had also been unsure of what kind of rock or soil surrounded the water. If it was some sort of impermeable rock around it, then fine. They could build a masonry dam. If not, well, then they would probably have to resort to a sand dam. But Sevana didn't like Option B whatsoever. Unlike a masonry dam, the sand dams had to be built in stages, over several days. A masonry dam could be built in one go, and right now, that's what everyone preferred to do.

Now that the soil was out of the way, the water exposed, they could finally get a better idea of what they were dealing with. Sevana extracted her see-through glasses from her pouch (a special invention of hers that let her see through *everything*) and put them on before peering over the side of the hole.

"Hmmm. I'm seeing bedrock."

"Impermeable?" Hube asked hopefully.

"It certainly looks that way. I cannot see any water in the rock itself."

All the men standing around her let out long sighs of relief.

Sevana raised her head and took a good look at the sky. She estimated another three, perhaps four hours of light left. "Hube, you think we can put the sub dam in today?"

He lifted his eyes to the sky, making the same calculations she had just done. "I think we might can, if you've got spells to harden cement with."

She gave him a cocky smile. "Actually, I do."

He grinned right back at her, revealing crooked teeth. "Then let's get crackin'."

The spring did not prove to be particularly large or fast-moving, so the dam they built was more than adequate for the job. The pool they'd constructed held up as well, although Hube calculated that it wouldn't be quite large enough to hold more than two days of water. They spent most of the next day constructing another timber pool and linking the two with a pipe to deal with overflow.

After that, of course, it came down to a waiting game.

Well, Sevana waited. Everyone else seemed intent on playing in the pool. Granted, with that crystal clear water coming straight from the ground, it was perfect to play in. But half the draw had to be Master's "toys." Not only were his toys floatable, but they were animated. He had dolphins, sharks, and even one miniature whale in there thrashing about. The kids had a heyday trying to ride them.

Not quite trusting Master to remember he had an eight-year-old "hammer" in the water with him when toys were about, Sevana sat in the shade of a large weeping willow, kicked back in her favorite portable chair, and just watched the show. If Sky started drowning, she'd levitate him out.

The two wolves, not interested in playing in the water, seemed intent to lay in the shade of a tree and catch a long nap. Sevana had no idea when they'd been introduced to each other, but considering the way that Gid had pillowed his head on Hinun's stomach, they were friends now. She laughed softly to herself when Hinun's feet started twitching. Now, what did he chase in his dreams? With him, it could either be rabbits or children.

Since she had nothing else better to do, she pulled out her Caller while she sat there. "Pierpoint."

It took a few seconds—judging from the sounds, Pierpoint had been startled by her call and dropped something breakable, or at least the crashing sounds and cursing made her think so. But he picked it up with only a huff and a slightly disgruntled look. "*Sevana.*"

"How expensive was it?" she couldn't help but ask, evilly amused by his frustration.

"*Quite expensive, thank you ever so much for asking,*" he growled sarcastically, brows beetled together. "*And to what do I owe this honor?*"

"I'm waiting on something so I thought I would update you."

Pierpoint's expression showed a mixture of relief to get an update and sardonic amusement that she *only* called because she had nothing else better to do. "*Pray, do continue.*"

She skipped the failed attempt and her interesting excursion to the other end of Kindin, starting with the solution they'd thought of and what they'd done so far. The two magicians had packed up and gone home already, and almost as an afterthought, she passed along the message that Aren needed to pay them. Pierpoint reached over and scribbled down a note to make sure that was done.

"*So at the moment you're waiting on the water to drain out of the fountain completely so you can remove the—what did you call it?*"

"Gadgick," she supplied.

"*Wherever did you get that term from?*"

"Jacen." Seeing his blank expression, she elaborated with a sigh, "Jacen Windau? Artifactor? Specializes in ancient artifacts?"

"*Ahhh. I know the man by rumor and reputation, but little else. You consulted with him, I take it?*"

"We did. In fact, I fully intend to give the gadgick to him once we've removed it. He's the one most qualified to deal with it."

"*Heaven knows I wouldn't really know what to do with it either. I'll assure the king that it will go to an expert. He was talking about destroying the thing.*"

As tempting as that idea had been for her, "No. We don't dare.

For one thing, we'll lose valuable information that we'll probably never have a chance of gaining ever again. For another, I'm not sure how tough that thing is. For all I know, it'll take throwing it into a live volcano."

Pierpoint arched a brow at her. "*A trifle extreme, don't you think? But I get your point. Regardless, I don't feel it's necessary if it's going to your friend. I'll inform Aren of all of this. How much longer until the gadgick can be removed, do you think?*"

"Hmmm, I think we can take it out either late tomorrow or the following day. The water is draining out of the fountain nicely. We're waiting for what little remains to evaporate just for the sake of caution." No one wanted to be marked for transportation again by getting wet like Sevana had.

"*I'll pass it along.*" He cocked his head slightly and half-turned to look behind him. "*Are they playing in the timber dam?*"

"They certainly are," she confirmed, uselessly considering he could see it for himself.

"*Is that safe?*"

"Probably not. Master's in there after all."

Pierpoint let out a short chuckle. "*He's mischievous in water, I take it?*"

"He's mischievous all the time," she corrected with a roll of the eyes. "Put him in water and he's an outright devil. Why do you think I refuse to go in there?"

He just laughed again, shaking his head. "*I'll go make the report to the king. Anything you want to add?*"

"Not a blessed thing."

"*Then keep us posted,*" he ordered before the Caller went still.

She looked up at the pool as she put the Caller away, scanning the water for a certain head of blond hair. In this area of mostly brunettes, she spotted him quickly. Sky had stopped clinging to the sides and now splashed around energetically, even flip-flopping and swimming the other direction on the turn of a penny. Ohhh? Master had done quite well drown-proofing the kid, it seemed. Good. She didn't need to worry about him anymore then.

Putting her hands comfortably over her stomach, she leaned further back in her chair, closed her eyes, and took a well-deserved nap.

Even with the nice, sunny weather it took a full two days for enough water to evaporate before they deemed it "safe" to go anywhere near the fountain. With the pitiful little puddles of water here and there, the gadgick didn't have anywhere near the power it needed to even activate itself, much less transport anyone.

Hube had said that the decorative piece on the very top of the fountain had been carried over here intact, the only piece that had been moved without being dismantled first. Sevana pulled out a wand and scanned the area just in case, but the results came up positive very quickly, confirming that the gadgick had indeed been enclosed in the top part. She'd spent her free time examining it from a distance and had a fair idea of how to get the gadgick out.

The fairy girl holding the jug of water looked pretty and all, but in truth, the design had a practical element to it as well. The jug she held had the perfect place to put the gadgick. In olden times, perhaps the gadgick hadn't been left in place all of the time, but instead put in there when it was needed. (Sevana certainly wouldn't have left it running all the time. The magical energy that wasted alone made her head spin.) The jug provided a place to put the gadgick where it didn't run the risk of being damaged or knocked over but had direct access to flowing water. The decorative stone grill over it simply sat in place, several notches in the jug's opening giving it stability and support.

The only real problem she had was reaching the jug. The fountain stood a good five feet taller than she. Even standing on a chair wouldn't give her the necessary height. But with the three-tier build of the fountain, trying to use a ladder would be beyond awkward. It really only gave her one option. "Sarsen, lend me a shoulder."

"You mean let me be your footstool," he translated dryly.

She gave him an impish smirk. Sarsen and Master had been too curious to let her retrieve the gadgick alone, so they had trailed after her when she announced her intentions. In fact, quite a few people from the village had shown up as well, although for what, Sevana had no idea. If they expected a show, they'd be sorely disappointed. Removing the gadgick would be anticlimactic in the extreme.

Sarsen blew out a breath and sank to one knee. "Fine, fine. Climb aboard."

She swung one leg up and around so she could sit on his shoulders, like a child getting a ride from their father or favorite uncle. Sarsen held on to both of her legs just below the knee, giving her some stability, then slowly rose back to his feet with a grunt of effort.

"You comment on my weight and I'll kill you," she warned him.

"Did I say anything?"

"I could hear you thinking."

"Children, no bickering in front of the clients," Master scolded them. His words would have gone over better if his tone hadn't sounded so amused.

They left Master at the base of the fountain as Sarsen carefully stepped closer, putting Sevana within arm's reach of the top section. She had to raise her hands high over her head to reach the jug, but she didn't have to stretch *that* far, and she could mostly see what she was doing. The stone grating had been there for so long, though, it had more or less wedged itself into place. She had to tug, firmly, in rhythmic pulls before it started to slowly grate its way free.

Expression tight in concentration, she put both sets of fingers through the holes of the grate and gripped firmly. The stone felt cold against her skin, and a little harsh, but not rough enough to be abrasive. Fortunate, that. She'd hate to scratch up her hands just getting this thing free. But she didn't dare use magic of any sort, not after what happened last time.

"Sev, I have to ask…" Sarsen hesitated, body tensing as if not sure how she would take this question. "Why did you end up on the far side of Kindin? What were you dreaming of to be transported to a primeval forest?"

She let out a snort. "What makes you think I'd remember the dream?"

"Well, the image had to be powerful enough for the gadgick to use it," he pointed out a tad defensively.

Sevana paused and turned to look at the top of his head. "I remember once, while we were both apprentices, that you dreamed you rode a pink, talking elephant across the Wasteland."

He stopped with his mouth hanging open, no good retort to be found anywhere. "Ah. Your point being that dreams don't make sense?"

"Nor should we expect them to." She shrugged as she went back to the task at hand, yanking hard. Stubborn little piece of...*ugh*. "There's a whole group out there that believes in dream studies, and the psychology behind it, but personally I feel like it doesn't really matter."

"So there's no rhyme or reason why you ended up in the woods in the dead of night."

"I blame it on Hinun," she responded mock-serenely.

"Why?" Sarsen seemed to find this funny as his shoulders jerked in a silent chuckle. "'Cause he isn't here to defend himself?"

"He was sleeping with me and no doubt dreaming of hunting in the woods."

"That sounds plausible and all, but it doesn't explain that smile of evil satisfaction you're wearing."

"Children," Master requested mildly from the bottom of the fountain, "Can you please focus?"

The grate finally came free, tumbling into her hand with nothing more than a last groan of protest. She almost lost her balance after expecting resistance and not finding any. Fortunately, Sarsen's grip on her legs kept her from toppling right over him and straight into the basin. Puffing out a breath, she righted herself again and put the grating next to a carved stone flower, propping it up temporarily. Then, very cautiously, she reached in with both hands and felt inside the jug. "I feel something cold and smooth. Not stone. Porcelain?"

"Can you pull it free?" Master inquired, tone betraying a certain amount of caution.

"I think so." She didn't feel any resistance at all this time. With her fingertips, she urged it to come out in slow degrees. When it came close enough, she grabbed it more firmly and pulled the top out of the jug entirely.

Well, well, well.

It certainly resembled porcelain, her tactical sense hadn't been wrong on that, but she'd never seen the likes of this before. It glowed faintly—thank all mercy she hadn't used magic—with crisp lines of white engraved into the light gray of the body. It looked stunning, really. Sevana thought of written incantations as practical things, not particularly visually appealing, nor were they meant to be. But this was both. One hand on the top of the gadgick, she slid it free completely, balancing the base with her other hand. Oh? It didn't have the simple cylindrical design that Jacen had shown her in his catalogue remnant. Instead, both ends flared out slightly, the interior of the gadgick completely hollow. Now that she could see all of it, she saw that the design around it was beautifully detailed. If she hadn't known better, she'd have taken it for some sort of vase.

"Well, sweetling?"

"There's still some residue of power left in it," she responded. "I'd be careful, if I were you."

"Straight in the box it'll go, then." Master had taken the caution of fetching one of his 'behave boxes' from his workroom before coming here. He'd invented them ages ago, as a young apprentice, but still used them to this day. Once something was placed in the box, it was cut off from all outside magic and would be obediently dormant until released again.

Sarsen slowly turned, facing Master, and she leaned forward just as Master lifted his box up. She put the gadgick directly into the box without anyone else touching it and he closed the lid as soon as she pulled her hands free. Sarsen barely got a good look at it during this process, but he didn't utter a word of protest. Then again, after everything that had happened, he likely didn't want to tempt fate by leaving it out in the open any longer just to satisfy his curiosity.

Master latched a few seals and buckles into place, making sure that it couldn't be casually opened, before he looked back at them with a satisfied smile. "We might have had a few bumps along the way, but the job is done."

"And thank all mercy for that," Sevana grumbled as she slid off Sarsen's shoulders and to the ground. "It's too late for any of us to get any work done at this point." It was, in fact, only a few hours until sunset. "Although I suppose I can remove the dam at the very least and let the fountain fill back up again."

"Replace the grill first," Master reminded her.

She flapped a hand at him. "Yes, yes. Are you leaving for Jacen's now?"

"Hmmm." Master thought for a moment before shaking his head. "I don't know the roads well enough to navigate in bad lighting. I'll wait until the morning."

She shrugged, as it didn't really matter to her either way. "Sarsen, if you'd pitch in? We might as well start the cleanup."

"Sooner it's done, sooner we can go," he agreed.

Sevana clapped her hands together loudly, raising her voice so the whole square could hear her. "Alright, folks! The problem's solved, the show's over, go on about your business!"

This made people give a shout of joy and they clapped in celebration. A slight smile on her face, she put the grill back in place with a wave of her wand before she climbed off the fountain's edge and headed for the dam. She just had one more thing to do tonight before she could be satisfied with a full day's work.

A guttural scream ripped through the night air, followed by the sound of tinkling glass as it shattered.

Sevana went from a sound sleep to an upright position in her bed before she could even get her eyes open. What in all the wide green world was that?! Hinun, who had been asleep across her feet, was already off the bed and tearing through the door, low growls coming out of his mouth as he sprinted. Even Sky awoke as she rolled quickly out of the bed, her bare feet slapping against the wooden floor as she snatched up a protective crystal and a wand.

"Master! Sarsen!" she called out, sprinting out of her room and into the dark hallway.

With all of the noise going on, several people had awoken and come out of their rooms to investigate. She had to shove one curious trader aside just to get through. Hinun let out a high-pitched whine from Master's room, and she knew in a flash of dread, just where the noise had been coming from. Swearing, she sprinted the distance and slid into the room.

Master sat on the edge of his bed, a hand to his head, blood gushing out between his fingers. The window nearby lay in a spray of broken glass all over the floor, and the room looked like a storm had blown through it. Not heeding the splinters on the floor, she went directly to Master, snatching up a towel from the washstand as she moved and pressing it against his head. "What happened?" she demanded, even as she used her hip to nudge a hovering Hinun out of the way.

"Thieves. But not your garden variety. These had a rather gifted magician with them. They'd nearly levitated the box out the window before I felt the magic and woke up." He winced and looked up at her. "Sevana. They've got the gadgick."

Just the thought of that artifact in the wrong hands made her blood run cold. A lot of evil could be done with it. Making a split decision, she turned to Hinun and ordered, "Get Decker. *Now.*" She'd need his tracking skills for this. Then she turned further and saw Sky hovering in the doorway, his eyes wide at the scene. "Get Sarsen."

The boy nodded and spun on his heels, disappearing in a flash.

"I can't believe he slept through all of this," Master said, almost as if speaking to himself.

She snorted, not one bit surprised. "Don't you remember that time the house was on fire? He slept right through that, too."

"I suppose his sleeping habits haven't changed since childhood." Master half-raised a hand toward the towel. "How bad is it?"

"Not that bad. It's just because it's a head wound that it's bleeding like this."

Sarsen stumbled into the room in the next moment, eyes wide in his face, his pouch in his hand. "Master! What in sweet mercy happened?"

"Thieves," Master explained again. "They were levitating the box out of the window when I woke up. I tried to stop them and they yanked the box forward, hitting me in the head, and then jerked it through the window glass."

Hence his head wound and the glass all over the floor. Got it. "Did you see any of them?"

"Not a soul. But they had to have a fairly high level of ability to be able to do what they did while remaining on the ground. It would take a seer spell to see through the building and work a levitation spell at the same time."

She understood that without the explanation. That's what made this whole situation so much worse. Sevana rose to her feet. "Sarsen. You deal with Master. I'll go after the thieves."

"Not alone!" both men protested simultaneously.

"I'll take Decker, Hinun and Gid," she assured them, already heading for the door. "I doubt any magician and his little band can handle an Artifactor prodigy, a huntsman, and two Illeyanic wolves."

"Sweetling," Master called after her. She stopped in the doorway, half-turning to see him. He grimaced a smile. "Be careful. For my sake."

Careful? She'd done far more dangerous things than chasing down a group of stupid thieves. But she gave him a sloppy salute to reassure him—otherwise she feared he would try to follow along, despite the head injury.

As she stepped out of the room, she found Sky huddled near the doorway, arms wrapped around himself. "Sky. Stay with Master and Sarsen, help them if you can. This time, you can't follow me."

He looked up at her with solemn eyes. "You're not afraid?"

"What? You think they're more dangerous than a water dragon?" she scoffed.

The boy blinked, thinking that through, and then a fierce smile took over his face as he put the danger into perspective. "Take no prisoners."

She returned the wolfish smile. "You bet."

By the time Decker arrived at the inn, Sevana was more than ready to go. She had gotten dressed in the darkest clothes she owned, put several useful things into her pouch, and strapped on not only her sword, but her long dagger as well. If it came down to a fight, she was more than ready for it.

Decker's stallion pulled to a sharp stop in front of the inn, two wolves in his wake. The huntsman looked as if he had thrown on the first clothes at hand, although she noted with approval that he also had several weapons strapped to him. "What happened?" he demanded before the stallion could come to a complete stop. "Your wolf was frantic to get us here."

"The gadgick has been stolen."

Decker could not have been more surprised if she had smacked him in the back of the head with a club. "WHAT?!"

"You heard me. I'll explain the details as we go, but we're already a good thirty minutes behind them and losing ground fast." Turning to the two wolves, she pointed toward the east side of the building. "I believe the thieves stood over there to do their work. Get a scent, if you can." Hinun might not be able to pick out their scents from the rest of the villagers'—after all, he'd only been here a few days—but Gid could.

Both wolves leaped lightly onto the porch and went directly to where she indicated, their noses to the ground, tails wagging slightly as they searched.

Sevana grimaced, but bowed her head to the inevitable and extended a hand to Decker. "I'll ride with you."

He quirked a brow at her. "You're not going to ride your flying thing?"

"I can't see the ground well enough from the sky to do any tracking," she explained with limited patience. "And it attracts too much attention. If we discover later that we need to ambush them, we won't be able to with me flapping about up there."

"Good point." He grabbed her hand and kicked one boot free of the stirrup, letting her get a good foothold to swing aboard with. Fortunately, his saddle design had enough room to accommodate two people, if barely. She felt a little squashed between him and the cantle, but she could still breathe. She wrapped both arms around his waist in a firm grip, already knowing that by the end of this mad chase, she'd be saddle-sore and cranky. If this wasn't such an emergency, where she couldn't go back to Big and get one of her other vehicles, she'd *never* consent to climb onto a horse.

Decker put his boot back into the stirrup. "Looks like they have the scent. Gid, Hinun, you sure? Yes? Then lead on."

As soon as the stallion moved, Decker's weight pressed back into her a little more, although he kept such a good posture that she didn't feel squashed. Conversely, she felt reassured by the closeness, as she didn't feel comfortable up here at all. Considering that she flew about in the air on a regular basis, the height from on top of a horse shouldn't bother her at all. This rationale didn't help her an ounce. She eyed the distance to the ground and fought an uneasy coil that wrapped around the base of her spine.

The wolves couldn't go too fast without risking losing the trail, of course, which limited their pace to a trot. At this speed, they left the village fairly quickly, exchanging cobbled streets for packed dirt that softened their hoof beats slightly.

The highways at this midnight hour were completely deserted, the only light coming from the half-moon in the sky. Both wolves and horse must have known the road ahead well, as their pace didn't falter. Sevana felt the slight chill of night air along her exposed skin and fervently hoped that the thick jacket she wore would be enough to combat the cold. She hadn't grabbed a cloak for fear that it would prevent her from easily accessing either her magic pouch or her weapons.

"Alright, explain," Decker ordered without turning his head.

"Not much to tell," she admitted morosely. "Master said a thief with good magic ability tried to levitate the box with the gadgick out of his window. The magic woke Master up, he tried to grab the box, the magician used it as a weapon to hit him in the head, and then he broke the window getting the box out quickly. Master never saw his face or got a look outside. He kept saying *thieves*, though, so for some reason he thinks there's more than one person."

"Maybe he heard multiple people run away?" Decker suggested.

A plausible theory, and likely the answer. Sevana hadn't thought to question it until just now.

"But how did they know about the gadgick to steal it?" Decker asked in true confusion. "You just got it out of the fountain this afternoon!"

"What, are you joking? Bel and Aren classified this thing as a *national emergency*. We had multiple people from all over come to help us, even if only short term, and then leave again. Rumors, I'm sure, spread like wildfire about this thing." If anything, she should have realized that thieves would likely target it and taken precautionary measures. After all, she had thieves that tried to raid her mountain on a consistent basis. Wouldn't an ancient, powerful artifact be a more attractive lure? She mentally kicked herself for the oversight.

Decker let out a groan. "You're right. So, a magician thief. Or a magician that thieves hired for this one job. Is that common practice?"

"More common than I care for. The black market adores anything magical, and the higher quality it is, the easier it is to sell. The gadgick will fetch a pretty penny if they can get it to the right dealer."

"And, ah, why do you know so much about this?"

"The first year I was in business, I didn't have any anti-theft protections up and some fools raided my storeroom. It was quite the adventure getting everything back." The original thieves had paid for the stupidity as well. She'd made sure of that.

"So you've dealt with this before."

"I've never had to track someone down in the middle of the night before, but yes."

"If it came down to a fight between us and them, then…?" he trailed off, glancing over his shoulder at her. Why he bothered, she had no idea. In the pale moonlight and with trees shadowing the road, she could barely see anything at all.

"A silly question, Decker. Of course I would turn them all into toads."

For some reason, this made him smile. "Of course. What was I thinking?"

"More importantly, how fast do you think we can catch up with them?"

"Now, that I can't tell you. It depends on where they're going. Right now, we're heading straight north, but that can't last long. This road dead ends and forks off in two different directions—west toward Kindin or east toward the coast. The coast offers them a quick escape route to Belen, one that will be hard for us to immediately follow as we don't have a ship on hand."

Sevana would bet her left hand the thieves would choose to go to Belen. It boasted one of the largest black markets in the world. In fact, it was there that she had found most of her stolen goods years ago. But they might well choose to go into Kindin instead, as it offered its own variety of markets, so she shouldn't be too hasty in making assumptions.

"No other trails they can choose?"

"Oh, this place is riddled with game trails. It depends on how well they know the area, how prepared they are for pursuit. I would think that if they knew about the gadgick, they'd know who was tasked with taking care of it." He sounded grim. "I imagine that everyone knew the Artifactor prodigy, Sevana Warren, had been sent here by the king to deal with this situation. In their shoes, I'd do a lot of preparation to handle you before I ever came to steal the gadgick."

She growled wordlessly. Decker's logic was impeccable in this case and she couldn't disagree with any part of it. In their shoes, she'd likely have several traps and at least one bolt hole, if it came to that, to evade their pursuit. With the magician they had, they might very well be able to escape detection by her, depending on how skillfully they worked their magic.

Only one thing really weighed in her favor: she had a pair of Illeyanic wolves tracking them down. That magician might be able to camouflage things to where she couldn't magically detect them, and he might be able to cover their tracks at a certain point to where even Decker couldn't follow, but he probably hadn't taken the wolves into account. It would be another task completely to throw *them* off the scent. Or so she hoped, anyway.

They kept riding at a ground-eating trot that made miles pass under them. With only glimpses of the moon overhead, and no clock on her, she couldn't say how much time had passed. Her aching backside firmly maintained that it had been at least a decade since she'd climbed on board. Grimacing at the discomfort, she tried to grip the horse's sides with her legs and readjust her position. This did and didn't succeed. "There's no way to tell if we're catching up, is there?"

"Not until we actually catch sight of them," Decker confirmed. He turned his head slightly toward her. "You're fidgeting. Getting sore?"

"I'm not used to riding a horse." She decided to leave it at that.

"Well, with all of those magical flying devices you have, I

suppose that makes sense," he allowed. "Bear with it. We're making good headway, I think. In fact, I'll be surprised if we don't catch them by dawn."

"And, ah, how far away is dawn?"

"A good three hours yet."

So they'd already been riding like this for two hours? She thunked her head against his back and groaned. And she had to put up with this for another *three hours?*

"You'll survive," he assured her drolly.

Probably. "I'm taking every ounce of my discomfort out on those thieves' hides."

"I won't stop you," he promised in dark humor.

Up ahead of them, the wolves slowed to a walk and then stopped altogether, their noses up in the air and pointing to an area off the road that looked to be dense with virgin forest. They stopped as well, the horse blowing out a sigh of relief to finally have a chance to catch his breath. Sevana put her hands on Decker's shoulders and used him to lever herself up so she could properly see. "Hinun? What are you sensing?"

The wolf let out a long whine, taking two cautious steps toward the side of the road.

"What?" Decker looked at his own wolf, who didn't seem to know what to think of the situation. "You're not smelling what he is?"

"It's probably not a scent at all," Sevana said absently, her eyes straining to see in the dark. "Hinun is sensitive to magic after living with an Artifactor for so many years. I think I'm seeing what he sensed. It's faint, but there's an aura of magic over this area."

"A trap?"

"Off the road?" she countered. "I would think you'd put the trap *on* the road. But I really can't tell from this distance. I barely see it at all."

He stiffened his arm and gave her something to balance with as she slid off the horse. Hinun looked uneasy about this thing, whatever it was, so she trod cautiously. The wolf might not understand magic the way they did, but he certainly had good instincts about it. If he didn't trust it, she wouldn't either. She came up to stand at his side, drawing first a crystal that emitted a soft glow of light so she could have a proper view of the area. It lit up everything in a pale yellow, throwing things into a sharp chiaroscuro of shading and light.

Hmmmm, something looked strange about this. Very strange. The trees directly in front of her, exposed to strong mage light, looked flat, almost two-dimensional. The trees off to either side looked like exact duplicates, something she hadn't been able to see until she stood this close. One, two, three…five trees were mirages based on some of the surrounding trees.

"This area isn't real," she said, outlining it with her free hand. "It's either a trap meant for us to fall into or a bolt hole for them to hide in. I can't tell which."

Decker dismounted as well, one hand resting on the sword hilt belted at his side. "Which one are you inclined to think it is?"

"A trap," she said frankly, not taking her eyes away. Something about this didn't look quite right, not compared to the skill she'd already seen from this magician. In fact, part of the spell seemed to be…leaking? "Gid doesn't smell them going into there, right? Hinun doesn't seem to be either, he just sensed the magic. And the way this is set up is almost shoddy, in a sense. Like they had designed it to where it would have *just* enough of a magical presence that I would detect it."

"And come in close enough to fall into it," Decker finished darkly. "Well, well, they are clever, aren't they."

"Not clever enough to outsmart a wolf, thank mercy. But they certainly caught something." She rubbed at her chin and stared harder. Now that she saw the spell, she could see through it to a certain extent, although the inky darkness kept the details hidden.

"Something?" Decker parroted, peering into the woods himself.

A piercing cry split the night air, the sound like an angry bird of prey calling out in challenge.

"Ah…was that…?"

"A griffin," Sevana confirmed for him. "At least, I'm seeing a large body with wings and it certainly looks like a griffin."

"Those idiots trapped a griffin in there?" he demanded incredulously.

"Likely not on purpose. Traps like this are devilishly hard to set because you can only set it to trap a certain amount of creatures or races before you hit a limit. He likely set it to entrap beings with sentient intelligence, as that's the easiest way to mark humans apart from animals. Griffins are intelligent enough to fall into that bracket."

Decker looked unnerved by this, as well he should be. Griffins did not have a natural propensity for being benevolent toward humankind to begin with. They wouldn't attack humans without provocation, but they weren't inclined to get along with them either. You had to win a griffin's respect first before ever trying to deal with them, and that was challenging.

While this situation had 'danger' written all over it, it also came with a great deal of opportunity. She rocked back on her heels and thought about it. "Decker, how far are we away from that split in the road?"

"About a half-hour or so, why?"

"And are there game trails that can get us ahead of them, if we know which way they went?"

"Well, of course, but it's impossible to know…" he trailed off as he picked up on where these questions led. "You think you can get him to cooperate with us if you free him?"

"I don't see the harm in trying." She shrugged. "If he's not in the mood to bargain, I'll contact Sarsen and have him come up and undo the trap. It won't hurt our flying friend in there to be trapped for a day or so."

Decker shifted from one foot to the other, ill at ease. "I heard griffins are hard to deal with."

"That's an understatement. But I think I have the right motivation for him to cooperate at the moment." Rooting through her bag, she found a vocal wand and put it to her throat, projecting her voice to a more audible pitch. "Honorable griffin. I am Sevana Warran, an Artifactor."

The thrashing on the other side of the trees abruptly stopped.

"**Artifactor**?"

"Indeed. I am in pursuit of the men that set this trap and ensnared you. They are evil and we wish to punish them."

"Then free me. Undo their work."

"I certainly am willing to, but my efforts come at a price. Will you aid us in hunting them down? I will consider it a fair deal if you do."

A weighty silence descended as he mulled this over. Finally, he responded, "**What do you wish of me**?"

"It won't take long," she promised. "Let me ride on your back and see if I can spot them in the air. If we know which road they took, we'll know how to get ahead of them and can catch them sooner."

Another weighty silence before he capitulated with ill grace, "**Fine. Undo this wretched spell.**"

She grinned in victory.

The spell didn't take much to dismantle. Spells that camouflaged didn't take a lot of power—that's how they were able to evade magical detection in the first place, by using more natural power and less of the human element. But that also meant that if push came to shove, any magician worth their salt could break it easily. All Sevana did was switch wands to one with more power in it, and with a sharp slashing movement, commanded, "∥ ∫⅄ ∥ ⏜⌒⏝"

The trap dissolved as if it had never been there, revealing a small clearing instead of the line of trees that had been there before. The griffin lost no time in leaping free of the clearing and landing on the road, coming in close enough that he spooked both wolves and the stallion. The wolves quickly backed up, coming in closer to their respective humans in a clearly defensive posture. The stallion just jerked at his reins, trying to leave the area altogether. But most animals would when faced with an angry predator their own size.

The griffin didn't appear to either notice or care about their reactions. He just shook himself from head to tail, wings flaring as if he had been locked in a cage instead of a clearing. Sevana pursed her lips in a silent whistle. My, my, my, what an amazing specimen. In her mage light, his eyes shone like polished glass, and even under all those glossy golden feathers she could see muscles ripple and contract as he moved. He looked to be a young adult, old enough to have his full body, but just barely. It could explain why he fell for the trap, as well. He didn't have the experience yet to recognize when an area looked suspicious.

After another full-body shake, he looked at her squarely. "**Well, Artifactor, climb on. I wish to get this over with**."

"And, ah, how do you propose that I stay on?" she asked him. After all, she didn't have a saddle or anything like that, and she'd seen griffins fly before. They could put falling stars to shame with their speed.

"That is your business."

Right. Obviously she wouldn't get any help from that quarter. Shaking her head, she reached in her bag and pulled out two charms, which she stuck on the inside of her thighs. She put the mage light away at the same time, as it would interfere with his night vision and give away their position up in the air.

"Um, Sevana?"

"I'll be fine," she assured Decker, hoping she didn't lie. She looked the griffin over with a calculating eye and decided to sit at the base of his neck, right in front of his wings. It seemed the best spot, anyway. With a bit of a running start, she hopped up onto her stomach—why did he have to be so *tall?*—and swung both legs around so that she could sit up properly. His feathers felt smooth and prickly at the same time, depending on where she gripped, but she found a likely spot to hang on to. As soon as she did, she activated the charms on her legs, which gripped tightly to his sides. Thank all mercy she had sticking charms in the bag. Hopefully they would be adequate to the job at hand.

Settled, she directed, "We need to fly north."

Without a word, he spread his wings, and with a few running steps, took off into the air. Air blasted her in the face, whipping a few strands of hair out of her braid to slap her in the face. She didn't dare lift even one hand to drag them free. It felt as if she *barely* had a secure perch on his back. Sticking charms or no sticking charms, if she made it to the ground in one piece, it'd be a miracle.

The air up here felt far colder, and at the speed they flew, it felt like icicles formed inside of her lungs. She kept her mouth closed as much as she could and breathed through her nose, but it didn't seem to help much.

"Where?"

Peering downward, she tried to see the ground. It looked like nothing more than pitch darkness to her, most of it semi-bristly. "We're looking for a group of men travelling fast."

The griffin didn't respond, just took off in a short dive that brought them closer to the ground, speeding them ahead. Sevana had to trust his eyes, as she couldn't see a single thing, but a griffin's night vision should be able to see every mouse as it moved down there.

He did one slow, lazy circle, and then stopped in midair, hovering with gentle beats of his wings. "**I see nothing.**"

She blinked. "Nothing at all?"

"There are no humans down there," he confirmed darkly. "Woman, you are sure of the direction?"

"The wolves were the ones tracking their scent. I didn't detect any magic that would have confused them." She pondered that for a moment. "I suspect they have a bolt hole of some sort prepared to evade our pursuit. It's apparently closer than I would have guessed. How far can you see?"

"**Far.**"

She rolled her eyes. Really? That was the best answer he could give her? "Down both the east and west highways?"

"**Yes**."

Well, they couldn't be *that* far ahead to disappear completely out of a griffin's sight. No, they had to have a bolt hole fairly nearby. "Do you see any areas that look…strange? Like the area that trapped you."

"I cannot see human magic."

Ahhh. That explained why he was trapped within it. Well, staying up here any longer would serve no purpose except to freeze her even further. "Thank you," she said politely. With griffins, you were polite, or you were a mid-meal snack. "If you'll take me back now?"

"**That is all you wish of me**?" he sounded surprised.

"That's all I needed to know," she assured him. "If you can't see them from up here, then they're hiding nearby. Knowing that, I'll be able to find them."

He didn't respond, but his lack of response carried weight, as if he was thinking it all over. He turned and dove back toward where Decker and the wolves waited on them. It seemed that the return trip took half the time, which Sevana felt like saying a prayer of thanks for, as her hands felt so cold she didn't know how much longer she could grip anything. From now on, if she ever had to pursue anyone in the dead of night, she was wearing *gloves*.

The griffin landed lightly on the ground, wings fully extended, and stayed still as she undid the sticking charms and slid stiffly to the ground. With frozen face muscles, she managed a smile and gave him a bow. "Thank you."

For the first time, the griffin reciprocated the courtesy and gave a nod of his head in return. "**You make fair deals, Artifactor. I will remember this**."

Oh? Sounded like she'd just made a friend, of sorts. "I promise to track down the men that trapped you."

He gave a curt nod of the head, feathers bristling. "If I am nearby, and you need my aid, you may call on me. I am Clear Wind."

She gave an appropriate bow for the gift of his name. "I will do so."

With a last, piercing cry, he lifted off the ground again, sending gusts of wind swirling about them. She lifted her arms to shield her face in a defensive gesture, but as quickly as the air hit her, it disappeared as he took to the sky.

She blew out a breath. "Well. That was an adventure."

"What did you see?" Decker pressed.

"Not a blasted thing," she confessed frankly. "It all looked like various shades of black to me. But *he* said there weren't any humans moving about and a griffin's eyesight is not to be underestimated. He also said that he couldn't see anything that has human magic on it—"

"Hence why he got trapped?"

She gave a nod at his guess and continued, "—so it's likely they're holed up somewhere. Somewhere close, if they managed to get under cover this quickly. Hinun, Gid, it's up to you to track these gormless twits down." She didn't think she'd be able to see their true bolt hole. As much as it pained her to admit it, their magician's skill level was too high for him to make careless mistakes.

They remounted, with much pain and grumbling on Sevana's part, and set off. The wolves kept their noses in the air or dropped them to the ground now and again. After shivering for a full minute, she gave up and picked up the bottom of Decker's jacket, climbing her way underneath it.

Decker yelped as her cold hands touched his back and squirmed. "Sevana!" he squeaked. "What are you doing?!"

"Shut it. I'm freezing."

"What, you don't have warming spells or something?"

"Not on me," she grumbled against his back. Ooooh, so nice and waaaarm. Like a lizard finding a hot rock, she wrapped her arms around his stomach and snuggled in. The chill started leaving and she felt like purring in contentment.

"Happy?" he drawled.

"Mmmm-hmmm," she sighed.

"You realize your hands are freezing me?"

"Do I care?"

Decker muttered, "Apparently not."

They rode along in silence for several minutes. Eventually, Sevana started to feel too confined and stifled by being under the jacket like this. Most of her body liked being warm but it felt hard to breathe. After some internal debate, she gave up and climbed back out of the jacket and into the progressively colder night air. When she lifted the jacket up, Decker let out a hiss of protest. "What?" she asked in exasperation. "I thought you didn't like me under there."

"I don't, but every time you lift the jacket, a cold blast of air goes up my back!" He shifted one hand off the reins so he could tug his jacket back into place.

She shrugged, as this didn't bother her any, and asked, "How are the wolves doing?"

"Still going strong. They don't seem the least bit confused. Is it possible to duplicate someone's scent and lay a false trail?"

"Yes," she responded instantly. "But it's hard to do it in a hurry and make it credible enough to fool an Illeyanic's intelligence. Hinun especially will be able to tell the difference."

Decker gave a nonverbal grunt of understanding.

A thought occurred and she asked, "Have you ever hunted down men before? Thieves, murderers, that sort of thing?"

"Yes," he answered simply.

She didn't press him for details. She didn't need to. Huntsmen in any corner of the world were depended on for more than just game and furs. They also augmented the ombudsmen and whatever law enforcement might be in place. Sevana had joined in with such parties once or twice before on Milby's behalf because the criminal they chased had some sort of magical talent or device on them that a normal man couldn't safely handle. She knew exactly what Decker had experienced before this. The way he reacted to this situation, spur of the moment as it was, spoke a great deal of his history.

"Have you?" he asked her, as if he hadn't thought to ask this until she had.

"Oh yes. I've never had to do it in the dead of night like this, as I said earlier."

Decker mulled that over for a moment before saying slowly, "The more I'm around all of you, the more I realize that Artifactors are rather jack-of-all-trades. You seem perfectly capable of turning your hand to anything."

"We have to be," she agreed. "We cater to both magicians and those with no magic at all. We must think outside of the lines and inside of them. Being an Artifactor means that we are the most intelligent, the most creative, the most talented, because that's what you *have* to be in order to do the job."

"You sound so matter-of-fact about it." A timbre of amusement colored the words. "Even though you are renowned for being a prodigy."

"I don't believe in false humility."

He snorted a laugh. "Obviously."

Really, if she had a choice on whom to go into a rough situation with, she'd choose Sarsen, Master, Kip or someone else she'd known for years and trusted. But aside from the fact that she'd never fought side by side with Decker before, she had no complaints about him. In fact, he might be the better choice as he knew the land like the back of his hand. He'd been hunting and living in this area for decades, after all.

Their pace slowed slightly. She perked up and tried to look ahead, but really, she couldn't make out much. "Why are we slowing?"

"There's a ravine up ahead. It's shallow, as ravines go, but steep enough that I don't want to take it at any speed."

Scratch that—Decker was the *perfect* person to take into this situation. She'd have run right into that ravine and probably broken a few bones, to boot.

They slowed to a walk and within a few steps started to navigate the sloping sides of the ravine. In this season, it contained a good quantity of water in the bottom, but not enough to do more than cover the horse's frog. It barely even splashed any water on Sevana's boots. She said many a prayer of gratitude for that. What did hit her felt so icy cold that she was amazed it hadn't frozen solid yet.

It took bare minutes to cross the water to the bank on the other side.

Wait. Crossing water? Wouldn't that mean— "Won't Hinun and Gid lose the scent since we're crossing water?"

"Hmm? Oh, no. That's an old wife's tale, actually. Scent is stronger on top of the water. It's actually easier for them to follow it."

She blinked. Despite having been around Hinun for ten years, she hadn't known that. Of course, she'd never gone tracking or hunting with a wolf before either. "Really. So what does mess with their sense of smell?"

"Too many smells," he admitted easily. "If we followed them into a city, for instance, there would be no way for him to discern their scent from others. He'd get confused and lose the trail eventually. Even a village is a mite challenging. Fortunately Gid's very familiar with the village scents, otherwise we'd never have been able to follow them."

Sevana made a mental note of that for future reference. Using Decker for support, she leaned around him and checked on the wolves. They'd already climbed lithely up the bank and were back on the road on the other side as if nothing had changed, their eyes intently watching the humans following along as they waited for the slowpokes to catch up.

The stallion strained a little to climb back up to the road, but the ease with which he picked out a path said without words he'd done this many times before. They returned to the road without any mishap and kept going, the wolves silently leading the way.

Sevana blew out a heavy breath. She'd worked a full day and only gotten a few hours of sleep before the thieves had struck, and her body felt the toil of being awake and moving so long. She started wishing for a flat surface. A bed would be preferable, of course, but *any* flat surface would do. The only thing that kept her from turning around and heading back toward Chastain was the awful premonition of what an evil man could do with the gadgick in hand. That thing could transport whole armies, if it felt like doing so. The thought sent a chill racing up and down her spine.

Decker abruptly reigned into a stop and called, "Gid, Hinun, stop!"

The wolves skidded to a halt immediately and trotted back to him, their noses in the air in an inquiring manner.

"Ah, Decker?" Sevana saw absolutely no reason to stop. The woods around them had gotten a little thicker near the road than they had been, but other than that, nothing had changed.

"This doesn't look right." He stood in the stirrups and strained forward as if trying to get a better look.

Sevana became alert, straining her senses in all directions. She could smell the water they'd just crossed behind them, and the scents of pine trees and damp earth. No wood smoke, though, so it couldn't be that which tipped Decker off. Her ears heard the sounds of insects and bull frogs, but no other strange noises. In this pitch darkness, she didn't trust her eyes at all and quickly gave up on that.

"Decker. Nothing looks or seems out of place."

"Something's not right," he insisted. "This area doesn't look right."

She rolled her eyes to the heavens in a bid for patience. "We've been riding around in the woods for *hours* in pitch darkness with barely enough light to tell the trees from the road. How in mercy's name can you tell?"

"I know these woods. There should be a large clearing right after we cross the ravine."

Her strained patience evaporated, replaced with taut concentration. "How sure are you?"

"Sure." He dropped back into the saddle and turned slightly to look at her. "There should be a clearing off to the left. You think it's another trap, like the one before?"

A 'no' hovered on the tip of her tongue. She looked at the area with new eyes, questioning everything, but it still looked like normal forest to her. "No, Decker. If it was a trap like before, there would be something about it that would seem suspicious, something that would draw my attention. There's no magic aura here at all. If you didn't know the area so well, I would have kept on riding."

A feral smile stretched over his face. "Then this is likely where they're hiding?"

"I'd lay good odds on it." She turned to Hinun. "You smell them going off the road?"

The wolf let out a confirming huff.

Good enough for her. "How many, do you think?" she asked the wolf. "Ten? Less than that, huh? Alright, we can handle less than ten."

Decker looked at her cross-eyed, as if he didn't know what she based *that* conclusion on, but didn't question it. "So do you have a plan, Mistress Artifactor?"

"I do, as it happens." She rubbed her hands together in anticipation. "Let's play a little bait and catch, shall we?"

Sevana crouched a few feet away from Decker, both of them on the far side of the road waiting in ambush. She had her ears and eyes strained, waiting for any sign of the thieves bursting free from their hidey-hole.

The wolves had gone in nearly a minute ago with the aim to chase them out. Sevana knew that if two wolves—two gigantic wolves, at that—appeared out of the dark woods growling, *she'd* certainly run for higher ground. The thieves were clever, but they'd gone to great lengths to avoid fighting, which suggested they wanted to avoid conflict if they could. She and Decker both were wagering they'd run from the wolves rather than fight. Hopefully, they'd run for a clear path—the road.

But really, what was taking so long? She'd expected to hear or see something by now. Unless the wolves had found some situation in there that they didn't know how to handle and were taking the long way back? Or—oh, no. Maybe they'd run into trouble? Sevana started rethinking the idea of sending them into the unknown.

Two long howls pierced the night air, sounding unnaturally loud. It sent her nerves, already stretched taut, jangling.

"Something's wrong," she and Decker said in unison, bursting out of their hiding places and sprinting forward.

She ran for what looked to be an open space between two trees and felt disoriented when magic washed across her skin and she felt no resistance from the trees. Oh, the mirage, eh? Right. Wand in one hand, sword in the other, she kept moving at a fast clip, swiveling her head back and forth as she panned the area. No, no sign of movement at all. A feeling of unease grew in her chest. "HINUN!"

The wolf let out a yip of acknowledgement, and she followed the sound to him. He stood almost invisible in the open clearing, only his gleaming eyes giving her something to pinpoint him by. She intended to go directly to him, but at the last second realized something lay on the ground between them. Skidding to a stop, she raised a foot to step over it before realizing just *what* lay on the ground.

Bile rose in her throat as she stared for a long moment. A man? No, a *corpse*. Horrified, she quickly looked about the clearing. What she had mistaken for logs at first glance weren't. Under the weak moonlight, eight prone bodies lay deathly still.

Decker got over his shock faster than she, kneeling to check the body nearest to him. "I'd say he's been dead a good hour. I can't find any blood or obvious sign of injury, though. Magically killed?"

"There are several curses that can kill a man without leaving a mark on him," she answered past a dry mouth, not even really aware of what she was saying. "An hour. They've been dead for the past hour?"

"No wonder your griffin didn't see any signs of movement."

She slowly sheathed the sword, eyes roving the clearing again. "This is…"

"Disturbing?" Decker finished.

"Creepy. I was thinking creepy." In fact, she would like nothing better than to turn and leave immediately. But first— "The box. Do you see the black box that has the gadgick?"

"No, but it's hard to see much of anything. It might be blending in with the ground."

Or more likely was taken. The only explanation for this scene that her mind could think up was that there had been a falling-out among thieves and the box had been taken by the murderer. Nevertheless, they looked diligently. Without needing to worry about discovery, Sevana now freely used mage lights to brighten the area. But it was to no avail. The box didn't turn up at all.

Decker leaned down, resting on one knee, and put his hand on the grass in an 'L' shape. "It rested here. See the indentation it left? We tracked the right group."

Tracker she was not. She didn't see anything that would tell him that, but took his word on it. "Hinun, Gid, can you find the scent of the man that left here?"

The wolves circled about in confusion several times before sitting down, clearly giving up. She swore several choice curses but didn't feel surprised. "He had time to mask his scent and erase any tracks. An hour would be plenty of time to a skilled magician. We're not going to find him tonight."

Decker grunted as he pushed his way back to his feet. "I must agree. What now? Back to Chastain?"

"For now." She rubbed at her forehead and hoped that the image of this scene wouldn't stick in her mind for long. Hoping for no nightmares at all would probably be asking too much. "I can't track this man, so he might well get away with this, but I might still be able to get the gadgick back."

"How?" he asked in puzzlement.

"The black market. I imagine our murderer friend will take it there."

Decker seemed less than pleased with this. "The nearest black market is in Belen. And it's *huge*."

"Don't I know it." She shrugged and waved the wolves to follow her. With the black box gone, she had no desire to stay in this unburied cemetery even a second longer. "But I have a contact there. I stand a better chance of finding it there than tramping blindly out here in the woods. Come along, Decker. We're not going to do any good standing around out here."

By the time that they made it back to Chastain, it was well past dawn. Sevana had gone from tired, to exhausted, to grumpy. Night owl she might be, but she still preferred to sleep every now and again! Besides that, even though the sun stood in the sky, it held no warmth. She'd retreated back under Decker's jacket after a while, unable to stand the cold anymore. He had to have been miserable too, as he didn't argue or complain about her snuggling, which meant he felt glad for the extra warmth.

Master must have been sitting in the main room of the inn, watching for their return, as they'd barely turned into the square when he appeared on the porch. She saw with relief that he'd cleaned the head wound he'd gotten last night and that a simple bandage sufficed to keep it wrapped. Painful as it might be, it wasn't serious enough to keep him off his feet.

Decker reined in to a stop in front of the inn, the stallion blowing out a grateful breath for finally coming to the end of the long night's trip. Sevana slid ungracefully to the ground, legs unnaturally stiff and sore from the many hours of being rubbed raw.

"Those don't look like victorious expressions to me," Master observed, eyes narrowed. "You didn't find them, I take it."

"Yes and no," she responded, moving in slow steps onto the porch. She could swear she heard her muscles creaking with every movement. "We found them. Or, what was left of them." Seeing his confusion, she quirked her mouth up into a humorless smile. "Apparently they had a falling-out of some sort, or they were ambushed, because when we caught up the whole ring of thieves was dead."

Master closed his eyes in understanding, looking as tired as she felt. "I see. The gadgick is long gone, I take it?"

She nodded confirmation. "Whoever did it knew how to cover their tracks well. Neither one of the wolves could pick up on it. We've only got one last lead to explore if we have any hope of getting it back."

He didn't need her to spell it out for him. "The black market. Yes, of course you're right. But which one? Kindin's or Belen's?"

"Belen's," she said firmly. "If I were a thief, I'd go there. They always get higher prices there, for one thing. But it's also faster to get to and a larger market than the one in Thirdcastle."

He opened a hand, palm up, that ceded the point to her. "Go ahead and rest. I'll prepare for the trip."

She cocked her head. "You're not going."

Master opened his mouth to protest but was interrupted by Sarsen joining them on the porch. He looked like he'd slept in his clothes—he likely had—and only the cup of hot tea in his hand gave him the energy to keep going. "Oh, you're back. No luck?"

"Do you see a string of bodies trailing in my wake?"

"Didn't expect any," he refuted, well used to dealing with her when she was severely sleep deprived. "Knowing you, without anyone around to stop you, you'd turn them all into toads."

Well, granted, she had been planning to do so. "When we caught up with them, they'd been killed and the gadgick stolen by assailant or assailants unknown."

Sarsen winced. "Which means we get to go hunting for this thing on the black market? Oh, Aren and Bel are not going to like that. Not one bit."

"Do I look overjoyed to you?" Sevana crossed her arms over her chest and glared at him venomously.

Sarsen, being a man of great wisdom, chose not to respond to that and instead offered his tea. She took it and drained it one gulp, letting the soothing and familiar taste warm her from the inside out. Ahhh, better. She no longer felt homicidal.

"Sweetling," Master started, clearly not liking the implications of what she'd said, "What do you mean I'm not going?"

"To be clear, you shouldn't go with me to Belen. I might be wrong, or jumping to conclusions, and the thief will choose to go to the Kindin market in Thirdcastle. In which case, we need to split up and search both."

"But why should you go to Belen?" he pressed, not following.

Shouldn't this be obvious? Oh wait, she'd never told him the full story about that, had she? "Because I've been to Belen before and I know where to go."

Sarsen, who had gone with her and knew the full story intimately well, snorted a laugh, which he tried to cover by faking a cough. Master darted a look between them, suspicions growing. "You've been to Belen before," he repeated neutrally.

"That's right." All things considered, she didn't feel like going into the full story right this minute. In fact, she wanted to get the details on this sorted so that she could crawl into a bed for a few hours and sleep. "So it's best I go to Harkin."

"Wait, sweetling, I don't understand why it's *you* that has to go!" Master protested, looking downright uneasy. "This is a black market. There are all sorts of scoundrels and rogues in that place. Even a magician would tread cautiously."

"I have to go," she maintained, tone firm.

"Sweetling—"

Her free hand slashed to cut off the rest of his protest. "Listen to me. *I have to go.* Not just because it's still my job to deal with the gadgick, not just because I'm afraid of what will happen if that thing ends up in the wrong hands. I'm the only person who has actually handled it and gotten a good look. Can you promise me that you could tell the real article from a well forged fake after only getting a brief look at it?"

Master opened his mouth, paused, and grimaced.

She nodded her head in grim confirmation. "I thought not. I need to go. Since Belen is the best place to unload this thing, I'll go there. On the off chance that I'm wrong, you go to Kindin as you're the only other person who had a look at the gadgick. Besides, I have a... contact at the Belen black market."

Sarsen's chest jerked as he struggled not to laugh. "Oh, yes. She does at that."

Master looked between the two of them, brows quirked in confusion. "Did I miss something?"

She rubbed at her forehead, feeling a headache coming on. Oh had he ever. "Do you remember that first year I was in Big? Before I taught him how to handle intruders properly and I had a group of thieves come through and steal a lot of things from me?"

He gave a cautious nod as the memory came back to him. "Yes..." he said slowly, tone tilting it up into a question. "You never did tell me the full story on that. Just that Sarsen helped you track the thieves down."

"Well, and we did, but they'd already unloaded everything at the black market in Belen. I had to contact the owner of the place to negotiate getting everything back." The twinges blew out into a full headache and she grimaced. "He's, well, um…"

"An ardent admirer of Sev's," Sarsen offered, finally losing the battle and chuckling.

She groaned and shook her head. "That's far too tame of a description. Anyway, if I show up on his doorstep looking for something, he'll bend over backward to help me. So this isn't as dangerous as you think it will be, Master." Just very inconvenient. The culture of Belen said that unless a woman was of a very low station, she should not run around unescorted. She either had to be in a party of women or in the company of a man. Sevana, to preserve her working reputation in that country, *had* to go with either Sarsen or some other male. She'd call Kip up here if she needed to—although it would be an unnecessary delay in a situation where time counted— but regardless, someone had to go with her.

Master didn't look the least bit reassured with her words. "Just who is this man?"

This would start a whole other round, but…. With a sigh she capitulated and said, "Count Romano Rizzo Conti de Luca."

His jaw nearly came unhinged. "de Luca?! He's famous for running one of the largest black markets on the eastern border of Mander!"

"I know," Sevana responded, taking a strangle hold on her patience.

"He's also a famous womanizer!"

"I know."

"You can't trust him at all!"

"I know," she snapped, patience evaporating. "Why do you think I'm taking Sarsen with me? It's not just because of Belen's backward cultural quirks. He can help me deal with that lecherous twit."

Master's eyebrows clearly expressed he did not like this situation, not one bit. Sevana hardly felt thrilled about it either. But what did he expect her to do, stay here while someone else went? It would be a mission doomed to failure. She had to go. There was no other option.

Standing around arguing about it didn't change that. In fact, the more she thought about the situation, the more plausible it seemed to take *Bounce on Clouds* and let Sarsen steer while she slept. Changing her plans on the spot, she ordered, "Sarsen, we leave in ten minutes."

"What about Sky?" Master asked pointedly.

Oh. Right. She had an eight year old to think of. Sevana was so accustomed to just going when she wanted to go that she had a hard time remembering that someone else needed her. She pondered the question for a full second before turning to look at Decker.

He didn't need her to ask the question aloud before he raised a hand in surrender. "I'll look after him while you're gone. How long do you think this will take?"

"If the gods have any mercy on me, not more than five or six days." Glad to have that situated, she turned back to Sarsen and repeated, "We're leaving in ten minutes."

"I'm already packed," he told her, laugh lines crinkling around his eyes. "But you're going to need to make a quick trip back to Big, aren't you? After all, you can't wear pants in Belen."

Aish. Another little quirk of the culture she'd momentarily forgotten. Growling out curses, she stomped off the porch, heading for her clock portal.

It took two days to reach Harkin, Belen by her skimmer, and Sevana shamelessly slept most of the distance. Sarsen woke her up at one point, making her navigate for about eight hours so he could sleep, but other than that, she rested as much as she could.

Where they were going, she'd need all the energy she could get.

They reached the outskirts of Harkin at sunset, which made the city rather pretty in bold strokes of oranges, golds, and dark browns. From the air, it almost looked picturesque. Harkin was one of the largest cities of Belen, second only to the capital, Windtower. Situated on the coast like this, it spread out in every direction so that its entire eastern section curled around the coastline. In some parts, even *over* the ocean as people expanded using houseboats and the like. She'd been in many a city that had grown faster than was wise, where the streets became a rat maze, but Harkin put most of them to shame. Then again, most of the trade of Mander went through Harkin at some point or another, legal or illegal, so it was no wonder the city grew every year.

Sevana leaned over the side railing and looked down, watching as the people scurried about in the streets, some of them taking notice of the flying skimmer above their heads and pointing at it. Turning her head slightly, she said casually to Sarsen, "You realize that we'll have to land on de Luca's roof. Otherwise we'll have waves of thieves try to steal the skimmer."

"Yes, I'm heading to his roof," Sarsen assured her. "Hopefully he'll recognize it's you before someone tries to attack us."

Oh. Right. He wouldn't know the skimmer. He'd never seen it before. Sevana had made it three years ago and de Luca hadn't seen her in well over four, mayhap five years. Hmm. Resigned, she pulled the Caller out of her back pouch and laid it on top of a flat palm, held at eye level. "de Luca."

The Count of the Black Market did not have an ounce of magical ability in him, but a man of his position and power could well afford a magical lackey. She knew that someone near him would have a Caller that would respond. It took a few moments before the Caller perked up, although it remained faceless because the speaker did not have a magical connection to it.

"*My dear Sevana! This is so rare, but delightful! You never contact me.*"

That was his smooth, cultured baritone though. He always sounded as if he were attempting to seduce her when he spoke. "This is more rare than you think. I'm coming toward your house."

A thud sounded, as if he had just dropped out of his chair. But then, the last time he had contacted her, she'd threatened to turn him into a mouse and give him to Baby to play with. He'd never in his wildest imaginations think she would come to him after that. "*You're HERE?*" he demanded incredulously, with all the excitement of a child with five birthdays' worth of presents in front of him.

"Almost," she responded. Right then and there, she promised herself that if she could get through this visit without killing the man or losing her temper, she'd indulge in a secret vice to her heart's content when she got back home. Bribing herself might be the only way to insure that they would all survive this surprise visit intact. "I'm coming to you via my flying skimmer. I need to land on your roof, so I'd take it as a kindness if you didn't have any of your magicians try to shoot me out of the sky."

"*Of course, of course,*" he assured her hastily. "*You! Pass the word that she's coming and to bring her to me with all due courtesy. Sevana, my love, I am thrilled beyond words at your visit. Dare I hope that you have finally decided to accept my proposal?*"

"The day that I decide to be one of your lovers, de Luca, is the day that I have lost all sanity," she informed him dryly. "No, I'm here for your help."

He audibly switched from potential lover to business man. "*In what respect?*"

It felt like chewing on moldy lemons saying this, but it had to be said. "Something was stolen from me, something very important, and I need your help to get it back. I am not sure, however, if you can even help me."

"*My love, for you, I will move mountains.*"

She was banking on that, too. Sevana kept an eye out and saw that Sarsen had found the right roofline and was mere minutes from reaching it. "I hope that in this case, it'll be enough. I will explain the particulars when I see you. For now, we're a bare minute from reaching your house." Although 'house' seemed such a wrong word to use. The man had a compound with a manor house in the middle, one which would put most palaces to shame, surrounded on all sides by normal sized homes meant to house his staff, guards, and guests. She'd always assumed that one of the red brick homes kept all of his mistresses as well, but she had never had that confirmed. Actually, she didn't care to confirm it.

"*Land in the center courtyard,*" he directed. "*I shall come out to greet you.*"

She caught Sarsen's eye and he nodded confirmation that he'd heard the direction. "We shall."

"*You keep saying 'we,' my dear. Who is with you?*"

"Sarsen."

He let out a long sigh. "*Surely you know that there's no need for a chaperone or another man between us?*"

"There's a need," she said firmly, shaking her head in reluctant amusement. The man just couldn't give up the idea that she might one day be his, could he. "Come out. We're almost there." So saying, she put the Caller back in her pouch.

Sarsen had a wry smile on his face as he carefully maneuvered the skimmer through the rooftops, avoiding crashing into any houses. "You have to give him this—he's devoted."

"Ha!" Sevana didn't believe this for a second. "He's only interested because I'm the only woman he's never been able to catch."

"Well, and there's that," Sarsen admitted.

Speaking of…. Sevana gave herself a good look from shoulders to toes. She'd brought her plainest dresses and skirts, not wanting to attract any male attention, but would this plan work? She wore an ink blue suede skirt, her normal white shirt and a dark gold vest. It was nice enough to keep her reputation as a respectable business-woman intact, but should hopefully be plain enough to not fire up any man's ardor. Her blonde hair had been tightly braided and wrapped around her head, also severely curtailed.

"You look fine," Sarsen assured her without any prompting.

"I'm not worried about looking fine, I want to look *plain*," she objected. "I don't want to encourage his attentions any."

Sarsen gave her quite the sardonic look for that. "Sevana, you could be dressed in a meal sack and it wouldn't deter him any."

Her shoulders slumped. Sarsen might very well be right on that.

The skimmer touched down in the courtyard with a slight thump and scrape as the wood settled against the stone tiles. She unlatched the side gate and stepped out, lifting one part of her skirt up a little to avoid tripping herself as she got down. Hmm, well, the place hadn't changed much since she'd last seen it. Belen's idea of fashionable architecture revolved around stone gargoyles, dramatic buttresses, sweeping rooflines, and an overall gloomy theme that made a house seemed haunted. The count, having no sense of taste whatsoever, simply went along with the current fashion, so his home looked perfectly suited to entertain a vampire or three. She shuddered just looking at it, half-disgusted and half-cold at the obvious signs of wealth.

Sarsen alighted to the ground with a soft grunt before coming to stand at her side.

Count Romano Rizzo Conti de Luca came out of the main doors of the mansion like a king greeting a foreign dignitary. Aside from the fact that he wore his curly hair short, so that it no longer touched his shoulders, he hadn't changed. He stood barely taller than she did, body slim except where the multiple layers of shirt, vest, and brocaded black jacket made him look bulkier. Really, he had a handsome face and a blindingly white smile that would make any woman turn her head. It was his rotten personality that ruined the whole package.

With arms spread wide in welcome, he came straight to her. "Sevana, my love! I am overjoyed to see you again!"

He really did look pleased to see her. If his smile got any wider, it would split his face in two. Seeing that expression, Sevana had a sudden bout of misgivings. From the side of her mouth, she muttered, "Can I change my mind?"

"No," Sarsen murmured back.

"Please? That expression scares me."

"I don't blame you." His tone added, *I would be, too, in your shoes.* "Just remember, you can turn him into a mouse if you need to."

She held on tightly to that thought as the count swooped in on her and grabbed her by the waist. He leaned in, obviously with every intention of kissing her, but Sevana had expected this reaction. With lightning quick reflexes, she released the wand from the holster on her arm, springing it into her hand, and pressed it into his Adam's apple. "Behave yourself," she warned him.

He froze, looking more than a little ridiculous in that half-swooping posture, and eyed the wand in her hand with misgivings. "Surely one little kiss wouldn't hurt anything."

"With you, it's never 'one little' anything," she refused firmly.

Sarsen came to her rescue and pulled her free of his arms, turning so that he half-stood between them. "de Luca," he greeted mildly, the smile on his face never touching his eyes.

"Vashti," the count greeted sourly. "You always get between us."

"It's a hobby of mine," Sarsen agreed blandly.

Sighing, he turned back to Sevana, eyes lingering on her. "You look positively radiant, my dear."

"And you haven't changed at all," she responded wryly. Funny, she didn't truly dislike the man, despite all his vices. He knew how to be charming. Most of the time, she just found his advances annoying. "de Luca, I don't have a lot of time to explain everything."

"Romano, please," he requested with a particularly charming smile.

She rolled her eyes. Patience. She'd promised herself she'd exercise patience. "Romano. This is very time-sensitive, so I'm not in the mood to explain everything over a glass of wine and a seven-course meal, alright?"

His dark eyes sharpened, once again switching from lover to business man. But then, he successfully ran one of the largest black markets in this area of the country without once being caught or fined by the Belen government, which took not only serious money but intelligence to pull off. He wouldn't lose his head entirely because of a woman, not even her. "Yes, you mentioned this before. How serious?"

"What was stolen from me can be highly dangerous in the wrong hands. I need it back before it disappears into some private collector's vault."

He offered her an elbow like a gentleman. "Then explain everything to me on the way to my office. We'll coordinate a search of the market from there."

Oh, how she wanted to ignore that offered elbow. But Belen customs restricted her from doing so and she'd hardly be stepping off on the right foot with the man if she started showing him discourtesy a bare minute after landing. With a long sigh, she put her hand through his elbow and allowed him to escort her in.

De Luca and his ever-present butler took off back inside the mansion, she and Sarsen keeping in step with them. As they crossed the courtyard, she caught sight of several dozen people all taking peeks at them. A few faces she recognized from her last visit here.

Shaking their stares off, she turned to de Luca and said, "The item was stolen three days ago. I believe the man who stole it is a magician of high caliber."

He quirked an eyebrow at her. "You believe?"

"I never saw him," she admitted sourly. "I chased after him, of course, but through some very nasty tricks he managed to evade me. I eventually hit a dead end in my pursuit which is why I came directly to you."

He let out a soft whistle. "Well, now *that's* impressive. This wouldn't have anything to do with the artifact you were taking out of a certain small Windamere village, would it?"

As expected of a black market lord, his information network was not to be discounted. "Yes, that's exactly what he stole. I'm not sure if he's taken it out of the box it was sealed in. We found no trace of the box where the trail dead ended, but that doesn't necessarily mean anything."

"Indeed, that is true."

Sevana was momentarily distracted as they crossed into the black and white tiled foyer. The walls were painted by masters in some of the darker fairytales, ceilings arching high overhead with a wrought black iron chandelier sparkling overhead. The foyer itself was so spacious that their footsteps rang like they walked through a tomb, the air cool against her skin. Sevana couldn't begin to comprehend how anyone could actually *live* in this mausoleum.

The count led them around the half-spiraling staircase and toward the back of the house. His office took up most of the ground floor, as several people worked at long tables, all of them coordinating information and trade agreements for the market. Stepping inside of his office felt like entering a war room, as everyone talked over each other, papers being handed off to others, all of it coordinated by specific officers. Sevana always felt upon seeing this flurry of activity that many a government could learn how to properly organize and run a country by just observing here for a day.

De Luca led them past all of this, without even a glance to either side, and through the open doors on the other side, into a comfortably intimate room with a small arrangement of chairs that looked remarkably inviting. Despite the modesty of this room compared to the rest of the mansion, Sevana knew without a doubt that *this* was the true hub of the count's little empire. Many a deal had been brokered in this room.

He escorted her properly to a chair and promptly took the one right next to hers, turning so that he was a scant few inches away. As long as he didn't try to capitalize on that distance, she'd let him hover.

Sarsen, prudently, sat on the other side of her.

"Now, no one could give me an accurate description of what this artifact looks like," de Luca continued with uncommon seriousness. "I only know what it *does* and you're right to be worried about it falling into the wrong hands, beloved. I've had multiple inquiries already from interested buyers and I wouldn't trust any of them to look after my worst enemy."

She rubbed her forehead, feeling the headache that had been brewing for the past three days start up in earnest. "Then let me describe it. It *was* in a black box roughly a foot squared with magical seals on it. If it's been freed of that box, then it looks rather like a porcelain vase, standing so tall—" she demonstrated its length with her hands, "—that is hollow all the way through. At either end, it flares out slightly. It's a light gray in color with beautiful white designs carved into the surface."

As she spoke, the butler was quickly writing this down into a small leather notebook. She took proper notice of the man for the first time. Really, it was easy to overlook him. Standing barely taller than his master, he had wispy hair and such a thin body that if he stood sideways, she was convinced he'd disappear altogether. What was his name again? Edward, Edmond, Edwin? Something like that.

"No magical glow or inherent power in it?" de Luca pressed.

"It did three days ago, after being active for months, but now?" She spread her hands palm up in a shrug. "After being in the behave box, it should be entirely dormant." That was the whole reason they'd put it into the box to begin with.

De Luca nodded to his butler—who likely ran the black market more than he did the house—and the man scurried to the next room over, no doubt to get people to start looking for something matching that description.

Sevana itched to go out and explore the market herself, but rationally she understood that sitting right here and waiting was really the better option. Nothing happened in the market without de Luca knowing about it. She could walk around that market and never find the gadgick. It's why she had come here to begin with.

De Luca captured one of her hands in both of his and leaned in slightly, a seductive gleam in his eyes. "While we wait, beloved, may I express how heartrendingly beautiful you appear to me?"

She rolled her eyes to the heavens with a fervent prayer that they find the gadgick soon. Otherwise she'd be forced to kill this idiot, self-imposed bribe notwithstanding.

"What say you, Sarsen?" de Luca asked with unnatural enthusiasm. "You've been doing nothing but sitting about on that flying contraption for the past two days, I'm sure you'd like to let loose a little."

Sevana's problem with the black market count never happened in the first few minutes of the exchange. At first he seemed normal, if overbearing, and perhaps a bit too overly familiar in his approach. Then again, with women often flocking to him, he typically didn't have to *woo* a woman so his skills had never really fully developed there. No, the problem she truly had always occurred about fifteen minutes after she was in his sphere of influence.

Almost perfectly at the fifteen-minute mark, de Luca came up with this harebrained scheme, and since Sarsen was handy, chose him to help put it into motion. "It won't be serious of course," the count pressed. "We wouldn't want any injuries. Just some light play to get the blood flowing."

Sevana silently asked any god that might be listening *why* she had to deal with this fool. Then she cocked her head to look at Sarsen, who looked not only perturbed at the idea of mock-sword fighting with his host, but also sorely tempted. (As well he should be. If Sevana had been in his shoes, she certainly wouldn't pass up on the opportunity to chase him around the yard while waving a sword about!)

De Luca obviously wanted to do this to show off his skills (he always tried to impress her) and thought that by showing up her friend, he'd become more reliable in her eyes. But he was a pretty duelist who had grown up with fine instructors who had never had to put his skills to the test. Sarsen, on the other hand, fought regularly with demons, goblins, rogues, thieves, and other threats of similar ilk. To call him a 'master swordsman' would be understating his skills. It would not be a fair competition, not in any sense.

Sarsen looked to Sevana for a second opinion, eyebrow slightly cocked. She shrugged and mouthed silently, 'Just don't kill him.'

His lips parted in an evil grin. "Alright, de Luca, I don't see the harm."

"Excellent." He rubbed his hands together in open anticipation before standing, his voice rising to call into the next room, "EDWIN! MY SWORD!"

Edwin! That was it. Sevana usually had a good head for names, but the man had so little presence that it made him completely un-remember-able.

Sarsen hadn't come in with his sword so he had to duck out to the skimmer and fetch his as well. It was probably best that someone go check on the skimmer at this point regardless. She had anti-theft and anti-tampering wards up around it, but that didn't mean that someone wouldn't try their hand at getting it. Sevana had never marketed this invention for the simple reason that she wasn't sure who to market it *to*. It took a master magician at the very least, who understood how to navigate, in order to fly the thing. Most magicians of that caliber already had other means of travel that they were far more comfortable with. But all that meant was that a very rare magical device sat in an open courtyard, and that was bound to attract unwanted attention.

Nothing appeared to have happened to the skimmer as Sarsen appeared untroubled when he came back in.

Within moments both men had their toys in hand and faced off with each other in the side courtyard. She stood in the doorway and watched, as a good trophy should, trying not to laugh at the whole situation. De Luca had pulled many a stunt over the years trying to get her attention, but out of all the things he had done, this one had to take the prize as the most ill-planned.

Both men drew their swords in a *shiiing* of sound as they cleared the scabbards and assumed a guard position. At first glance, it looked as if they were equally skilled. Then, without any signal whatsoever, de Luca leaped forward to attack.

For a 'mock-swordfight' the pace was a mite too quick. Sarsen parried the blows without any real effort, and while he was obviously paying attention, he didn't appear in the least interested in what de Luca would do next. They exchanged several feints and parries, giving and losing ground without consequence. Sevana shook her head slightly as she watched because even from here she could tell Sarsen was barely using a third of his true strength. This wasn't even a contest.

From the corner of her eye she realized that Edwin the butler hovered just behind her. Without turning her head she asked him, "Why does your master do things like this? He's too quick to jump into things. Instead of impressing me, he's going to get hurt."

The butler sniffed in offense. "The master is a highly capable swordsman."

She turned to give him a flat look. *I now see the problem.* Surrounded by people who only sung his praises, was it any wonder that de Luca had an overly inflated opinion of himself?

A gasp for breath jerked her back around. De Luca didn't have the stamina Sarsen did, but he clearly realized the gap in their levels. The smart thing to do would be to call a halt to this whole demonstration and ease out of a potentially embarrassing situation. But men who had their blood up rarely did the smart thing. Instead, in a frantic effort to win, de Luca increased the speed of his blows in a desperate attempt to get past Sarsen's guard.

She swore aloud and sprung her wand free of her wrist guard. At this rate, something would go very wrong very soon and she had best be prepared to shield one or the other from danger.

De Luca shot forward, sword slashing toward Sarsen's chest, but in the process he overextended and she could see the sudden realization as his eyes flew wide that he was precariously close to losing his balance. For a split second, time seemed to slow as her adrenaline kicked in. Sarsen blocked the strike, but in doing so, his

Honor Raconteur

sword was perfectly angled to slide along de Luca's sword and take the man's head off. His speed would be nearly impossible to stop.

"⸸◯⸸〰〰◯√" she commanded sharply.

Both men froze in place, helpless to do otherwise. Only their chests moved, dragging in air, and their eyes as they looked toward her.

"Alright, boys, playtime's over." She stalked forward and snatched both swords out of their grips before ramming them home into their respective scabbards. "No more sword fighting, mock or otherwise."

Danger passed, she undid the spell and holstered the wand.

As soon as the count could move, he grabbed up her hand and clasped it to his chest. With stars in his eyes, he crooned, "I knew it, beloved. You care for me above anyone else! That you would go so far to protect me—"

She ignored the prattling and tried to yank her hand free. To no avail, curse it. He might be thin, but he was stronger than she.

"—I will accept a scolding for such a senseless display," he finished hopefully.

Sevana heaved out a breath. "De Luca. Make up your mind. Do you want me as a lover or a mother?"

He blinked at her as if she had just asked a nonsensical question. "Why as a lover, of course. But you are so fierce, so brilliant in your anger that I find you awe-inspiring."

Oh. Is that why he kept doing stupid things, so she'd lecture him? Just how twisted was this man's way of thinking?!

"Alright, de Luca, behave now." Sarsen intervened and dragged her free of him. In this particular moment, she saw nothing wrong with using her friend as a shield and ducked behind him, letting him be exactly that. "You lost the fight so you can't monopolize her."

De Luca raised a hand of outrage to cover his heart. "You—you fiend! That was never a term of our duel!"

Sevana blinked, as this idea had never occurred to her. If she challenged him to a duel (judging from what she saw of his sword skills, she could probably beat him) and set the terms as he would not be able to court her from now on, would that work? She ran the possible scenario through her head and frowned at the conclusion. No, mercy take it, it probably wouldn't. He would either A) not agree as he would never be able to raise a sword against her, or B) view the whole fight as a 'scolding' and get meaninglessly hyped up about it to where she really would be forced to kill him.

Curses.

With evil delight, Sarsen wagged a finger at the count. "The loser should obey the winner. It's a natural law. Behave yourself around her, that's all I ask."

De Luca actually *pouted* and gave her a longing look. "My sweetness, this is too much to ask! After years apart, I finally see you, and I am not allowed to touch? Oh, the unfairness of it rends my heart."

With those sorts of acting skills, it was a shame he wasn't on a stage somewhere. "It won't kill you," she responded heartlessly.

His head lowered as he sighed. Then he perked up again. "Still, you love me enough to come to my defense and shield me from danger. I take that as a positive sign. I shall win your heart soon enough."

I should have let Sarsen behead him. She groaned aloud. Too late to realize that now.

From the doorway, Edwin cleared his throat. "Forgive the interruption, my lord, but we have received word that three articles matching Mistress Sevana's description have been located. I have their whereabouts written here." He held up a piece of paper in demonstration.

Three? Sevana blinked in confusion, but it didn't take her long to realize what had happened. "Forgeries? Already?"

"Forgeries at a black market are not a rarity, my sweet," de Luca responded as he accepted the paper from his butler.

"But *already?*" she objected, still astounded. "No one but Master and I really got a good look at this thing before we sealed it in the behave box. That means the gadgick has only been out, at most, for three days! Just how fast can these forgers work that they can make a fake artifact and put it on the market in *three days?"*

De Luca found this amusing as he turned a smile on her. "My dear, I can have a fake made of your flying machine done overnight if I so wish. These forgers are not to be taken lightly."

Obviously!

He skimmed over the parchment and frowned slightly. "Most of these are close by. Shall we go investigate it ourselves?"

That did seem the fastest way. "Fine."

He held out an elbow and waited expectantly. When she hesitated, that pout of his returned. "I won't go unless I can escort you."

"De Luca…" Sarsen said in warning.

The man sniffed and turned his head away. "I won't."

What, was he a child? It was *this* erratic behavior that she found so annoying. With a mental renewal of her promise to reward herself after all of this was over, she managed to get a stranglehold on her patience. Waving Sarsen down, she put her hand through the man's elbow. Really, if letting him escort her would get them in motion, she'd put up with it.

A brilliant smile lit up his face and he started for the main door with a bounce in his stride. "Excellent. Edwin! Form up my guards!"

Sevana reflected as they waited for the guards to arrive that it was better overall that Master hadn't come with her and instead gone to Kindin. If he ever saw how de Luca reacted to her, the count really *would* have been fish bait by now.

A four-man guard met them at the front doors and escorted them off the compound. The count had been very careful when he situated the black market. It was on property he owned, but something he had gained by a defaulted loan. It was a sketchy gray area that the law couldn't quite figure out how to deal with, or so he had explained once to her. The land was kitty-corner to the compound, within easy reach of him, and it gave him perfect access while also giving him a perfect excuse to ignore it, if the law ever came knocking.

Sevana couldn't help but feel that if this was Windamere, and not Belen, de Luca would never have gotten by with that legal loophole. Bel would have still found a way to shut the man down. A smile tweaked the corners of her mouth at the thought.

He noticed her smile and asked, "What amuses you, my dear?"

She shot him a quick glance, but didn't dare do more than that for fear of bumping into the narrow passageway in between estates. Why were they taking this alley route, anyway? It felt cramped and cold in here. "I was just thinking that if this was Windamere, and not Belen, my prince would have shut you down by now."

"Prince Bellomi? Ah, that's right, you lived with him for several months." He sighed as if upset. "I was truly jealous when I heard of that, you know. I was afraid you would fall for him."

"Romano." She gave him a flat stare. "He was *eight*."

"He was in his twenties and *looked* as if he were eight," he corrected, meeting her stare for stare. "And I understand he's both handsome and charming."

"You weren't there while he was learning *how* to be charming. I swear it was just like dealing with an eight year old."

"Your Princess Hana didn't think so."

"You didn't get to see that awkward courtship either," she retorted, although she laughed as she said that as it brought back memories. "Ohhh, if I ever wanted to make an easy million, I'd write a book about him staying with me. Parts of it were downright entertaining."

He quirked his brows at her, smiling at her smile. "Oh? Well, we have something of a walk ahead of us. Why don't you regale me with the story?"

If it kept him from sweet-talking her, gladly. She started from the beginning, what she knew of it, and weaved the story for him. Truly, though, she didn't pay a great deal of attention to what she said. What lay ahead of them took up most of her interest. She hadn't seen the market in four years, and in that time, it had grown significantly.

A good indication of the state of the world was the black and gray markets. The more unrest, upheaval and disorder there was, the more these two markets thrived as people were forced to go outside the law to buy the basic necessities. If this market was anything to go by, then Belen's economy was in very bad shape indeed. Four years ago, the various tents, booths, and vendors took up a city block or so. For a black market, it was sizable and it thrived with sound and activity as people went about their business. But it didn't compare to this. Now, Sevana would say it had grown five times over and covered at least three or four acres. The sounds of humans conversing, work being done, and goods being traded created such a din of noise that she had to raise her own voice to hear herself. But more than that was the smell. With this press of unwashed bodies and ill-prepared food, it stank to high heaven. She instinctively flinched.

"Oh, I have grown so accustomed to it, I nearly forgot." From a breast pocket, de Luca pulled out a vial and passed it to her. "Extract of orange. Place a dab under your nose otherwise you'll faint from the vapors."

She whispered a quick revealing spell as she accepted the vial, but nothing reacted, so it was indeed what he said it was. (Not that he had ever tried to drug her, but since she trusted the man about as far as she could throw him....) She dabbed a significant quantity under her nose before passing the vial back to Sarsen, who took it gratefully.

"I've tried putting some regulations in here to help with the smell," de Luca sighed in true aggravation. "But it's mostly the people here who are the problem, and what can I do? Say they must bathe properly before entering? I feel like an overbearing parent."

"They obviously need one." Sevana could still smell some of the stench past the orange extract although it helped significantly. It made her nose want to revolt and her stomach churn. Orange-scented rotting fish is what it reminded her of. How charming.

The tents lined up on either side, crammed together to take up as little space as possible, and were huddled so close together that there wasn't much of a path in between them. A crowd of people shifted through, literally shuffling along as it was impossible to make any real headway, with absolutely no breathing room whatsoever. Even with the guards around them, they were pressed together tightly, although the people who noticed the count's guards tried to move out of the way as best they could. Really, anyone that had issues with either enclosed spaces or crowds would have had a fit just looking at this place.

It seemed like they didn't make any progress at all, but soon enough de Luca turned toward a particularly garish tent of red and gold stripes and hailed the burly man working there with an upraised hand. "Master Yawas!"

The man looked up from the customer he was helping and his prominent eyes flew wide as he recognized who called to him. He instantly ducked into a respectful bow. "My lord! You honor me."

The guards forcibly shifted people aside so that she and de Luca could approach the table and stand directly in front of it. Sevana took in her first deep breath since entering this madness.

Extending a hand to her, de Luca purred out the introduction. "My fiancée, Artifactor Sevana Warran, has come to make an inquiry of you."

For that, she stomped firmly on his foot with the heel of her boot. He made a squeaking noise in the back of his throat in pain, teeth gritted. Her eyes shot to him in warning. "Make that introduction one more time, and I shall surely cut off *all* ties with you."

This threat panicked him more than anything else she had said before, and he put a hand to his heart and half-bowed in apology. "Take my words as nothing more than meaningless wind."

"I shall do so," she assured him coolly. To the waiting merchant—who, judging from his expression, seemed impressed by how she handled the count—she said simply, "I am looking for a magical artifact. We are told you have something in your possession that resembles it. It stands roughly this tall, is seemingly made of gray porcelain, and has white engravings on it?"

He bobbed his head in recognition. "Yes, my lady Artifactor, I know what you're describing. I received it this morning." He turned and rummaged in a box off to the side. "I wasn't quite sure I should put it out yet, as I didn't know the value of it, but I paid a pretty penny for it. My nephew's a magician trainee, and he said it had strong magic attached to it."

Well, that sounded promising, or it would if there weren't spells that could fake 'strong magic' just to rook people with. She waited with baited breath as he pulled out a wooden box and unwrapped the blue cloth to expose the item.

As soon as the top was revealed, she let out the breath she held in disappointment. While it was tall, and gray, it was nothing more than a cylindrical vase with pretty white lines in a swirling pattern painted on it.

De Luca waited anxiously for her reaction, but when she did nothing more than stare at it, he seemed to know without her saying anything. "That's not it."

"It's not," she admitted. Reaching out, she plucked the vase out of the box entirely and gave it a good, thorough look. "Master... Yawas, was it?"

"Yes, my lady."

"I hope you didn't pay too much for this, because if you have, you've been rooked."

Yawas' brows slammed together. "What is it?"

"It's a disappearing vase," she answered, studying the bottom of it, looking for a maker's mark. "It's used in magic shows, usually. You drop something in this vase, and it'll come out in its twin. I'm afraid that one is entirely useless without the other."

Yawas looked ready to murder someone right there. "And the magic my nephew sensed?"

"Oh, that's there," she assured him. "He wasn't wrong about that. There's nothing wrong with this vase. In fact, I'm sure it would function perfectly if you had the full set. But without its pair, it's only good for vanishing things into the great unknown."

"You bought this from an unknown supplier?" de Luca inquired.

"Yes, my lord," Yawas confirmed unhappily. "He left me with a name, which I bet now is fake."

"Make a report about him anyway and give a description," de Luca ordered. To Sevana he explained, "If I let bad dealers come in like this, then the level of goods will drop and the market will suffer terribly. It's hard to catch men like this, as they seem to only appear once and make off with what they can, but when I do catch them I make them pay dearly."

For good reason. Sevana approved of his methods although not particularly his reasons. She handed the vase back to Yawas and waved a hand. "Let's go to the next."

Sevana went through two more fakes in the next hour, each one better and more convincing than the last. The disappearing vase could very well be dismissed as a coincidence simply because it matched the description she gave and nothing more. But the next two had obviously been made to look like the gadgick. They had the right shape to them, the right color, but the designs weren't right. In fact, they weren't anywhere near right. It reminded her of an illiterate child trying to copy an adult's handwriting. They could more or less reproduce the same letters but it would come out sloppy and barely legible. The same could be applied to the fakes—the designs carved into the sides were beautiful but completely useless as far as magic went. Only a skilled magician would be able to tell the difference.

These fakes served as a magnificent red herring and annoyed her no end. They would, *of course*, be on opposite ends of the market as well. After so much walking, she felt a little footsore and the dabs of orange scent under her nose had ceased to work a good hour ago. In sheer self-defense, her nose shut down completely. She felt further aggravated that they had to go from one side and then trek all the way to the other just for another forgery. But as irritated as she felt, it did give her hope. For the forgeries to be this good, this accurate, the real gadgick had to have come through this market. If any luck were with her at all, it wouldn't have sold yet either.

With them in the center of the market like this, new information came through Sarsen's Caller via the magician that served de Luca. Sevana saw absolutely no point in trudging all the way back to the house only to have to wade through these crowds again later. Still, night had fallen hard over the land, and the only lights came from the bright moon overhead and the multitude of lanterns strung up to light the way. She well understood that the black market did more business at night than during the day, but actually seeing it in action was something else entirely.

She was jostled on one side—although the guard did his best to shield her—and slammed her shoulder into de Luca's. The count, having decent reflexes, caught her and steadied her about the shoulders. "Are you well, my dear?"

"Someone jostled me," she explained while straightening. "Is it my imagination or is this place becoming *busier?*"

"We're at the rush hour now," he responded cheerfully, the businessman in him glowing with greedy anticipation. "It'll be like this for some hours yet before it wanes again. Sometime around the pre-dawn hours it'll be much more peaceful."

Sevana felt particularly glad that she'd slept most of the way here. What was it about this job that came hand in hand with sleep deprivation? Even with Bel and a mountain full of guests, she'd had more than a nodding acquaintance with her bed!

Abruptly she realized that while she might have slept, Sarsen hadn't. She turned sharply to look up at him over her shoulder. Uh-oh. Far from being tired, he looked around with glassy eyes, an unnatural grin on his face, and did he just bounce on his toes? "Sarsen…"

He beamed down at her. "Hmmm?"

"You're dry-drunk, aren't you?" she meant that to sound accusing, but in truth she was nervous. Sarsen had a history of doing remarkably stupid and reckless things while in this state.

"No, no, I'm just strangely alert," he assured her.

That's what I meant by dry-drunk! She wailed internally. Her first instinct was to send him back to de Luca's and force him to sleep, but she honestly couldn't afford to. Who knew what kind of move the count would make with the pesky chaperone out of the way? She gripped her wand through the sleeve in reassurance. It was fine. This whole situation was fine, really. Nothing had gotten out of hand. If

Sarsen started something, well, she'd freeze the whole place and get him out of here before anything truly serious happened. Yes, alright. That was a good plan.

"Oooh, that looks fun." Sarsen went up on tiptoe to see over the crowd better. "Hey, while we're waiting for word of another prospect, I'm going to go try my hand at that."

That? She grabbed his arm with an iron grip before he could move an inch in any direction. "What's that?" she demanded.

"That," he said again while pointing somewhere off to the right. With this wall of people, she couldn't begin to figure out what he meant. "That person swallowing swords. I want to learn how to do that."

Her grip tightened. "*No.*"

He blinked down at her like a child denied a treat. "But it looks fun!"

"No," she maintained firmly. Sweet mercy and miracles, he thought swallowing a sword looked *fun?* What would he think of next?

"Then what about the other one? He's blowing fire out of his mouth."

She'd just had to ask, didn't she? "*No,* Sarsen. And if there's anyone over there sticking their head in a lion's mouth, you're not doing that either."

"Oh, you can see that?" he asked her ingeniously. "It's a beautiful lion but it looks very tame."

She slapped a hand to her head. "Listen to me. *Thou shalt not leave my side.* Your job is to be here as a chaperone, remember? You can't wander off."

He snapped his fingers in remembrance, acting for all the world as if for a moment he truly had forgotten his role here. "Oh, right. Right, right. Well, leastways I can watch, eh?"

Sevana breathed out a prayer of thanks. As off-kilter as he might be, he still retained enough sense to listen to reason, eh? Good, good.

De Luca took his eyes off of her long enough to truly study Sarsen. In a stage whisper he said next to her ear, "I've never seen him act like this before."

"None of us have gotten proper rest while on this job," she whispered back. "He's sleep deprived, and that's a very worrying state. He loses all sense of danger when he's like this." She said this in warning and hoped de Luca would take it that way. Earlier, with the sword fight, Sarsen had taken it easy on him and it had still almost ended disastrously. Right now, if challenged, she had no way to predict how Sarsen would respond.

Her warning did not have the effect she intended it to. The count seemed intrigued by this information and she could see the wheels turning in his mind. In an effort to distract him, she turned the conversation to an entirely different topic. "Why forgeries?"

He blinked, mentally switching tracks, and looked back at her. "Pardon?"

"Why forgeries?" she repeated, glad her hook worked. "I understand that forgeries are good for making money and that there are some who make a full career out of it. But wouldn't it be considered foolish to have multiple forgeries of the same thing in the market at the same time?"

"Ahh, I see your point." In an effort to keep them from blocking the road and thereby becoming squashed, he urged the group back into motion as he spoke. "You see, my dear, money is only part of the reason. I haven't made a study of it but I have spoken to many forgers during my time, and it seems to me that their motivation is resentment."

She had just broached the subject to distract him, but that last sentence intrigued her. "Resentment?" she parroted, surprised. "What do they resent?"

"On that, the list seems endless. They resent others' wealth, their abilities or training, the fact that these people once possessed the genuine article of whatever they are forging, the fact that their skills can *only* create forgeries, etcetera." Pleased to have her genuine attention for once, he preened a little under her eyes. "In truth, they tend to be people that are simply unhappy with life and resent everything. But they also conversely take pride in making a forgery so exact, so skillful, that even an expert eye can be fooled." He let out a soft chuckle, expression smug. "Although they certainly haven't been able to fool you."

"It would take a master magician to make a forgery that would even stand a chance against me," she informed him dryly. "No matter how excellent their skills, these things have no magic in them and can't be imbued with it at all."

"Oh? Is that why it only takes you a glance to tell?"

"That's why."

From behind her, she heard the muttered voice of de Luca's magician coming through Sarsen's Caller. She half-turned, as much as she could, and tried to listen as the report came through. The Callers had never been particularly loud in volume, which was a feature that she hadn't thought to change until now. Usually she used them in fairly quiet areas, after all. But in this noisy, crowded place she could only catch about half of what was said even though she stood barely a foot away.

Sarsen nodded and put the Caller back in his pouch. "He says there's another report in about a vendor selling not one, but three of them. They match your description perfectly, and what's more, the story the vendor tells is that this comes from Chastain."

Her attention sharpened. No one before had told a story of how the piece came to the market or where it was originally found. But this person actually claimed *Chastain*, a remote village that most people in even Windamere wouldn't recognize by name. "Where?"

"Southeast quadrant, on the very last row."

She let out a groan. Of *course* it would be on the polar opposite side of where she stood now! Well, no help for it. She lifted her chin, squared her shoulders, and started forward. "Let's hope this is the person we're really looking for."

With a great deal of shoving, calling ahead to clear the path, threats, and some judicious use of elbows, the guards managed to clear a path through the crowds. Sevana didn't even bear the brunt of this path-blazing and she still felt a little knocked about by the time they reached the southeastern quadrant. Whatever de Luca paid these men, they deserved a raise.

The last row didn't have *quite* the crowd that the rest of the market did, not from a lack of good products—from what she could tell through glimpses—but simply because the customers coming in through the main gates hadn't yet filtered down to this section. Given another hour or two, it would likely pick up. But right now it had some breathing room for anyone shopping in the area, and Sevana felt more than grateful for it. It was almost worth the battle to get here.

All of the men around her stood taller than she, which blocked most of her view, so she turned and asked Sarsen, "Do you see them?"

"Hmmm," he said noncommittally as he scanned the area slowly. "Ah! There they are, all three of them lined up in a neat little row."

Three. That still puzzled her even after thinking about it on the walk over here. Why three? Wouldn't it be more valuable if he played it off as just *one* to sell? Or was the forger going off the principle that quantity was better than quality?

De Luca presented her to the vendor's tent with a flourish, an anticipatory smile on his face. "I am Romano Rizzo Conti de Luca."

The vendor's eyes flew wide and he immediately ducked into a bow, although it looked jerky, as if he wasn't in the habit of doing so. "My lord! I am honored by your presence. The name's Rabi."

Rabi, eh? He looked more Kindin than Belen to her eyes, somewhere between forty and fifty although it could be the scrawny build, rough skin, and bloodshot eyes that made him seem so. Her eyes didn't linger on him long as the artifact copycats drew her eyes down to the scarred wooden table of wares. She picked one up and gave it a close scrutiny by lamplight. Hmmm? Interesting, this was a far better copy than the others. Lifting another, she compared them side by side and realized with a start that one of them was actually a closer replica to the original than the other. Almost as if with each forgery, the maker was getting better.

Her eyes honed in on the vendor's hands and clothes, looking for any evidence of the suspicion that had just lodged in her mind. It took her bare seconds to find it—specks of white and gray paint. Her mouth stretched into a feral, satisfied smile. *Found you.*

With a slice of her hand, she knocked over all three pieces, sending them to the ground hard and fast enough that they broke on impact. The porcelain shattered in a tinkling of sound and made everyone jump back instinctively to avoid the shards. She didn't. One hand flicked and caught the wand as it snapped out of its holster, and with the other she grabbed Rabi by his shirt and yanked him in close. "Where is it?"

"M-my l-lady, I have no idea what I've done to offend—" he stammered out.

She raised her wand and put it directly in his line of sight and growled out in a menacing voice, "*Where is it. This is not a question, Rabi. I recognize these trinkets of yours for what they are—excellent forgeries. They bear such a close resemblance to the original, in fact, that it would be impossible to have made them without the original on hand to study. So, where is it?"

The man's breath stank to high heaven and his eyes rolled like a wild animal trying to figure out how to bolt.

"Forgive the late introduction, goodman," de Luca continued pleasantly, as if they were chatting over tea. "This is my close friend, Artifactor Sevana Warran."

Rabi let out a choked sound of pure fear.

Her lips stretched even further, baring more teeth. He had every right to be afraid. After the weeks of pent-up frustration, followed by a wild goose chase that put her back in *that* fool's sphere, she felt the need to pound on something until she felt better.

"Do you understand now? I will curse you so that you will never have any peace, or rest, or sanity until the day you breathe your last unless you *tell me where the original is.*"

"It's h-h-here, right here," he assured her brokenly, wiggling free and squirming until she finally released him. Then he fell to all fours and scrambled to a back corner, curtained off from view, although he appeared barely a second later with a very familiar black box in hand. When he shifted the curtain aside, however, she saw in openmouthed dismay that he had not made a simple three copies as she thought, but had a whole production line behind that curtain. From this viewpoint, she counted a good two dozen lined up on some upturned crates, all of them in various stages of completion.

He hastily brought the box to her and set it on the table before scrambling backward again, anxious to put some distance between them although with the confines of the small tent he couldn't manage more than four feet. Sevana tucked her wand under one arm and touched the behave box, springing it open. Huh? Strange, it shouldn't open that easily. Turning the box slightly, she saw that it had been forced open on one side and so could no longer close properly. Ah, of course. They couldn't magic it open so they used brute force, eh? Made sense.

Lifting the lid, she took a good look inside before daring to lift the gadgick free. This time, she had no doubt it was the original before she even touched it. It still radiated a trace amount of magic even though it had been sealed away for so many days.

Sarsen leaned over her shoulder for a better look. "That's it."

"That's it," she agreed with a breath of relief. Eyes narrowing, she looked back up at Rabi. "Where did you get this?"

"A-a strange man offered a trade for it," he answered with nervous looks between her and the count. "He said it was too famous to trade in Windamere. I heard the story, knew what it was, so gave him a good deal. My lord count, I followed the tenets!" this last he said in a plaintive wail.

De Luca spread his hands in an apologetic shrug. "He does have a point, my dear. A black market would cease to be altogether if he weren't allowed to broker deals like this one."

Rationally, she understood that. But it was the culmination of having to work so hard to get this gadgick free, then have it stolen from her, and then have to come all this way to a place she hated and have to track it down *again*. "If you think I'm paying you for something that was stolen from me, you're barmy," she informed him tartly. In fact, just the idea that he would do so made her boiling mad. Putting the gadgick back in the box, she shoved it into Sarsen's hands before ordering Rabi, "Kneel. *Now*."

Too scared to do anything else, he dropped to his knees and

cowered. Sevana had no idea what expression she wore just then, but it must have been something as even de Luca, with his twisted mind, looked impressed. Ignoring her audience, she focused on the forger/ vendor. "Let's be clear on this, Rabi. It's not the fact that you took on a stolen product that bothers me. This is, after all, a black market. I *expected* it to show up here."

He looked hopeful at her words and gave a ginger nod.

"No, I'm angry with you for a different reason entirely." Pointing her wand at the nearest section of gadgick wannabes, she blasted them into dust, making everyone jump. "Do you know why I'm mad? No? Allow me to explain. I have spent the past *four hours* crisscrossing this mad labyrinth searching and being fooled by *your* fakes when it could have been prevented."

Just the thought ignited her anger all over again and she blasted another section of the pottery, making white dust fly everywhere. Rabi lost five years of his life and started shaking nervously, no doubt wondering when that wand would turn on him. "Your greed, your selfish desire to flood the market with *dozens* of these has already wasted hours of my valuable time—" BLAST! "—and would have wasted even *more* time if I had gotten here any later! I might very well have spent *years* tracking every one of these things down if I had been delayed by even a few days!" *Blast!*

"B-but my lady Artifactor," Rabi dared to argue even though his voice shook. "I didn't steal it from you!"

"I know that!" she snapped at him. "I'm just taking it out on you!"

The count whispered behind her back, "Is she always this unreasonable when she's angry?"

"Always," Sarsen whispered back. "But she's worse when she's sleep deprived. Be thankful that she slept on the way up here, or this section of the market would likely be in tatters."

With a last blast of the wand, she destroyed any trace of what was left of the fakes. She didn't feel particularly satisfied by it, but her temper had cooled enough that she wasn't tempted to blast Rabi too. With a huff, she turned on her heel and headed back for the skimmer.

"We're done here."

De Luca, laughing, lengthened his stride in order to catch up with her. "My love, you are simply dazzling when you're angry!"

She shot him a glare. "You're paying for that."

"Of course," he assured her as if he hadn't been expecting anything different.

"Sarsen, is that thing properly secured?" she asked, not slowing her speed any.

"It is," he assured her. "What now?"

"We're going directly to Jacen's from here," she said firmly.

De Luca let out a squawk of protest. "No! You can't just leave only hours after having arrived!"

Her eyes cut to the side to regard him suspiciously. Why did he sound as if he had ulterior motives in saying that? Wait, what was she thinking? Of *course* he did! She never had any intention of staying the night at his mansion anyway, but after that, she felt particularly glad they'd found the gadgick on the first day of the search.

"Romano, I don't dare dawdle. The last time I waited for the morning before transporting that thing, it was stolen that night. With me being this close to a black market, the odds of it disappearing while I sleep are even *worse*. No, we're leaving now and it's going straight into the hands of someone I trust."

He gave her puppy eyes, silently imploring for her to stay. With complete ease, she ignored him.

"And after that?" Sarsen asked. "Back to Chastain to finish up the job?"

She nodded confirmation. "And after *that* I'm collecting a certain boy and going home."

Sky's hand trembled in hers, his eyes wide as he looked all around. He might not have any magic in him, but he didn't need it to see that he had stepped into an unworldly realm. The very air glowed, and the trees and plants grew in vibrant hues that no human saw naturally. Even the scent was different, as if a fine perfume had been sprayed through the forest.

"Are you sure we should be here?" he whispered.

"No, we really shouldn't be," she told him seriously. "Or at least, I shouldn't be. We've been in Fae territory for some time now, and they don't like outsiders coming this close. But because I have you in tow, they're curious, and they're letting me approach without warning me off."

He gulped nervously. "How'd you know?"

"I can sense them." They possessed a very different kind of magic, but to her senses, they were like lit beacons surrounding her on all sides. But she hadn't lied to the kid—as long as she had no ill intent and she had a young child in tow, they would let her approach.

It had been a week since her rather interesting trip to Belen and her retrieval of the gadgick. She and Sarsen had delivered it safely into Jacen's eager hands, and with a sigh of relief to have *that* out of the way, went back to Chastain. After spending two days on cleanup, she had finally won free and clear of the job. Of course, that was when the real trouble began. Just remembering it gave her a headache.

Decker—henceforth known as 'the rat fink'—had led a campaign to give her an Illeyanic pup. Even though she'd explained multiple times that she had a grumpy old mountain lion that would *not* look favorably upon a puppy invading his territory, they'd insisted she take it anyway. Decker trotted out all sorts of reasons and assurances that convinced the whole village it was a splendid idea to where it made it impossible for her to refuse with either good *or* bad grace. Sky hadn't helped matters either, as he had happily scooped up the puppy and cuddled with it while she argued.

In the end, she'd given in, wondering how in the world she'd deal with Baby when she returned. Then, after all of that, the rat fink further embarrassed her by doing something he knew she wasn't comfortable with.

He had hugged her.

With a mischievous smirk on his face he'd swooped in, grabbed her up in a tight bear hug that lifted her feet off the ground, and before she could hex him, put her down again and danced off. Of course, when he got by with it, the whole village seemed to find that a grand way to bid her farewell and they'd done it *too*.

"Sevana?" Sky looked up at her askance. "Are you mad?"

"I'm just remembering all that insane hugging I had to fight off to fly back here," she grumbled.

He cocked his head, still not following. "But aren't you happy people like you?"

"They didn't hug me because they liked me, they did it to see me flustered and blushing."

He mulled that over for a second before he shook his head in disagreement. "Only people who really like you tease you."

The simple truth of that hit her strong enough to where she actually paused for a moment. Teasing, eh? Sevana was blunt and not really comfortable with demonstrative touchy-feely things, which usually isolated her from people. But if she viewed the teasing as a sign of being *liked*…well, who wouldn't be happy about that? Smiling a little to herself, she shook her head and kept walking.

They'd stayed in Big for a few days before coming out this morning for two very good reasons. The first was that Sevana was simply exhausted after traveling all over Mander in a simple three and a half weeks' time and she just wanted to be home for a while, surrounded by familiar things. But she'd also been uncertain about leaving the still-unnamed puppy alone with Baby. Her cat had not been happy to see him. Granted, he was never happy after she was gone for any length of time as he preferred to have her nearby. But it was worse when he saw the puppy in tow.

The first day he'd snarled and snapped and did his best to force the puppy out. Then, for some strange reason, she'd woken up this morning to find the puppy snuggled in against his side as they napped. She'd expected a truce to be worked out at some point, but this exceeded expectations. Not that she minded. If Baby took on the role of mentor, it meant she wouldn't have to train the pup, which took a load off her shoulders.

Still, she had a suspicion that Big had stepped in and worked things out while she wasn't looking. The mountain did things like that. Big had a soft spot for anything young and vulnerable and liked to take them in. She and Baby were prime examples of that. He had been all in favor from the very beginning of taking the puppy in.

Her young guest had been delighted to see the two getting along, of course, but he also understood when they stumbled across the scene that they had no further reason to delay their trip to the Fae. Sky, understandably, felt nervous about this whole adventure, but after everything he had seen in Big, it didn't overwhelm him as much as she thought it would. In fact, mixed in with the nervousness was a healthy dose of curiosity and anticipation. He kept up with her admirably as they hiked the very long trail deep into Fae territory.

They took the same trail that she and Bel had traveled down so many months ago, stepping in and around ancient trees that dwarfed most houses. Finally they went around a bend and came to a small pond that looked very familiar. This was where she had stopped last time, and where a certain Fae man had met her. She stopped in the same spot again and called out in a clear voice, "Hello."

The same Fae that had taken Bel stepped out from a hidden doorway, the air shimmering, looking the same as he did back then. He wore a light blue coat today with white trousers underneath, but his feet still had no shoes on them, his blond hair tied off to hang over one shoulder. He looked cautiously optimistic as he approached them, his bare feet making no sound on the grass as he walked.

"Artifactor. I did not expect to ever see you here again."

She smiled at him wryly. "I bet not. The boy you took last time grew into an adult and chose not to return. However, in the course of my latest job, I ran across this child. He fits your requirements, I believe. He's without kith or kin, is young, and has no human magic on him. He desired to meet you and see if you are interested in adopting him."

The Fae seemed intrigued and he knelt on one knee to put himself eye level with Sky. "Young child, you wish to become Fae?"

Sky licked his lips nervously. "Sevana's told me about you, some. I don't know about becoming Fae or not, but I want a family. Sir," he added as an afterthought.

The Fae's eyes gentled into a soft smile. "That is reason enough, I think. That is the core of what we are—family. We are praised and feared as magicians, but in truth, all we truly do is live so that we are in sync with the world's energies. You are nervous about changing?" he didn't need an answer, as he seemed to know what Sky felt just then. "I was too, in the very beginning. But it's not a frightening experience, or an unwanted one. Living here gives you a sense of completion that a human rarely finds."

Sevana had a few choice words she wanted to say about that, but bit her tongue. This was not the time or place for an argument.

Sky searched the face in front of him, brow furrowed. "So...it's my choice? I mean, you don't mind taking me?"

"Mind?" he repeated, faintly shocked at the question.

"Oh, you're making a mess of this!" a female voice said in exasperation. From the other side of the pond, a door opened—again, seemingly from thin air—and a woman appeared. She had the same style of clothes, although hers were in a deep, shimmering green, her hair elaborately braided around her head. With quick footsteps, she skipped over the water's surface as if it were solid ground and came directly to Sky.

Sevana blinked at her, nonplussed at this abrupt appearance. This Fae's…wife? Consort? From the way she casually leaned against him to kneel in front of Sky, they had some sort of close relationship, so Sevana guessed wife. She could tell Sky felt overwhelmed by the woman's beauty, as a slight flush came into his cheeks as he stared up at her.

"My dear child," she said to him with a warm smile, "My name is Ailana. This is my husband, Lorin. You are a handsome, sweet boy, and we would be blessed if you chose to stay with us. Don't you wish to do so?"

Sky nodded, dumbfounded. But then, she could have suggested throwing him into the pond and he'd have likely nodded in agreement. He was so star-struck by her, most of what she said likely went right into one ear and out the other.

She lit up—literally, her aura became almost blinding for a moment—and reached out, scooping him up into her arms. Sky gasped at the sudden movement and grabbed her around the neck for balance. But once there, he liked being so tightly hugged by the beauty and gave her a shy smile.

"You're mine, then," she told him firmly.

"And mine!" Lorin protested.

Giving a musical laugh, she ignored her husband's pouting and turned to Sevana. "Artifactor, I thank you many times for bringing my son to me. If, in the course of your work, you find other children that are like him, will you bring them also?"

So, not content with just one child, eh? Having no problem with bringing them orphans, Sevana just shrugged. "I will. As long as you understand I want favors in return."

Lorin understood her perfectly and gave her an elegant nod in confirmation. "We will find ways to repay your kindness."

Good enough for her. She looked at Sky, who seemed somewhat befuddled with this abrupt adoption but beyond happy at the same time. "Well, Sky, I'd wish you luck but I have this feeling you won't need it. So instead, I'll say enjoy your new life."

A grin wide enough to reveal two missing teeth split his face.

"Thanks, Sevana. Really, thanks."

"Don't mention it." With a salute to him, and a proper bow to the Fae, she turned around and left the way she had come in. She had a bounce in her stride and a wide smile on her face as she walked. Some people would likely question her decision on this, giving a child over to the Fae to raise, but in her mind, human society had already had their chance to take care of the kid and they'd failed miserably at it. The Fae would raise him with all the love and care he should have had from the beginning. She had no qualms leaving him there or bringing other children here in the future.

Pleased with herself, she hummed a ditty and enjoyed the feeling of a deed well done.

Dear Reader,

Your reviews are very important. Reviews directly impact sales and book visibility, and the more reviews we have, the more sales we see. The more sales there are, the longer I get to keep writing the books you love full time. The best possible support you can provide is to give an honest review, even if it's just clicking those stars to rate the book!

Thank you for all your support! See you in the next world.

~Honor

Honor Raconteur is a sucker for a good fantasy. Despite reading it for decades now, she's never grown tired of the magical world. She likely never will.

In between writing books, she trains and plays with her dogs, eats far too much chocolate, and attempts insane things like aerial dance.

If you'd like to join her newsletter to be notified when books are released, and get behind the scenes about upcoming books, you can isit her website or email directly to honorraconteur.news@raconteurhouse.com and you'll be added to the mailing list. If you'd like to interact with Honor more directly, you can socialize with her on various sites. Each platform offers something different and fun!

Other books by Honor Raconteur
Published by Raconteur House

♫ Available in Audiobook! ♫

THE ADVENT MAGE CYCLE

Jaunten ♫
Magus ♫
Advent ♫
Balancer ♫

ADVENT MAGE NOVELS
Advent Mage Compendium
The Dragon's Mage ♫
The Lost Mage

WARLORDS (ADVENT MAGE)

Warlords Rising
Warlords Ascending
Warlords Reigning

THE ARTIFACTOR SERIES

The Child Prince ♫
The Dreamer's Curse ♫
The Scofflaw Magician
The Canard Case
The Fae Artifactor

THE CASE FILES OF HENRI DAVENFORTH

Magic and the Shinigami Detective
Charms and Death and Explosions (oh my)

DEEPWOODS SAGA

Deepwoods ♫
Blackstone
Fallen Ward

Origins

FAMILIAR AND THE MAGE

The Human Familiar
The Void Mage
Remnants
Echoes

GÆLDORCRÆFT FORCES

Call to Quarters

KINGMAKERS

Arrows of Change ♫
Arrows of Promise
Arrows of Revolution

KINGSLAYER

Kingslayer ♫
Sovran at War ♫

SINGLE TITLES

Special Forces 01
Midnight Quest

Crossroads: An Artifactor x Deepwoods Crossover Short Story

Sovran at War ♫

SINGLE TITLES

Special Forces 01
Midnight Quest

Crossroads: An Artifactor x Deepwoods Crossover Short Story

*Upcoming